THE DEVIL'S FIRE

MATT TOMERLIN

Interior art by Brendon Mroz.
Flintlock pistol by pzAxe/Shutterstock.com

www.TheDevilsFire.com
Matt Tomerlin on Twitter: @MattTomerlin

ISBN-13: 978-0615916507
ISBN-10: 0615916503

"There is nothing so desperately monotonous as the sea, and I no longer wonder at the cruelty of pirates."

James Russell Lowell

1

KATHERINE

Katherine Lindsay pressed her legs against the bulwark and peered into the cold blue waters of the North Atlantic, hoping to locate her supposed beauty within the rippling reflection that gazed back.

An emaciated figure, pale skin, and ordinary features were a tax on her self-esteem. Bodices did not accentuate her breasts as nicely as most of the women she knew. She had received no shortage of flattering remarks, all of which she credited to the striking mane of red hair that curled naturally about her head and spilled down to her waist, forging an illusion of beauty by cloaking her less interesting traits. It was a wicked burden of tangles that she fastened as best she could, but the wild tresses were as much a curse as they were a fiery splendor.

Her aggravation was heightened by the miserably cold and wet environment of the ship, a three-masted merchantman that her husband had lovingly christened, "*Lady Katherine.*" It was a cramped place, beset by the pungent aroma of damp wood and the tangy flavor of salt, both of which mislaid their initially agreeable virtues after the first week at sea.

The journey had been inescapably dull. She ventured on deck in late afternoon to admire sunsets, whenever the sky was not obscured by storm clouds. She had grossly underestimated the need for reading material, and swiftly finished what few books she had brought with her. The stark contrast of life aboard a merchant ship frequently prompted her to dwell on the simple pleasures she had entertained each day in London.

She marveled at how easily *Lady Katherine's* young crewmen accepted their lives. They numbered seventeen and were aged twenty to twenty-five. They kept to themselves and spoke of her in hushed, gossip-ridden tones. She loathed the way they hungrily leered at her, as though they had never looked on a woman before. She saw them as animals in a zoo, indifferent to the chivalries of civilized society, motivated only by appetite.

She missed tea parties with her friends and conversations that consisted of nothing more than extravagant jewelry and rich husbands. She was born to a middle-class family and had wisely married into wealth. She instantly took a perverse kind of delight in her new surroundings, and that included fitting in with the wives of her husband's friends. She had never really considered herself one of them, but she had convinced them beyond a shadow of a doubt that she was. Fickle though they were, after only a few days at sea, she longed desperately for their mindless banter.

Katherine was nineteen, and her attempts to produce a child with Thomas had been unsuccessful thus far. This proved a scandalous concern for friends and relatives, but she remained happily optimistic. Thomas had three brothers. All of them were married, two of them with children. The mortality of the Lindsay family line was not at stake, therefore Katherine and Thomas were not under any immediate pressure to preserve it.

Thomas was a handsome man with nicely tanned skin and fine blonde hair, which Katherine believed to be thinning. Her friends were certain that his apparent balding would prove to be a hindrance on their relationship, but Katherine had not fallen in love with Thomas for his looks. She adored his nonchalant attitude towards life. He was not the type of man to angrily combat the problems that came his way; he simply worked around such nuisances calmly and peacefully.

When he announced that he would sail his merchant ship to America, Katherine demanded in no uncertain terms that he take her with him. He endured a week's perseverance, which began each day before breakfast and ended long after supper. She told him that she wanted to see more of him, having been too often deprived. While this was indeed true, it was also true that she longed for adventure, and there was nothing more adventurous than a voyage at sea.

After getting her way, she dared not grumble of the voyage's monotony, as she was certain that Thomas would only remind her of her prior diligence. She knew it would be pointless to bellyache, and she did not want to prove just how womanly she could be. The anticipation of seeing America helped keep her complaints at bay.

Katherine's journey ended two weeks earlier than expected, in the late days of September, in the year 1717. A week's worth of densely clouded skies had finally given way to a clear day. She basked in the unusually warm weather, ignoring the wandering eyes of her husband's puerile crew.

She wore a saffron mantua that was derived from expensive silk that hugged her shoulders and plunged to her cleavage. A splendid floral design was brocaded into the bodice. The skirt, which was an extension of the bodice, was parted at the front and looped to the sides by buttons and cords, revealing a flounced petticoat underneath. Thomas occasionally came to her side to offer a tender comfort, sliding his hands along the silk of her dress, as he liked to do, before promptly returning to his duties.

It was Katherine who spotted the ship on the horizon, broad on the port bow. She underestimated the weight of her upper torso and pitched over the rail, feet lifting precariously into the air. She flailed her legs until her toes touched the deck. When she steadied herself, a sweeping wave of nausea blurred her vision. She focused her gaze on two distant black dots on the horizon, squinting until the dots merged into one. The indistinct blemish gradually formed shapes she recognized: a hull and sails.

The sea was a desolate place, and she was positively giddy at the prospect of meeting new faces. Maybe there was a woman aboard who would join her for dinner before their ships parted ways. That would temporarily ease her boredom. She alerted Thomas immediately. After a glimpse through his spyglass, he kept a curious silence. She didn't like to bother him when he was contemplating, but impatience got the better of her.

"A merchant ship, you think?" she inquired placidly.

"Most probably, dear," he replied. "I can't see her colors with the sun behind her."

"Colors?"

"Her flag," he said, a little too sharply. "We'll know what she is when we see her flag."

She furrowed her brow at the briskness of his tone. She wanted to spin on her heels and retreat to the cabin, so he would regret speaking to her so curtly. She had to remind herself that her husband's duties as captain far outweighed his matrimonial sentiments, at least for the duration of the voyage.

Still, she made a mental note to scold him when next they were alone.

They watched the ship for an hour, until the sun began to set at last. When the vessel was near enough to discern the particulars, Thomas leaned close to Katherine and said, "She's a brigantine." The vessel had two masts, square-rigged fore and topsails, a fore-and-aft rigged spanker abaft her mainmast, a triangular main staysail between the foremast and mainmast, and a jib that stretched from foremast to bowsprit.

Katherine asked, "What does 'brigantine' mean?"

Thomas set his jaw and fell silent.

She squeezed his arm. "Thomas?"

"Brigand," he said finally.

The sun ducked beyond the horizon and the sky turned a variety of colors, from brilliant orange to deep purple. Goose bumps riddled Katherine's flesh as the air took on a sinister chill. The closer the brigantine came, the colder the air became.

A crewman's breath prickled the hairs on the back of her neck, and she turned with a start. His face was a ghostly shade of white and his eyes were wide, unblinking saucers, staring at the brigantine. Several more had gathered round, appearing equally distressed.

She looked to Thomas, who was studying the ship through his spyglass, and said, "What is it?"

He handed her the spyglass. "See the flag on that ship?"

She peered into the eyepiece and guided the spyglass until she found the mainmast, and then scaled it to the top, where a massive black flag thrashed in the wind. Broad at the center was the frightful image of a blood-red heart, impaled by a white cutlass.

"Pirates," Thomas concluded with a grimace.

"Do we run?" said a crewman, his voice trembling.

Thomas gave no reply. Katherine wasn't sure her husband had even heard the man. Seeing him so uncharacteristically despondent left a hollow feeling in the pit of her stomach.

A blast sounded from a chase gun on the forecastle deck of the brigantine. Water exploded in a billowing plume on the port beam.

Katherine backed into Thomas's chest. She felt his hands cling to her waist, as if he feared losing her over the edge. He released her and returned to his crew, shouting orders that she didn't understand. She was so fixated on the brigantine that she was only distantly aware of the crew's frantic activities behind her.

Thomas ordered, "Hard to starboard!"

Katherine was thrust against the bulwark as the helmsman tilted the ship into a sharp evasion. The dull emptiness in her stomach gave to a severe jolt of pain. A second report exploded from the chase gun, and she stared dumbly as a plume erupted directly in front of her, spraying her with seawater. She was blinking the saline sting out of her eyes when she heard her husband bellow:

"HEAVE TO!!"

This prompted frightened gasps from several crewmen.

"Do it!" Thomas shouted. "They outgun, outman, and outmaneuver us ten to one and more."

Lady Katherine's bow was aimed against the wind, with no small amount of fuss from the sails. Katherine braced herself as the ship was wrenched to a sudden halt.

The pirate brigantine approached at such a startling speed that, for an alarming instant, Katherine thought its bowsprit would rake across the deck and split her in half. The brigantine tilted sharply and ran parallel to *Lady Katherine*. Each snap of the brigantine's sails sounded with the fury of a thunderclap.

Protruding from the bulwark were six cast-iron, four-pound cannons. Swivel guns were mounted on the quarterdeck and forecastle. Scattered across the decks were what Katherine wagered to be a hundred pirates.

Before she could absorb further details, Thomas seized her firmly by the arm and whisked her to their cabin. "It won't last long," he assured her, "but keep yourself concealed beneath the bed, you hear me?"

She nodded.

"I love you," he said. He closed the door before she could echo his words.

It was six hours before she was discovered underneath the bed.

The night began with five rapid thudding sounds, followed by three loud clacking noises, and a violent tremor of feet pummeling the deck. She heard domineering shouts from the pirates and submissive responses from Thomas's crew.

Several pirates spilled into the cabin, laughing and cursing. She glimpsed only their feet. Some wore boots, but most were barefoot. Through a hole in the heavy quilt that was draped over the bed she watched as they thieved most of her clothes and jewelry. They took whatever piqued their interest and left, their boisterous laughter lost in the roaring pandemonium that had enveloped the main deck.

After what she presumed to be two hours, she heard a loud scuttle and a subsequent shriek that was abruptly cut short. A riotous commotion lasted for nearly five minutes before it broke into uncontrollable fits of laughter. For the next hour she was left to ponder Thomas's fate. Her mind played out a relentless torrent of ghastly possibilities, with Thomas meeting a grisly fate in every one of them.

And then, with a glorious flood of relief, she heard his voice. Her eyes burned. She squeezed them shut, refusing to allow any tears to burst free; there would be time enough for that later, when she held him in her arms again, and the present ordeal was nothing more than a memory.

Thomas was conversing with a man whose voice had a distinctive air of authority. As this man spoke, the pirates gradually calmed. Katherine found herself transfixed on the voice, even though it was far too muffled through the cabin walls for her to distinguish words. He possessed a tranquil tone that she rather liked, and she temporarily forgot her peril while listening to him.

Thomas and the man with the fair voice eventually ended their conversation, and the pirate uproar started anew. This went on at some length, and the cabin remained empty over the next few hours. Gradually, the clamor outside grew even louder, and the unmistakable sound of a shattering bottle prompted her to wonder if the pirates had discovered the cases of wine in the cargo hold.

The endless ruckus numbed her senses, and she found her eyelids growing heavy. The deck seemed to stretch away from her. Her vision thinned to narrowing slits that soon receded into darkness.

The door was thrust open, and the ruckus outside flooded the cabin like a tidal wave. Katherine lifted her head before opening her eyes and smashed the crown of her skull against the underbelly of the bed. Her eyes shot open in accordance with the jolting pain.

A pair of buckled shoes marched deliberately for the bed. The man who wore them reached down and tore the quilt away, spoiling her hiding place. With the velocity of a striking snake, his hand shot under the bed to grasp Katherine's hair, dragging her painfully from cover.

"This ship's treasures never cease," said the man with the voice that she had liked so much. But his pleasant enunciation was no match for the hunger in his eyes.

The death cry Katherine had heard earlier belonged to one of Thomas's crew. He had been viciously taken apart by a cutlass, and it looked as though the desecration had continued long after he had perished. His head was connected to his neck by only a few threads of muscle, and his right leg and left arm had been hacked off completely.

The rest of the crew looked exhausted but uninjured, apart from one man whose right eye was badly bruised. Thomas had been placed in a direction that prevented her from seeing his face, and she assumed that his hands were bound at his front.

The man that had discovered her seemed unwilling to part with her for the duration of the night. She tried not to contemplate his intentions. She was afraid to speak to him or ask any questions. She deduced that he was the captain. He was a clean-shaven, ruggedly handsome man with raven hair that fell on broad shoulders. He wore a long, gold-buttoned, dark blue coat over a loose-fitting white shirt that was tucked into brown trousers. A red sash was wrapped around his waist, into which he had inserted an impressive flintlock pistol with gold accents. Over the sash, a large black belt dipped toward his left side, weighted by a cutlass with a jeweled hilt.

In contrast, most of the pirates were dressed in as little as possible. Many of them did not wear shirts and had rolled their trousers up to their knees. Though a few wore boots, most seemed to prefer walking barefoot. Some wore brightly colored bandanas. They each brandished a single cutlass, and anywhere from one flintlock pistol to three, fastened at the waist by silk sashes.

The majority were white, but Katherine also counted several black men. The blacks seemed less boisterous and far more attuned to their duties than the whites. She couldn't be sure of the ratio of whites to blacks, as the pirates would continuously descend below decks in rotations, and she would too easily lose track of them.

Lady Katherine had been hitched to the enemy ship by grappling hooks, and the pirates had set planks across the two ships. This accounted for the thuds and clacks she had heard earlier that night, just before the pirates boarded the ship. Presently, they were rolling barrels of gunpowder across the planks onto their ship. Between every few barrel runs pirates would carry across crates, food, bales of silk, spare sails, anchor cables, and rigging. They were stripping the ship of anything of remote value or potential use.

The sun greeted a cloudless sky, but Katherine took no joy in it. She was famished beyond reason, wanting more than anything to embrace Thomas. She felt dreadful for all the times she had yelled at him over matters that now seemed trivial. She wondered how he dealt with so rebellious a wife, while other women unquestionably accepted the circumstances their husbands provided. Thomas treated her like a princess, better than any of her friends' husbands had treated them. She did not deserve such a man.

The plundering lasted until midday; it took the pirates that long to transfer most of *Lady Katherine*'s cargo to their ship. Katherine's knees grew so weak that she finally seated herself on the deck without bothering to ask the captain's permission. He glanced impassively at her.

She started to wonder if this madness would ever end. She didn't care about *Lady Katherine*'s lost cargo, so long as it meant the pirates would peacefully be on their way. Losing so much would have repercussions on Thomas's business, but that was the last thing on her mind. She told herself that everything would be fine. Thomas had forged an acquaintance with the captain earlier that night. As long as they did what was ordered, they would survive this ordeal with a remarkable story to tell.

However, the dead man, whose corpse had already started to putrefy in the sun, was impossible to ignore. What could he possibly have done to deserve such a fate? Had he tried to run? Where did he think he could have gone? *He was stupid,* she rationalized. *He made a stupid mistake and died for it. An example of what will happen to the rest of us if we don't cooperate.*

As midday neared, ominous grey clouds gathered rapidly on all sides of the horizon, but the sky above remained as bright and blue as ever.

The pirates rolled the final barrels of gunpowder across the planks. Most of the crew had ventured back to the brigantine, leaving a small garrison on *Lady Katherine*. The captain left Katherine's side and approached Thomas. Thomas tilted his head and greeted the man with an uneasy smile. The captain took on a surly demeanor that seemed to catch Thomas off guard. "Is something amiss?" Thomas asked gently.

"You might have obliged our first cannon fire," replied the captain. He rested his hand atop the pommel of his cutlass and gestured to the black flag at the peak of his brigantine. "I have a reputation to preserve, you understand."

"But sir!" Thomas protested. "You promised you wouldn't harm anyone else!"

The captain's emotionless expression held. "I promised I wouldn't harm any of the *crew,* beyond that unfortunate young man over there, and I will uphold that end of the bargain. However, I said nothing of sparing the ship's *captain.*"

In the blink of an eye, the captain unsheathed his cutlass and plunged the blade into Thomas's chest. Thomas choked blood and clutched the captain's shoulder. The captain slapped his hand away and ripped the cutlass from his chest.

The blade flashed crimson in the sunlight before it was swiftly returned to its sheath. Thomas managed a glance in Katherine's direction before collapsing facedown onto the deck. His blood spread in a puddle beneath him, and he did not move again.

Katherine loosed a bloodcurdling wail that would have rattled a banshee. She sprung to her feet and lunged for Thomas, but was held back by the sweaty hands of two pirates. She fought to move forward, her legs going through the motions but advancing her no further, feet slipping on the wet deck. She shook her right arm free and slammed her elbow into one pirate's nose, spurting blood from his nostrils. She spun, aiming a fist at the left pirate's jaw, but it did not connect. The man ducked and caught her midsection. He lifted her up and carried her kicking and screaming to the captain, dropping her in front of him. She sprawled gracelessly onto the deck.

"Watch yourselves, mates," chuckled the pirate with the bleeding nose. "This lass has spirit."

The captain smiled charmingly down at her, as though he hadn't murdered her husband only a dozen seconds prior. She scrambled onto her hands and knees and smashed into his legs, thinking she might knock him off his feet, but she might as well have tried to topple a statue. He gathered a handful of her hair and dragged her across the deck, toward the planks that connected the two ships. She kicked at his legs and punched at his waist as he hefted her onto a plank. When her mightiest struggles proved pathetically ineffective, she reached pleadingly to *Lady Katherine*'s crew. Two of them stared woefully at her; the rest did not even hazard a glance.

"Help me!" she shrieked. "Help me, you cowards!" At that, the two who had been watching her turned away. "You bloody cowards!" she shrieked, voice breaking.

She frantically searched for an escape. The train of her dress snagged on a splinter, and the captain's feet nearly flew out from under him. He gathered the skirt in his hand and tugged vigorously at it, until the train started to tear. As he wrestled with the dress, Katherine looked to the sea below the planks, wondering if she could dive into the water and escape between the two ships. Unfortunately, the pirates would probably shoot her before she could make her way to safety, and even if they missed, she didn't fancy herself much of a swimmer.

By the time she understood the futility of her situation, the train ripped free of the splinter, and the captain hefted her off the plank and deposited her unceremoniously onto the deck of the pirate brigantine. The pirates slid the planks back onto their deck, and the brigantine started to pull away from *Lady Katherine*. She scrambled to the bulwark, fumbling beneath the bustle of pirates, and pulled herself up for a final glimpse of her former home. She was contemplating leaping over the rail when the captain snatched her and dragged her kicking and screaming toward his cabin. He shoved her inside and slammed the door, leaving her alone.

The cabin was dimly lit by a couple of milky windows at the stern. After her vision adapted to the darkness, she saw a small round table in the center, a desk on the starboard side, and a dresser and cabinet beneath the windows. An oversized bed filled much of the port side. The cabin was cramped and the pathways between the furniture were narrow.

She went for the desk first, opening all of the drawers except the top one, which was locked. She tugged at the handle, figuring that something important must have been concealed within, but eventually gave up on it. She moved to the dresser, but found only undergarments and useless trinkets.

She heard a number of voices out on the main deck, but only when she heard the word "girl" did she stop to listen. Individual comments were too difficult to distinguish amid the angry rabble, until one man loudly made clear the general feelings of the crew: "Bad luck, the lot of them . . . worse yet on a ship. How's this one any different?"

She shuddered as she considered the implications. Her worst fears were confirmed when a pirate with a gruff voice bellowed, "Let the sharks work through her troubles," followed by a deafening roar of laughter and cheering. There were more comments still, most of them detailing gruesomely ingenious tortures.

Another man said, "Better to put her at a stove. I haven't had a decent meal in ages."

"At a stove, or *on* it. Whichever tastes better!"

Thankfully, the captain bombastically proclaimed, "I'll not give the woman to the sea till I have determined her worth!" And then he chuckled. "Nor would I wish her ravaged by stove or otherwise!"

There was no further discussion on the matter.

Katherine fell to the deck, overcome with feelings of dread. Her stomach gave to convulsions, and she gasped hoarsely for air that would not come. Warm streams of tears rolled down her cheeks and touched her lips. She squeezed her eyes shut and prayed that while they were closed some miracle would spirit her back to London. Back to her friends. Back to her husband.

A plethora of memories assaulted her.

She saw Thomas on the day they were introduced as he reached to help her from a carriage. She stumbled purposefully into his arms, doing her best to make the misstep appear genuine. Their lips brushed, but they did not kiss. They stayed like that, his hands around her waist, her red mane enveloping his face like a veil. Their faces flushed and they broke into a set of shy giggles.

She saw Thomas with his arm slung across a park bench,

awaiting her approach with a fervent smile. He stood and took off his hat and embellished a bow, sending her into a spasm of bubbling laughter. They strolled through the park, coming to a small bridge that formed an arch over a tiny stream. It was here that they kissed for the first time.

She saw Thomas on his knees, presenting her with the most spectacular diamond ring she had ever seen. She knew it had cost him a fortune. She was fraught with words, struggling to explain to him how much he meant to her, and that no mere diamond could possibly compare.

She saw Thomas on their wedding day, more debonair any man present. He held her cheeks and drew her to him until their lips pressed together. Everything seemed to melt away around them, and she wanted the moment to last an eternity.

She saw Thomas dead on the deck of *Lady Katherine*, facedown in a widening pool of his own blood. The blood spread until it filled the deck and cascaded over the sides. The ship hemorrhaged into the sea like an open wound, dyeing the water crimson.

Katherine opened her eyes.

Regrettably, she had not been spirited back to London. She remained trapped in a cabin that belonged to her husband's murderer. But she was no longer devastated or afraid. Instead her eyes were fixated on the first thing they saw.

The answer had been right in front of her all along.

Above the captain's desk was a painting of a brigantine at sea, and mounted underneath it were two polished cutlasses with intersecting blades.

2

GRIFFITH

The chill winds cut deep into his skin and purged the warmth from the marrow of his bones. After nearly two decades at sea, Captain Jonathan Griffith had never developed a tolerance for the mounting cold that washed over the Atlantic as the winter months drew near.

As he stood on the forecastle deck, a cover of grey clouds filled the mid-afternoon sky, and only a few blemishes of sapphire were visible through the narrowing gaps. The threat of a rainstorm or worse was imminent.

Winters along the east coast of North America were known to freeze ships in their docks with layers of ice so thick that their hulls might as well have been mounted in brick. As a result, merchant shipping slowed to a virtual standstill.

Griffith took it as a sign. Tomorrow he would call for a vote with the proposition of sailing to the West Indies. The hold of his ship, *Harbinger*, was bloated with barrels of gunpowder, bales of silk, expensive wines, chests full of women's jewelry, and countless other treasures. It had been an extremely lucrative year, and there was no better place to spend the winter season than the warm, crystal waters of the Caribbean.

However, Griffith's mind drifted far beyond the fleeting pleasures of a single season. While the men were content to spend every piece of eight on whores and spirits, Griffith quietly hoarded his money for a greater purpose. He would live out the rest of his days under the warm sun, devoid of cares, on a plantation in the West Indies. He would die an old man in his bed, and history would not recall his fate.

Before this dream could be realized, he needed that elusive final plunder; the legendary kind of plunder that covetous pirates recounted in hyperbolic tales around raging bonfires. It was out there somewhere, waiting to be plucked from the sea, and taking it would be no simple task.

Griffith was sick of captains who valued their lives above their cargos; surrenders effortlessly achieved because their goods were not worth dying for. He sought a captain whose life was secondary to the treasure in his hold. It would be a grand battle, he knew, and the outcome would decide his destiny.

But something had been missing. He had never been able to place it, and it wasn't until yesterday that he realized what his grand scheme lacked. It had been an aberrantly warm day for late September, and out of that warmth sprouted a gift from the sea herself.

The bountiful plunder of *Lady Katherine* had topped off *Harbinger's* hold, but a treasure of greater value now lingered in Griffith's cabin. Never in his many travels had he set eyes on such a creature. He could have sworn she was a mermaid changed into human form. Her fiery hair and porcelain skin enchanted him. The sight of her made him feel something in his chest that he had never experienced before; a kind of rising swell that he was hard-pressed to describe.

When he first beheld Katherine Lindsay, he had a vision of her on his future plantation, gliding through the tall grass in a sundress, moving toward him with open arms and an evocative smile. He desired her more than anything in the world, and he knew that his life would not be complete unless he possessed her.

He suffered no remorse for killing Thomas Lindsay. Griffith knew when he was being lied to, and Lindsay's cooperation had been too easily earned, betraying the subtle nuances of a man with something to hide. Edward Livingston, *Harbinger's* quartermaster, murdered one of Lindsay's young crewmen, hacking the body to pieces in front of everyone. Griffith swiftly apologized for Livingston's "rash actions" and insisted that the quartermaster had acted of his own accord. It was a technique he commonly employed when dealing with merchant captains, and in most cases it was more effective than torture.

When Lindsay gave the name of his ship, *Lady Katherine*, Griffith glimpsed an uneasy shift in the man's eyes. He couldn't put his finger on it, but he was convinced that there was something valuable at stake; something that Lindsay would not dare reveal. Later that night, Griffith easily discovered her rather uninspired hiding place. He knew instantly that she was the woman the ship had been named after.

Taking the woman prisoner was the first time he had acted without first consulting the crew, and his drastic actions perplexed even him. Bringing a woman aboard a ship was bad luck, and everyone knew it. On most ships it was a forbidden offense, sometimes punishable by death. But he was the elected captain, and he had led the crew to countless victories. They had come to trust him with their very lives, which afforded him a certain leeway.

He had set their initial grievances at bay, but he worried

that a week's voyage or less would rekindle their concerns. Like birds, they reacted negatively to slight alterations in their environment, blindly accepting their circumstances so long as nothing changed. They maintained tried-and-true patterns, and obstacles in their path were almost always met with force.

A recent incident was fresh in Griffith's mind. A crewman had nicely opted to take over the duties of a man who had overslept after consuming an entire bottle of rum the night prior. When the late-sleeper finally arrived to discover that his position had been filled, he was overcome with jealousy. He shoved his dagger between his replacement's shoulder blades. Livingston secured the murderer before anyone could retaliate, and, after a month's incarceration in the hold, he was stranded on the first island they happened across.

Thinking back on the incident made Griffith to wonder if keeping the woman in his cabin, which the crew frequented almost as often as he, might prove to be a similar such obstacle. There was also the problem of taming her. She obviously wouldn't warm to him after he had murdered her husband.

His mind was riddled with plaguing questions, and he hadn't uncovered any answers. His entire piratical career had been one of intricately executed plans. "Any problem can be fixed into a plan," his father used to say. Of course, his father's plans probably hadn't included a gambling addiction that had prompted him to sell his Tobacco farm in Maryland and spend what little coin he had left drinking himself to death. With no inheritance to speak of, and fearing a similar fate, Griffith signed on to a merchant vessel that mainly supplied flour to the West Indies. The decision had changed his life forever.

Any problem can be fixed into a plan. Despite his father's many failings, Griffith had lived by the wisdom of those words. However, he now found himself leaping into a treacherous situation with open arms, minus strategy. His father's life had taken a downward spiral under a bout of pure impulse. Would his be no different?

Griffith shook his head, hoping to clear the doubt that muddied his thoughts. He considered returning to his cabin to check on the girl, but thought better of it.

"I need a plan," he muttered to the wind.

Like the waters they cruised, the pirates were a blur of infinite motion as they tended to their respective duties. The mottled contrasts of their various ethnicities were indistinguishable at this bustling pace, and the ship was of a single mind.

The crew numbered ninety-two, and most of them had reached their mid-twenties. The whites were mostly Englishmen from London and Bristol. Most had come from British merchant ships that Griffith had plundered here and there. Nine of them had been with Griffith from the beginning, including Livingston.

Livingston had proven to be the perfect choice for quartermaster. Aside from Griffith, he claimed no friends, and therefore could not be accused of bias when settling disputes between the men. He was a tall, barrel-chested man with a darkly sunned scalp that he shaved weekly due to thinning hair. He had a strong jaw and hawk-like eyes that missed nothing, set beneath thin eyebrows and a weathered forehead. Most respected him, and those few who didn't were at least wise enough to steer clear of him.

After many years in the West Indies, *Harbinger's* crew had gained several Jamaicans and Bahamans. The majority had been recruited from the port at Nassau on the island of New Providence. Griffith had also drafted a handful of American sailors from a merchant vessel he captured off the coast of New York, six months prior. They were a spirited bunch that cared naught for their lives as legitimate merchantmen, and they eagerly joined the pirate crew without requiring any additional incentive.

Nearly a third of the crew was black. Most stemmed from slave ships, gladly accepting pirate life as an alternative to lifelong servitude under potentially cruel masters. While some pirate captains saw this as their opportunity to capitalize on the slave trade, Griffith didn't have the stomach. Seizing a slave ship was always accompanied by horrors best left unspoken of.

The blacks were hard workers, and Griffith was grateful for them, but he found them difficult to relate to. He wasn't even sure how many of them spoke English, aside from key nautical terms. Some made appearances at parties on the main deck, providing strangely entertaining dances for the whites, but mostly they kept to themselves. And the whites allowed them no say when it came to votes. "The monkeys don't need a vote," Livingston argued. "They're happy enough to be freed of shackle."

There was a group of seven blacks who were called, simply, the "Seven." They had mutinied against their captors aboard a ship named *Baraka*, which was later discovered by *Harbinger*. There was an animalistic ferocity in their eyes. The largest towered over seven feet tall. No one talked to them, not even the other blacks, unless it was utterly necessary.

There were several elite cliques aboard *Harbinger*, often marked by various talents. The aptly named "Musketmen" were five Englishmen who carried muskets. Of them, none was a finer marksman than young Louis Robertson.

The Americans were a class all their own. Presently, Griffith found four of them enjoying a tobacco break at the gunwale. Nathan Adams, the youngest of *Harbinger's* crew, leapt from his seat and took Griffith's hand in his, shaking it vigorously. He had a sandy-colored mop of thick hair that made many balding pirates jealous, apart from those who proudly sported hairless scalps, and his attractive young face was enhanced by a week's worth of blonde stubble. He was a good-natured boy, and even the more hardened pirates had taken a liking to him.

"Oy there, captain," he said nervously.

"Nathan," Griffith smiled. "What's on your mind, lad?"

"Me and me boys was wondering if this dreadful cold will never end?"

Griffith glanced over Nathan's shoulder and saw the young man's companions leaning forward in eager anticipation of the answer. Of course, the cold was just beginning, and Nathan, having lived on the East Coast for most of his life, certainly knew this.

"I can hardly stand it myself," replied Griffith. "Tomorrow we alter course, and, if the vote calls fair, we set for warmer waters."

A massive grin lit Nathan's boyish face. "Certain it will, captain. Certain it will."

When the sun had dipped to the horizon through a breach in the clouds, Griffith found himself standing before his cabin door. He was no more confident of how to proceed than before. He turned away and looked toward the bow. The fiery rays of the setting sun reddened the circumference of the gap in the clouds, and looking at it made him think of *her* hair.

"Katherine," he whispered, testing the name on his tongue; the name he'd guessed without being told.

And then, as if struck by lightning, he realized what he had been missing all along: Thomas Lindsay had inadvertently given his wife away. If the girl thought that her husband had revealed her hiding place in order to save his own skin, she would curse his memory! The lie would be easily fortified by Griffith's unaccountable knowledge of her name, and he doubted she would come to the conclusion that he had guessed it on his own. Of course, it was a risky plan, especially if he had been wrong about her name all along, but it was all he had going for him.

He felt a little silly for having doubted himself. There was something about this woman that sent his mind reeling, as though he were blindly feeling around in the dark.

"Any problem can be fixed into a plan," echoed his father's voice, clear in his mind, despite the many years removed. There was strength in plans, and plans required deliberation. He had deliberated long enough.

He faced the door and checked himself, smoothing his clothes and pushing hair out of his face. He took a deep breath, opened the door, and stepped into the cabin.

The blade blinded him as a flash of sunset reflected off it. He felt a sharp pain in his left arm, and sudden pressure knocked him off his feet. The girl's slender silhouette stepped in front of the door.

Instinctively, he kicked out a heel and felt it make contact with her shin. She screamed and fell backwards. The blade crashed to the deck with the clang of steel against wood, and he was on top of her before she could retrieve it. He scooped up the cutlass and grinned, victorious.

Her knee caught his groin. He gagged for air as the hollow pain reverberated into his stomach. She clawed at the hand that held the cutlass, trying to pry open his fingers and wrench the blade free. He smashed his forehead into her cheek. Her head snapped away and rebounded against the deck. She groaned and tried to roll over.

His mistake was thinking she was done. He took the briefest of moments to relax his muscles, which is what she must have been waiting for. Her mouth opened and she rose up to enclose it around his right ear. She bit down with the brawn of a steel trap, her teeth ripping through the fabric of his ear. The pain spiked through his skull like a flower that blossomed needles instead of petals. When he pulled away, he saw that she had a chunk of his earlobe in her mouth with blood cascading down her chin. Before he could fully comprehend the horror of the moment, she spit the lobe into his face.

He fell away from her, wiping blood from his eyes. The pain in his groin no longer mattered as the intense throbbing from his severed ear resonated through his head and splintered into the muscles of his neck.

The woman was starting to get to her feet when Griffith felt something hard in his grip and realized that he was still holding the cutlass. He summoned all of the energy left to him and swung the weapon in a great arc. The blade smashed into her scalp with a satisfying spray of blood that was warm on his face.

3

LIVINGSTON

When Edward Livingston opened the door, the waning light fell upon what looked like a slaughterhouse. The girl was facedown, with blood oozing out of her head. In the dim light he wasn't sure where the blood ended and her hair began, but he was certain she was dead.

Next he saw Captain Griffith's legs; the rest of him was blanketed in darkness. Livingston stepped over the girl and dropped to his knees beside Griffith. A large chunk of the captain's right earlobe was resting on his collar, and a lengthy gash had been carved into his left arm, bleeding profusely.

"What in Hell?" Livingston exclaimed.

"That fire-haired whore," Griffith responded with a wry smile. "She very nearly killed me."

Livingston gritted his teeth. He had known the girl was trouble from the moment he'd laid eyes on her. He stood and returned to her body. "Are you dead, bitch?" he demanded. When she didn't respond, he emphasized the question by digging the tip of his boot into her ribs. She didn't budge. He kneeled beside her and put two fingers to her neck. Happily, he found a pulse. He would take great pleasure in torturing her for what she had done to his friend. He recalled that one of the crew had suggested putting her on a stove. He rather liked that idea.

"Patch her up," Griffith croaked. "And fix her to the mainmast. If it's death she desires, she'll find it there."

Livingston cocked his head. Had Griffith lost his mind? The girl had plainly tried to kill him. She'd taken a good portion of his ear, sliced open his arm, and surely would've done worse if she hadn't been overpowered, and the most creative anguish he could think of was a few measly days in the sun?

"Captain," Livingston started to protest.

"She'll be lucky if she lasts the night," Griffith interjected. "The fight she put up . . . you should have seen it." Livingston noted a disturbingly proud glint in Griffith's eyes. "She's earned a chance, don't you agree?"

"No," Livingston growled. "She's had it with chances."

"Five days," Griffith said, cutting him off. "If she lasts that long, she'll have earned her life."

Livingston's teeth gnawed at the inside of his cheek. He knew better than anyone that a dispute was best settled between the two people it involved and no one else. He could have overridden the captain's request and hurled the girl to the sea before she regained consciousness, but he did not wish to sully their friendship.

"Five days," Griffith persisted.

Livingston sighed. He was suddenly aware that the cabin had grown dark, and he turned to find several of the crew shadowing the door, struggling to see over one another.

"Bring Thatcher," Livingston told them. "Captain's hurt."

The crowd dispersed instantly.

A minute later, Thatcher shuffled in, ushered along by two of the crew. He attended first to Griffith. Livingston did not know the surgeon's age, but he was certain the man was at least a score older than any of them. He was also the fattest, though he had lost much of his girth since they'd recruited him. He was a bald man with a massive head that was perpetually sunburned. No matter how long Thatcher remained in the sun, his pale skin never seemed to tan properly. He was always sweating, even on cold days, and he smelled awful. He was constantly complaining of illness, embellishing his woes with a guttural cough that that made everyone wince.

Livingston secretly yearned for Thatcher's passing, so he wouldn't have to put up with his awful stench and endless bleating. However, he knew that *Harbinger* was badly in need of a surgeon. Accidents of a wide variety were common to a ship and crew of this size, and Livingston was thankful, now more than ever, that Thatcher had persevered, against all odds.

The slice in Griffith's arm was not as bad as it looked. The cut was long, but not very deep. Livingston offered the captain a bottle of brandy to get him through the operation as Thatcher stitched the wound with a curved needle from his weathered canvas case.

Livingston watched nervously. He habitually stroked his head, sliding his palm over the stubby bristles of hair, from front to back, then back to front. His hand encountered less resistance than he remembered.

Thatcher was finished with the arm in a few minutes, but the earlobe was another matter entirely.

"Just sew it back on," Livingston suggested.

Thatcher responded with a withering look.

"What?" Livingston shrugged. "The skin won't know no different, will it?"

Thatcher sighed. "Her teeth made a bloody mess of it. It's

mutilated. I'd have better luck fastening a pig's ear in its place."

"Give it here, then," Livingston said, holding out his hand. Thatcher slapped the lobe into his palm.

"I think I can make do without it," Griffith said, averting his eyes from the severed ear. "Patch up the hole and have done with it. And get that cursed thing out of here before I lose my supper."

"He won't hear from it!" Livingston protested, gesturing with the lobe and flinging trickles of blood across the cabin.

"Unfortunately, I hear you just fine," Griffith drawled.

Thatcher poured some of the brandy on Griffith's wound. Griffith wrinkled his brow and hissed through clenched teeth. Thatcher wrapped a bandage around the ear and then sat back to admire his work, as though he'd just accomplished the Mona Lisa. Then he took a hefty swig the brandy, wiped his lips, and burped.

"See to the girl," Griffith instructed.

"The whuh?" Thatcher said, genuinely perplexed.

Griffith indicated the body just beside the Thatcher.

"Oh," the surgeon said. He sighed exasperatedly.

Livingston saw his opportunity to chime in. "Griff's lost too much blood. Makes no sense to bother with that wench."

"I agree," Thatcher replied with an excessively sympathetic expression. He arched his neck for another swallow of brandy.

Griffith snatched the bottle away and seized the surgeon by his fat throat. "Patch up her skull before her brains come out all over the deck."

Thatcher nodded timidly. "Don't need to yell. I heard you. And it's not as deep as it looks." He moved to the girl and began cleaning her scalp. "Won't make promises, though."

"Patch her up," Griffith snarled, "or find yourself pitched over the fucking side."

Livingston enjoyed that thought, but would have suggested

throwing the girl over instead. Thatcher, as reprehensible as he was, had pulled his considerable weight.

A half an hour later, Livingston found Griffith resting his arms on the gunwale, staring pensively out to sea. The sun was no more and the sky had darkened prematurely due to the storm clouds that enveloped it.

The captain looked smaller than normal, with his arms tucked close and shoulders hunched, a bandage around his arm and another wrapped around his head, concealing his ravaged ear. Here was a man who, as far as Livingston had known, was incapable of bleeding. He had served with Griffith for most of his piratical career, and in all that time he had never seen the man injured. However, the first woman to be brought onboard *Harbinger* had spilled more of Griffith's blood in a matter of seconds than he had probably shed in a lifetime.

Livingston never much liked women; a disposition which had originated with his own mother. She used to shriek so loudly that his father would slap her until she stopped. Violence always seemed to shut her up eventually. As Edward entered his teenage years, his mother turned her vile shrieking on him, bemoaning his budding resemblance his father. His father gave him permission to "smart the bitch" when he so desired, instructing him with a broad grin and a wink, "If she thinks you're so much like me, show her just how much you are." It took Edward a while to get used to hitting his mother, but soon he grew to like it, and it wasn't long before he exercised his newfound power with reckless abandon.

One day, shortly after Edward had turned fifteen, he struck her so hard that she fell against a table and cracked the back of her skull. Her eyes went dull, as though what little intelligence she possessed had drizzled out of the wound. After that day, she had a terrible time stringing proper sentences together, mixing the words in odd ways. She never shrieked at Edward again, and that suited him just fine. His father congratulated him in succeeding where he had failed, and they shared many laughs as they watched her stumble about, trying to make sense of simple things.

As for his love life, Livingston had enjoyed the pleasures of countless whores, and had promptly forgotten each of them, save the most recent. So the cycle would continue until the day he died. Women were endlessly complicated creatures, and he had no desire to demystify them. So long as he found them in whorehouses, he would be content with their station in life.

Whatever madness had possessed Griffith to bring the girl aboard was beyond Livingston's comprehension. If Griffith needed a whore so badly, he could have found one in the taverns of New Providence. Was Livingston the only one who had seen the inherent danger?

"Dunno why I'm worried," he said, alerting Griffith to his presence. "With the old coat seeing to her, she's good as dead."

"I want you to take a vote on the morrow," Griffith said. "We're returning to the Caribbean."

Livingston was assailed by visions of blue skies, crystalline waters, and the plump breasts of whores. He suppressed a rush of joy, for he meant to uphold his solemnity. "Glad to know we still call votes," he muttered.

Griffith turned and regarded him with narrow, probing eyes. His raven hair tossed gently in the wind. "You're not happy."

"You figured that, eh?" he said. The faintest hint of a smile betrayed him.

"These damned clouds," Griffith said, aiming a finger at the sky. He was never very subtle at changing the subject, nor did he attempt to be. "Can't see any bloody stars."

"There's much you don't see," Livingston noted, not about

to let his friend drift from the topic at hand.

"What does that mean?" Griffith balked, caught off guard.

"That sorry excuse for a bachelor's wife," Livingston replied, shaking his head.

Griffith returned his eyes to the sea. "What about her?"

"Damn your daftness, man, have you had a glimpse at your ear lately?"

"I tried," Griffith grinned, "but my eyes stubbornly refuse to bend in that direction."

"Not the time for jests."

"I don't want a lecture."

"Neither did you want half an ear!"

"I was careless," Griffith admitted with an innocent shrug.

"Finally, you talk sense!"

"She won't live. You said it yourself. Why worry?"

Livingston lingered a moment, watching his captain gaze across the ocean, seemingly without a care in the world. The bandage around his ear said otherwise.

Thatcher had mended the girl's wound with sewing so crude that Livingston thought her lucky for having so much hair to obscure it. No one would know the scar was there unless they went digging through that wild shroud of tresses; not that she would live long enough for a scar to form.

Thatcher stood and faced Livingston, revealing blood-soaked hands. The surgeon wiped sweat from his brow, leaving a streak of red across his forehead, mottled with sweat. He looked positively appalling.

Livingston stared in awe at the wobbling fat of Thatcher's cheeks. He was dimly aware that the surgeon was talking to him, but, for the life of him, he couldn't hear words. He was entranced by every ripple of Thatcher's drooping skin. He wanted to prod him with his cutlass, as he had done to pigs when he was a boy. Thatcher's squeal would probably bring back memories.

The only three words that Livingston heard of the surgeon's analysis were, "She might live."

Livingston allowed himself a smile. "We'll see."

"Well," Thatcher suggested, "there's always the chance of infection."

"Amongst other things," Livingston noted. "It's a big ship for such a little girl."

The surgeon's gaze drifted to the girl's limp form, and for an instant Livingston thought he glimpsed the vaguest hint of compunction in that fat face. It passed quickly. "I'm done here."

Livingston pointed to the door, indicating that Thatcher was free to take his leave. The fat man lumbered out hastily, closing the door behind him.

Livingston dropped to the deck beside the girl to have a look at her pale face. She was prettier than any whore he'd ever bedded, but far too skinny for his taste. Her hair was by far her defining feature, scattered about her head in a spidery tangle. Livingston couldn't help but touch one of the strands, twirling it between thumb and forefinger.

He glimpsed her cleavage through the plunge in her dress's neckline. He placed a hand on her chest and slid it beneath the bodice, cupping one of her breasts. He squeezed sharply, causing her to stir. Her lips parted, but her eyes remained closed.

"Don't worry, girlie," he hissed. "Not near enough meat on you for my liking. Not where it counts, anyhow. I've seen more on a chicken, and I'd wager it tasted fairer."

Her right eyelid twitched. Could she hear him? He hoped so. He hoped his taunts would echo into her dreams.

"Do yourself a favor and die fast. Your life is through, one way or another. Quicker you catch on to that notion, the better."

4

THATCHER

No matter the weather, Douglas Thatcher was always hot. The pirates constantly complained of the chill of the Atlantic, but he knew nothing of it. All he knew was that they were sailing for the Caribbean, and that it would be very hot.

He gazed across the endless sea that he had once thought so beautiful. Now it was plain and dreary, and he longed for a sandy white beach, a patch of grass, or even a mound of dirt; anything solid that he could set his foot upon without sinking through. The ocean was an infinite prison, its beauty a cruel jest that taunted him like a naked woman beckoning from beyond a thick, impenetrable pane of glass. This prison needed no bars, for there was nowhere to go.

Thatcher dabbed at his wet forehead with a grimy handkerchief, the initials E.B.T. barely discernible within the filth. When his father had given it to him, the handkerchief had been white as snow, the embroidered letters shiny and gold; a parting gift to a son who had dutifully followed in his father's footsteps without quarrel. Smiles were rarely shared between them, but Douglas knew that his choice of career had not displeased his father. It was two years since last they spoke, their words polite yet brief, as always. His father had not looked well, having contracted a fierce malady from one of his patients. It was now Thatcher's eighth month aboard the pirate ship, and he was certain he would never see his father again.

Thatcher had become a surgeon in order to attend hard-working young men on accident-prone merchant vessels. A cruel twist of fate had forced him into helping murderous thieves who preyed upon innocent sailors. A collapsing yard-arm had killed *Harbinger's* previous surgeon during a severe storm. The pirates went several months without medical aid, and when they captured the British merchantman, *Jasmine*, finding a new surgeon was their first order of business.

Edward Livingston had pried a young man's fingernails off one by one with a pair of pliers until at last he divulged the identity of the ship's surgeon. After losing three nails, the unfortunate young man aimed a gnarled bloody finger at Thatcher and kept the remaining seven.

Looking back, Thatcher often wondered if the boy blamed himself, or if he had simply banished the incident from memory and moved on with his life. He hoped for the latter. He bore no ill will against the boy. How many fingernails would Thatcher have yielded before giving in? He doubted that he would have made it past the first.

Jasmine's captain, a stern man named Harrow, had done nothing to halt Thatcher's abduction. Thatcher and Harrow had exchanged nothing more than brief courtesies during the voyage, and Harrow probably saw no reason to stick his neck out for a man he hardly knew.

It wasn't long after Thatcher's conscription that *Harbinger* happened upon another unlucky vessel. Thatcher could only watch in sickened fascination as youthful American sailors were too easily recruited into a dreadful cult, as though their entire lives had escalated toward that moment.

The youngest and most promising was Nathan Adams, a bright-eyed lad with boyish good looks and a perpetual grin. He brought several of his fellows along with him, easily peer-pressuring them into joining the devil's ranks. They snickered and prodded each other like little boys who knew they were up to no good. "What would father think?" one of them had said, nudging his brother with his elbow and winking merrily.

The pirates took an instant liking to young Nathan, even Thatcher, who generally avoided socializing whenever possible. Nathan had been the first to step forward when the pirates called for volunteers. "This lad was a pirate long before he ever met one," Captain Griffith had said, slapping a beaming Nathan on the back.

Livingston kills with weapons, Thatcher mused, *Griffith kills with kindness.* The latter was far more deadly. How many promising young men had sealed their fates while trying to impress this man?

Thatcher saw his younger self in Nathan, albeit a far more dashing variation, and despite his aversion to the boy's self-appointed vocation, he exchanged cordial words with him as often as possible. While in Nathan's company, he offered subtle quips of disapproval towards piracy, hoping to plant the seeds of distrust. The boy would chuckle and nod, though he never seemed truly cognizant of the surgeon's sincerity.

Thatcher cut short his blather whenever Nathan's best friend Gregory Norrington was near. Gregory was known to repeat anything he heard. Nathan and Gregory's camaraderie was beyond Thatcher's capacity for understanding, as they were polar opposites in morals and wisdom. Gregory had a knack for opening his mouth and saying exactly the wrong thing at exactly the wrong time, while Nathan always knew exactly what or what not to say. Nathan had the uncanny ability to adapt to whatever company he found himself in.

Thatcher had not been gifted with such a talent. He was finding it increasingly difficult to mask his contempt. His destiny was no longer in his grasp. His fate belonged to a malicious people he dared not offend. It wasn't that he was frightened of death; he was terrified of tortures he would endure before death finally claimed him. These devils had recruited him under threat of such torments, and now he realized that he had accorded to the wrong bargain. At the time he had thought only of forestalling pain. *Do whatever they ask, and they won't hurt you. You wanted a life at sea, well this will have to suffice. Just do whatever they ask*

The pirates had not tortured him. They welcomed him and fed him, and some of them even thanked him when he fixed their injuries. But he was suffering nonetheless. A slow torture, far worse than any he could have imagined, was etching away at his mind and soul, bit by bit.

Lately he found himself contemplating the afterlife, which was very unlike him. One day he became obsessed with finding a Bible, frantically scouring the hold until he was exhausted. He had never bothered with religion, despite years of church-going. Even at a very young age he shared his father's passion for human anatomy, and he spent most days in church with a medical book in his lap, pretending to read scripture.

There was no Bible to be found. If God existed, he had turned his gaze from *Harbinger* long ago. God had more pressing issues to busy himself with than men who willingly chose a life of corruption and murder. These were no longer his children. They belonged to another.

Thatcher was gradually losing much of his physique as well.

The extreme temperatures that seemed evident only to him burdened his cumbersome figure. He was convinced that he had oozed thirty pounds of fat through his sweat glands alone. He had also lost much of his appetite in favor of an unquench-able thirst. The pirates worried that he would drink all their water and rum. Several of the less cordial pirates liked to gossip about his smell, loudly enough for him to hear. Thatcher was not aware of any stench, but enough pirates had commented on it that he had no choice but to take their word for it. He concluded that people had simply been polite to him his entire life. As far as most pirates were concerned, the civilities of standard society were a joke.

They reminded him daily that he was not one of them, and he was thankful for that. It would have been so easy to forget who he was, like slipping into a deep sleep, but their malice jarred him back into consciousness.

Around their fires they drank and they sang and they cursed both God and Satan, accepting neither. They swarmed over their victims' decks like oversized bees with a ravenous lust for cargo rather than honey. Rarely did Thatcher see them return without blood on their hands.

He felt more sympathy for the girl in the captain's cabin than he would ever reveal to Griffith, Livingston, or any of the crew. She hadn't the slightest inkling of the arduous journey she was about to undertake. She would cling to hope for as long as possible, against all odds, and in the end the only hope to remain would be that of a quick, merciful death.

Thatcher cursed his sympathy. He should have let her die. He should have refused to help her, suffering Griffith's wrath in order to spare the soul of an innocent. It had been a second chance. A third would be too much to ask for.

He was a slave to his cowardice. He had not saved the girl; he had merely prolonged her torture.

He cursed life and its inane desire to persist, despite all the terrors of living. He knew that none of it would matter in the end, but his phobia of pain was far more dictatorial than his grasp of logic.

He was tired of life.

He was tired of choices.

He was tired of being hot.

5

NATHAN

Nathan Adams scaled the rigging to the dizzying summit of the main topsail. One misstep would have sent him plummeting to the main deck below. If he was lucky, he might find himself tangled in the ratlines. The danger sent invigorating chills through his body. He craned his neck to take in the overcast sky. He felt close enough to reach up and draw in the clouds with a few swishes of his fingers.

A sharp wind tugged at his shirt and breeches, reminding him of his precarious perch. He made the mistake of looking down. The world spiraled beneath him. Swirling blue waters stretched for endless leagues in every direction, and the ship seemed a faraway blot in the midst of it all. For that fleeting moment he understood how small the ship was in comparison to the rest of the world. He squeezed his eyes shut and did not open them again until both nausea and enlightenment had subsided.

When his senses returned he opted to distract himself with

the task at hand: inspecting the yards for weaknesses and the main topsail for tears. His muscles were tense and his heart was racing, but a few deep breaths calmed his nerves and stilled his trembling hands.

He worked at a leisurely pace, not wanting to finish his chores too swiftly. The crew's labor had slowed considerably in the two days since the plunder of *Lady Katherine*. Tomorrow would bring the beginnings of a tedium that would not end until *Harbinger* reached her destination. The majority of Nathan's time would be spent playing cards with his American brethren. Others were generally more than happy to join in, particularly when Nathan's best friend, Gregory, was on hand. Gregory had yet to win a single game, but he boasted as though he was a force to be reckoned with. The pirates happily obliged his swagger, welcoming him to games with mock trepidation.

They weren't allowed to play for money on the ship, since money was too often the pretext for deadly quarrels. Griffith and Livingston believed that every man should leave the ship with no more or less than any other. What a man did with his wages once he set foot in port was his own business.

Nathan had been born into wealth, though he dared not relinquish that potentially controversial fact. When he arrived on *Harbinger* he was very well spoken, but he had since dulled his vernacular to blend with the crew.

He never knew his mother; she died giving birth to him. His father owned a successful ship building company and partook of the trading business. He was an overbearing man who wanted the best possible education for Nathan, no matter the cost. A professional tutor was hired to live at the house, and Nathan was forced into his studies while his father was ever away on business.

Whenever his father came home, and those times were

thankfully few and far between, Nathan would reiterate his aspiration to serve aboard a merchant ship. His father was adamantly opposed to the idea, warning of the dangers Nathan would find there. "I won't lose a son," he insisted, "to a falling yardarm, or worse still, pirates."

"I should be so lucky," was Nathan's internal reply. He had been fascinated with pirates all his life. They led injudicious lives that were a mockery of his father's strict ideals, as well as a burden on his pocketbook, due to their weekly raids of his merchant ships.

In the late days of March, Nathan took leave of his father, escaping the mansion that had become his prison. A bout of pure impulse hurtled him across town, straight for the docks, and he signed on to a merchant ship named *Getty*, where he made fast friends with Gregory and several others. The ship departed from New York and, after a week at sea, she was intercepted by a sleek brigantine.

When Nathan first glimpsed *Harbinger's* black flag, with its skewered heart, he struggled to keep a perverse grin from betraying his true joy. He couldn't believe his good fortune. The sight of the pirates sweeping aboard with their cutlasses only heightened his ecstasy. He didn't think to be frightened.

He signed what they called their "Articles of Regulation" as soon as the papers were presented to him. Several of his friends followed suit, including Gregory, who would follow him to the grave.

Captain Griffith was delighted with their enthusiasm.

Nathan's excitement did not subside. It was his sixth month of pirating, and he had yet to see the Caribbean. Since his recruitment, the ship had not strayed from the profitable trade winds of the North Atlantic. Livingston had tallied a vote that unanimously favored *Harbinger's* return to the West Indies, and the ship was presently headed in that direction.

Nathan swelled with anticipation for the legendary brothels of New Providence, which the older pirates never stopped going on about, and they weren't shy in surrendering details. At twenty years of age he was eager to conclude his virginity. The sooner he arrived in the Caribbean the better. He was a good-looking young man, and his various duties had toned his muscles. By all rights he should have romanced his share of women by now, but he hadn't seen land in as much time as he'd spent on the pirate ship, and before that he had spent most of his life bottled up in a mansion. There was only one woman aboard *Harbinger*, and that was one more than most pirate ships tolerated, and she was presently tied to the mainmast.

When Nathan finished mending the topsail, he started the long climb down the ratlines. He reached the bottom and hopped onto the main deck. He cautiously approached the mainmast, hoping for a closer look at the captive. Ropes were fastened around her ankles and wrists, allowing her only a few feet of leeway. She was sprawled on her side, and her great mess of hair was matted against the deck, as though each lock had become permanently fixed within the seams of the planking. He circled her until he could see her face, which was bright red from sunburn. Her eyes were open but staring at nothing in particular. She had thrown up all over herself, with chunks of half-digested food stuck to her chin, and her head was resting in what had spilled onto the deck.

Nathan swallowed his revulsion and ducked beside her to say, "Hello, miss. Are you alive?"

She blinked.

He reached out to slide a strand of hair away from her face. Her eyes teemed with ferocity and her lips peeled back from her teeth. He jerked his hand away before she could catch his finger in her teeth. Her jaw snapped closed with a jarring clack.

Curled fingers grasped for his face, her hands flanking his head, suspended by the ropes that bound each wrist. And then, as though released by an invisible puppeteer, her arms fell limp and she collapsed to the deck. Her eyes rolled back in their sockets, and the lids closed.

He sat there for a moment in shock. Though the bandage wrapped around the captain's head clearly concealed a grisly wound, Nathan had not believed the rumor that the girl had bitten his ear clean off. After glimpsing the animal ferocity in her eyes, he was thoroughly convinced.

"Almost got at you, didn't she?" came a condescending voice from behind him. Nathan turned to find Livingston approaching with an uncharacteristically broad grin on his face. "Now you know why the others steer clear."

It was true. The pirates had given the girl a wide berth. Whenever they climbed the mainmast, they started from the opposite side. Nathan wondered why she hadn't been placed at a less integral location.

"She's a biter, that one," Livingston said. His grin vanished as he knelt beside the girl. He grabbed a handful of her hair and twisted her head back. Her mouth dropped open and her eyes were thin slits. He felt her neck for a pulse. "I'll wager her cunny's dried up worse than a rotten prune." He released her hair, and Nathan winced at the sickening sound her head made as it smacked the deck.

"It's smart she's made herself a reputation," Livingston said as he stood. "We'll see what three more days makes of her."

That night, while the pirates were playing cards and drinking heavily on the forecastle deck, Nathan sat on the gunwale with a spare sail in his lap and an untouched bottle of rum at his feet. He set the end of his sewing needle against the leather palm that protected his hand and pressed the needle's tip through the hemp of the sail. With thumb and forefinger he plucked the needle and pulled the waxed cotton thread through to the other side.

As he idly patched the sail, his gaze fell on the lone figure at the mainmast. She hadn't moved in the last hour, and he was beginning to wonder if she was even breathing. He hadn't seen anyone make deliveries of food or water to her in the past few days. Were they just going to let her die there? A man was one thing, but this was a woman.

He had witnessed his share of creatively grotesque tortures in the past months. Such methods were generally implemented only when someone was foolish enough to withhold crucial information. It was always effective.

What was the point of inflicting such pains on a woman who had nothing to offer? Her husband had been murdered and she had been stolen from her ship. Nathan thought it completely understandable that she would fight back. It was a natural instinct, and he saw no reason to punish her for it.

He admired Captain Griffith. The man had never failed to lead them to victory. As far as Nathan was concerned, the captain's nautical strategies were nothing short of brilliant. However, he wondered how so meticulous a man could allow himself to be temporarily overwhelmed by something as simple as a girl, much less lose an ear to her.

Of course, he did not share these musings with his shipmates. Even though they might have been pondering the same issue, they would never admit it. They would either laugh at him or think him dangerous for sympathizing with a woman. As far as they were concerned, the girl was a hazard. They would be relieved when she perished.

As Nathan studied the girl for movement, a sudden howl of laughter rose from the deck. For the first time in sixth months, they disgusted him. He sprung from his seat and let the heavy

45

sail slide down his legs. He snatched up the bottle of rum and hopped down to the main deck. He uncorked the bottle and knelt beside the girl. "Hello," he said.

Her eyes blinked open. She wrinkled her brow. She looked at him for a moment before turning away.

"Are you thirsty?"

She spun on him like a waking lion. He fell on his ass and fumbled to keep from spilling the rum all over himself. He glanced about to make sure no one had seen his clumsiness. Thankfully, no one had.

The girl's eyes rapidly brimmed with desperation. "Water?" she rasped.

"The water's all gone bad," he said. "Rum is better. Keeps you warm."

He offered her the bottle, which she greedily accepted. She took a hefty swig, arching her long neck, and rum trickled down each side of her mouth. It was a while before she let the bottle part with her lips. She dropped it and muttered, "Thank you."

"It's fine," he said. "Are you hungry?"

She shook her head.

"You're sure? I might be able to scrounge some—"

She cut him off. "No!"

He winced. She rescinded instantly, attempting a grateful smile. The result was pathetically endearing. "I'm sorry," she said.

"What's your name?" he asked.

Her gaze was fixed past him, eyes widening. She turned away. Nathan glanced over his shoulder. Captain Griffith was strolling his way. Nathan stood and managed a rigid smile. "Captain."

Griffith laughed. "You're not in the King's Navy, boy. No need to go stiff. This ship is as much yours as it is mine. You should know that by now."

Nathan's shoulders sagged. He smiled sheepishly.

"You're welcome to make friends with whomever you wish. But be warned. Some choices are wiser than others."

"She was thirsty is all," Nathan explained.

"Of course," Griffith said. He gave Nathan's shoulder a pat and continued on his way.

"I brought you some cackle-fruit and hardtack," Nathan said, offering her a pewter plate with eggs and a biscuit.

The girl warily regarded the eggs. "How'd you manage those?" she asked hoarsely.

"We keep birds below. Hordes of 'em. Horrible stench. Most are dead and dying, but I picked out one of the healthier ones just for you."

She took the plate and nibbled at the eggs. He watched her, pleased that she had accepted the gift. It had been twenty-four hours since he'd last approached her. "Might I ask your name?" he hazarded.

"Katherine," she said between bites, gradually shoving larger portions in her mouth.

"Nathan," he said, extending his hand. Her eyes flashed from the plate to his hand and he instinctively jerked away.

"I won't bite you," she said. By now she was stuffing the eggs down her throat. She finished them and went next for the biscuit. She took one bite and frowned in revulsion. She dropped the biscuit and handed the plate back to him. He offered her another bottle of rum, and she swallowed a fair share.

"You're looking better," Nathan offered.

She glared at him.

"Didn't mean offense."

"Save your food next time, Nathan," she said, turning away.

"I'll be back tomorrow. And the day after. And the day after that."

"I don't want there to be a day after that," she said.

He was thankful he couldn't see her face, because he knew from her quivering tone that she was ready to cry.

"Now now," he said, setting his hand on her shoulder. He didn't even see her turn. One moment she had her back to him, and the next her face was in his. Tears streamed from narrow, red eyes, her nostrils flared, and her mouth was twisted in a vicious snarl. She could have bitten his nose off if she wanted to.

"What do you want from me, Nathan?" She growled his name like it was a curse, her croaky voice amplifying the effect. "You figure I'll spread my legs for you because you did what's expected of a common human being?"

He was dimly aware of laughter behind him.

"If you were truly a man, you'd cut these ropes." She shook the ropes for emphasis.

The laughter grew.

It seemed an eternity before he was able to find his voice again. "I can't do that, Katherine."

"Then you're nothing more than another bloody pirate. Do not bring me food again." And then, as if the statement had taken with it all the energy she had, she diminished, her scowl fading as swiftly as her temper. She turned away.

As he stood, Nathan felt heavy, as if his shoulders carried the weight of an anchor. Turning his body was like twisting a spoon in molasses. He faced the laughing crowd. Many were clutching their bellies for lack of air, faces beet red.

Nathan retreated to the cramped confines of the lower decks, fighting a bombardment of contrasting emotions. He was crushed and infuriated at the same time. His pity for the girl had potentially damaged his standing with the crew. In front of everyone, she had spit his sympathy right back in his face.

He hurled the pewter plate across the hold, followed closely by the bottle of rum. Two hens scrambled to avoid being clobbered. The plate landed harmlessly and the bottle shattered noisily. "To Hell with her!" he screamed at a hen. The animal curiously cocked its head at him.

He closed his eyes and took a few deep breaths, emptying his mind and then filling it with the happiest images he could conjure. He imagined the Caribbean in all its glory. Green islands surrounded by white beaches. He imagined a whorehouse packed to the brim with beautiful strumpets. He imagined himself in the arms of a large-breasted whore, in the privacy of her room. That was the only manner of woman a pirate need associate himself with.

Anything more was complicated.

6

KATHERINE

Blood streamed in thick rivulets from the raw abrasions that encircled her wrists. She had spent five days at the mast, and she was convinced she would not live to see the sixth. She had endured both sun and rain, each offering an array of vile anguishes.

Her face was so red from sunlight that she worried her cheeks might crack like a dry lakebed if she parted her lips beyond a thin line. Her esophagus felt like the inside of a hornet's nest. Every muscle was on fire. The slightest stir of movement pulsed excruciating pain throughout her body.

The laceration in her skull ached, and she felt lines of stitches when she ran her fingers over the wound. What little she recollected of the violent events in the cabin came to her in brief flashes. She remembered the coppery taste of blood oozing from a fleshy pulp that rolled in her mouth. For a time she couldn't recall what she had bitten off the captain's head, until one day she saw him walking the main deck with a bandage covering his ear.

Her once exquisite mantua was unsalvageable. The fabric was spotted with dark bloodstains, and the short train and petticoat ended in shreds. One of the loops of the skirt had come undone and now hung gracelessly over her right hip. The dress looked as much a mess as she did.

Apart from Nathan Adams, the pirates had avoided her. She guessed that biting off the captain's ear had established her as dangerous. However, the fear that they would surrender to their desires was always a threat in the back of her mind. She wouldn't have the energy to fend them off if they tried.

She was particularly wary of the seven black men who kept in a group. She knew when they were talking about her because they would indicatively jut their massive chins in her direction from time to time. The tall one eyed her in a strange, dubious fashion, while the others would discuss her in their native tongue and chuckle. They laughed with their shoulders; their facial muscles seemed incapable of conjuring a smile.

She hadn't suffered the slightest guilt over her treatment of young Nathan. She had no doubt that he wanted only one thing from her. She was convinced that there was not a single well-intentioned man among the entire crew.

An hour after consumption, she threw up the food he had given her, and continued to retch long after there was nothing left to purge. Either she was sick from heatstroke or the young pirate had given her spoiled food as a prank.

Sleep came infrequently and never lasted longer than an hour. She was slumped in an awkward position that rendered comfort impossible. She was constantly stirred into consciousness by the cyclical claps of the sails and the snoring of pirates, who slept wherever there was space on deck. On rare occasions when she gave to exhaustion she had unusual dreams that incorporated the strange ambience of the ship.

In one dream she was a bird, and the flapping of the sails became the sound of her wings as she soared high above the ship until she was awash in the cool currents above. The moon was full, and she decided it was as good a destination as any. With several thrusts of her great wings she propelled herself into the heavens, but the moon grew no larger. When she looked down she saw that she hadn't ascended as far as she'd thought. The ship was close, the tip of the mainmast nearly grazing her heel. She glimpsed her human form at the foot of the mast. The entire ship was on fire, and the blaze swept in on her. She woke before she was able to determine her fate.

Another night, when the pirates were especially rowdy, their howling resounded into her dreams. She found herself in the midst of the crew. They were naked and salivating, and their cocks stood erect as they fell in on her. She was swathed in the stench of their sweat-drenched bodies and the suffocating heat of foul breath as their fingers grasped at her clothes. Her mind was unable to comprehend what would happen next, and she was thrust into consciousness.

The dawn of the fifth day brought with it skies so blue that, for a fleeting moment, all of her troubles seemed insignificant. All the pain and trauma of the past several days vanished and gave to the beauty of a cerulean world above that was tangible only to creatures gifted with feathers. Her mind lifted from her body and ascended into the azure canopy. She was unaware that her eyes had rolled back in their sockets and that her muscles had loosened of tension. She was oblivious to the hustle and bustle of the pirate crew that moved about her as fervently as the ocean. There was nothing but blue sky. She rose further than even her fanciful dreams had allowed, and the sky dimmed as daylight faded swiftly into night. Shimmers of light appeared. The stars were brighter than any she had seen from the ground, and there were so many.

A sudden sting in her chest prevented her from admiring the beauty for long. She inhaled sharply and felt a stab of pain in her lungs. She took another involuntary breath, this one sweeping fire through her veins. And then her eyes flashed forward and her muscles tightened. The noises of the main deck exploded in her ears.

She was back at the mainmast.

Her peripheral vision caught the glint of something shiny. She tilted her head and saw the black-haired captain approaching with a gleaming cutlass in hand. She instantly recognized the weapon as the cutlass she had brandished against him. How appropriate that he would now kill her with it.

She closed her eyes and forged an image of Thomas in her mind. Again she thought of him on their wedding day, kissing her as they took their vows. She felt the texture of his lips on hers. She had opened her eyes just a tad to see if his were closed. His were open as well, thin slits, stealing a glimpse. She chuckled, puffing air into his mouth.

Death did not follow.

The ropes slithered apart, severed by the cutlass, and she fell onto her hands. The captain was silhouetted before the sun, features shadowed. Standing beside him was an obese man whose face was also indistinguishable. The captain nodded to the man. "Take her to my cabin and clean her up. Check her scalp and make certain there's no infection."

The stout man grunted a reply and bent down to help her to her feet. By the time she was up, the captain was gone. The large man helped her toward the cabin, and she focused on russet planking beneath her feet as she walked. Relief washed over her as she was ushered inside the darkened sanctuary, removed from view of the pirates.

"Douglas Thatcher," said the large man as he closed the door of the cabin. "Ship's surgeon." He moved past her, not making eye contact. His features slowly came into view as her eyes adapted to the dim light. "Sit on the bed."

"I'd rather not," she announced stubbornly, and was taken aback by the rasp of her voice.

"I'm sorry?" said Thatcher as he lifted a bucket of water.

"Well, that's the captain's bed, isn't it?"

"So?"

"So I'd rather not."

Thatcher brought the bucket over to her. "Sit on the deck then, though I should point out that it also belongs to Captain Griffith. As does the mast you've been tied to all this time."

"Griffith?"

"You haven't been formally introduced, I take it."

"What's his first name?" she asked offhandedly.

"You might ask him," Thatcher replied. "Now have a seat, if the bed won't do."

She sat on the deck and the surgeon knelt beside her. He parted her hair and ran a chubby finger over the seam. He mumbled something under his breath and frowned.

"What's wrong?" she said. "Is it infected?"

"No infection. You're fine." He seemed perplexed. He drew a sponge from the bucket and started for her arms, and then hesitated.

"I can do it," she insisted. She snatched the sponge away and squeezed the fluid onto a filthy arm. She scrubbed vigorously. She caught a whiff of the pungent liquid that saturated the sponge and recoiled with a frown. "What is this?"

Thatcher stood. "It's not water, if that's what you mean."

"Rum?"

"Cleans as well as anything," he shrugged.

"Barbarians," she whispered. She scrubbed at her chest, shivering as rum streamed down to her stomach.

"Well, I'll leave you to it," Thatcher muttered, clapping his chubby hands.

"I could use some clothes. I'm sure your lot has stolen many lovely garments."

Thatcher's discomfiture evaporated as he spun on his heels and proclaimed, "I have stolen nothing, madam! Do not include me in piratical activities!"

"You are a pirate, are you not?" she replied, hoping her smirk made it obvious that the question was rhetorical.

"Are *you* a pirate?" he countered.

"Don't be daft!"

"What are you then?"

She started to say, "A wife!" but realized that was no longer true. The implication of the question overwhelmed her. The one person that made her important was dead. There would be no more tea parties, no more masquerading as a woman born into wealth, no more servants to attend to her every whim, no more freedom of will. Thomas had made her someone, and now all of that was gone.

"If you're not a pirate, what are you?" she exploded in frustration, her voice breaking.

"A surgeon," he replied without the slightest hesitation.

Infuriated by his calm temperament, she aimed an accusing finger at him. "You sympathize with pirates, therefore I deduce that you, sir, are a pirate!"

He chuckled slightly. It was a sad, sardonic sound. "Is that what I am?" She wasn't sure if he had directed the question at her or himself.

When she was finished cleaning her chest, the sponge was brown with dirt. She tossed it away. "This won't do. I require a proper bath."

"Oh really? In front of a hundred pirates?"

She scoffed. "Surely you have a private bath on this ship."

"If only," he exclaimed with an extravagant roll of his eyes that was decidedly feminine.

She shook her head in disgust. "I shouldn't be surprised. I shouldn't be surprised by anything anymore."

Thatcher nodded his agreement.

"If you're not a pirate, as you claim, how did you come to be on a pirate ship?"

"Right," he said abruptly, clapping his hands again. "You can take care of the rest, then?"

"Answer my question." She studied him narrowly. "You don't resemble the others. Not physically, anyway."

"Why thank you, I think."

"Perhaps one day you'll feel inclined to share your story with me."

"Should we live that long," he quipped with a sad smile. He gave a curt nod and took his leave.

Katherine picked up the sponge and dipped it into the bucket. She hiked up her tattered skirt and scrubbed her legs until they were almost white again. She scrubbed her face as well, which drew the most dirt into the sponge, along with some crusty peels of skin. She had to rinse the sponge several times before it stopped coming away dirty. When she finished, she wasn't quite spotless, but she was a good deal cleaner than when she had started. However, now she stank of rum.

She stood and wandered around the cabin, reacquainting herself. Her sore legs were unaccustomed to walking. She felt as though she had never used them, and they wobbled like thin planks of wood. She spent a few minutes steadying herself.

She caught her distorted reflection in a bottle of wine in the captain's liquor cabinet and was shocked at the redness of the face that stared back. She tried to adjust her hair, but it was an unsalvageable greasy mess.

She walked to the painting of the brigantine behind the captain's desk. There were two hooks beneath it where the cutlasses had been. She doubted he would leave anything even remotely sharp within her immediate vicinity after what she had done to him. She also doubted that she would have the strength to try anything so rash a second time. It had nearly killed her the first time. If she failed at a second attempt, the captain would finish the job for certain.

She would have to bide her time. She wondered how long she could hold out. Time was a treacherous enemy on this ship. There were too many hazards, some of which she had already experienced firsthand and barely survived. How long before her luck ran out?

She was certain of only one thing: her crying was done. She had shed enough tears.

She stretched, her entire body shuddering, and she realized the great fatigue that gripped her muscles. She didn't want to think anymore. She'd had five days to do nothing but think and she was sick of it. Her mind was as drained as her body.

The captain's bed on the far side of the cabin was extremely inviting. She found herself drifting toward it in a daze. *I'll just have a closer look at it,* she told herself. *It's quite nice. Soft blankets. Maybe just a touch. Very soft indeed. Silk, in fact. And the pillows . . . so very soft. Mmm. I could die in them.*

She was plunging into the soft blankets and pillows before she knew what was happening. She stretched out in the warm sheets and rolled over. Her eyelids were too heavy to hold open any longer.

As Katherine rapidly drifted out of consciousness, she dimly recollected that, for some reason or another, she had meant to steer clear of the bed. For the life of her she couldn't remember why she would wish to deny herself something so comfortable.

7

GRIFFITH

Griffith's excuses for avoiding his cabin were wearing as thin as the purple hue on the western horizon. He rarely ventured out on deck after dusk, especially on cold Atlantic nights, and this was a particularly frigid night. A canvas of bright stars speckled a black and cloudless sky. The crew had grown quiet, perhaps as a result of their captain's presence, and the ship glided through gently rippled waters. A light swishing, quiet yet constant, mingled with the soft creaking of wood and the intermittent sweeping of sails.

Harbinger was slowly descending the East Coast of North America. She would hug the coast until she reached Florida, at which point she would break for the Bahamas.

At midday Griffith calculated the latitude with a quadrant. Afterward he spent a fair portion of the day studying charts that he had obtained from various merchant vessels over the years. The charts were elegant works of art, but Griffith was often frustrated by their geographical imprecision. More often than not the curves of the coast differed drastically from what the charts presented. He sometimes became so discouraged that he would rip a chart to shreds and throw the pieces into the ocean. Due to this crude process of elimination, only the most accurate remained.

After finishing with the charts, Griffith happened upon the ship's cooper. The man reiterated what Griffith already knew; the water supply was exhausted and food was dwindling. Over the past several months the barrels of provisions that had once filled much of the lower decks had gradually decreased, while booty had increased. All of the pigs and cows had been eaten and only one goat remained to provide milk. The majority of the chickens and geese had been stricken with a deadly malady. The cooper suspected that several ailing crewmen had been infected with this disease. Thus far, fourteen had taken ill. Griffith and Livingston convinced them to keep from their duties until they recovered. One man had died the day before *Harbinger* intercepted *Lady Katherine*.

After speaking with the cooper, Griffith went below decks to check on the ailing men, only to find that their conditions had worsened. If the malady didn't kill them, the lack of water and food surely would.

The problem, he grimly concluded, would work itself out naturally. He didn't like having to think this way, but years of seafaring had given him little choice. Losing crewmen to various illnesses was as natural to him as the boundless waves that the ship crested each day.

Griffith ascended from the clammy depths of the lower decks and joined the healthier members of his crew above. They were presently living off dried meat, hardtack, and eggs from the few hens that had maintained their health. He trusted that his crew would survive the journey to the West Indies. This wasn't the first time they had found themselves absent water, and it gave them a worthy excuse to glug spirits all the more recklessly.

However, Griffith was growing weary of stale biscuits and tough jerky. He would have given anything for the tender meat of a Caribbean turtle or a stout mug of ale. He didn't care for the dryness of white meat, but even a hearty breast of chicken would suffice right about now.

It was twilight when Griffith found Livingston securing a cannon that had come loose on one side. It was not unlike the quartermaster to attend to lesser duties on his own, to make certain they were "done proper." Griffith informed him of the ship's pressing need for provisions. Livingston indicated that he would pass the information to the crew on the morrow.

Griffith took his leave and wondered what more he might find to do. It had been a productive day. The work had kept his mind off Katherine Lindsay. She had tried to kill him, nearly succeeding where the most dangerous of men had failed. For the first time in his life, he was afraid. Of all the dangers in the ocean, he was afraid of a girl.

Before releasing her from the mainmast, he had removed all potential weapons from his cabin, leaving nothing for her to wield against him, though he seriously doubted she would have any strength left to try anything. And there was still a chance that she would die of her injuries.

So why was he apprehensive?

The silence of the crew, he realized. It was unnerving. Was his fear plain for all of them to see? How well did he conceal it? How long could he stay out here in the cold, with their eyes fixed on him? Perhaps Livingston was right. Perhaps he should have killed her. Perhaps he should have saved himself the trouble and just left her at the mainmast to die.

The very thought twisted his stomach in knots. He would have left a man to such a fate without a moment's hesitation or subsequent regret, and he had done so many times before, for lesser crimes than Katherine Lindsay's attempt on his life. Why was this so difficult?

He realized, suddenly, that he had never taken the life of a woman. This should have been obvious, but it was something he hadn't been required to consider until now. Men went to sea knowing the dangers inherent, and left their women on land where they belonged, sparing them a plethora of dangers. If a man died at sea, Griffith saw no tragedy in it, for he knew the risks when he set out.

A woman did not belong out here.

It was Thomas Lindsay who brought her to sea, he reminded himself. *The blame is his, and it died with him. All that remains is the frightened, wounded creature in your cabin.*

He entered the cabin with a pewter plate of jerky and hardtack in one hand and a cutlass in the other. Neither was necessary.

The girl was fast asleep, breathing heavily through a gaping mouth, her body twisted awkwardly with one arm behind her back, the other spread out across the bed, and a bent leg crossed over a straight leg. The dress she had worn since her capture was as ragged as her hair. Her skin was an angry shade of red and her lips were blistered. The hollows around her eyes were black, reminding Griffith of the dying men he had visited earlier in the day. She was a faint shadow of the beauty he had first gazed on.

He knelt beside her and watched her stomach rise and fall. Her eyes vacillated beneath twitching lids. He set the plate on the bedside table and crossed the cabin to his desk, where he fell into the chair and leaned back. He put his heels on his desk, crossing one leg over the other, and stretched his arms, interlocking his fingers behind his head.

He fell asleep before he could appreciate how exhausting

the day had been. The day's exertions carried into his dreams. He dreamed that he was still toiling with the crew, studying charts and discussing provisions.

It seemed that he dreamt for several hours before he awoke to find the cabin filled with smoke. His eyes stung. He blinked until tears lined the lids. He felt a strong pressure in his lungs, as though someone was sitting on his chest. He sprang from the chair and searched frantically for the source of the smoke. He swept through the cabin, unable to see two feet beyond the swirling haze. He stumbled several feet and bumped into a bulkhead before deciding it best to evacuate. He felt along the wall until his fingers brushed over the groove of the door.

He hesitated. He was forgetting something.

The girl!

He shook his head, damning his stupidity, and thrust himself into the smoke. He pushed through for several paces, the cabin seeming larger than he remembered. The fumes burned at his eyes, forcing the lids to squeeze shut involuntarily. When he opened them again, he saw that the bed was on fire.

He made the mistake of gasping. The sudden inhalation sucked ash into his lungs, and he crumpled to his knees in a fit of coughs. The air was cleaner below, giving him a chance to recover his breath. He spared a second glance at the bed and saw that the fire that consumed it was now spreading toward him along the deck.

He glanced around, reacquainting himself with the cabin. Once he was sure of the direction he had come, he scampered for the exit on all fours. He continued until his head slammed into a slender pair of legs. They were hard and resolute, like steel poles firmly rooted in the deck. He peered upward, scaling the legs as they curved into a pair of slender hips, glistening with sweat. He continued upward, past a naked waist, past small but firm breasts, past a slim, elegant neck, past a sharp jaw and unsmiling lips . . . until finally he met the eyes of Katherine Lindsay.

She was taller and sleeker than he remembered. Her hair was on fire and each truss writhed like a serpent. Her skin was white as ivory. Her eyes were obsidian. A terrible grin split her face, revealing a set of razor-sharp teeth.

She must have thought him pathetic on all fours, because she started to laugh. Her chest heaved with every giggle and her hair billowed until the flames touched the roof. The overhead was set alight by an outward spreading blaze that rolled over the beams like water over stones in a brook. Wooden planks cracked and popped as the flames chewed away at them.

She extended a hand, fingernails stretching into long and shiny black claws. Her awful giggles transcended her, echoing throughout the cabin and mingling with the roar of fire until it seemed that the flames themselves were laughing at him in a hellish chorus.

He beheld a tiny man entrapped within in her black eyes. Imprinted on the man's face was an expression of stark terror. Griffith was overcome with pity for the sniveling little man, and in turn saw his pity reflected in that man's face. As the fire encircled the doomed man from behind, he felt the flames lapping at his own back with claws as sharp as those that were closing over his head.

He screamed.

He woke with a start that nearly toppled him from his chair. He righted himself by dropping his feet from the desk to the deck. His boots pounded the planks too loudly, and he checked to see if he had woken the girl.

She was still asleep on the opposite side of the cabin. The bed was not on fire. The cabin was not filled with smoke. Thin trails of soft morning light spilled in through the foggy windows to highlight particles of dust.

The cabin ensnared a morning chill that was a welcome contrast to the burning fury of his nightmare. Griffith allowed himself a small chuckle at the vividness of his imagination. He had suffered hideously creative nightmares as long as he could remember, often waking in a cold sweat. Before she died when he was only six years old, he remembered his mother racing in and sitting at his bedside to calm him. She would always light a single candle before leaving, but the flickering light only made matters worse, scattering dancing shadows along the walls, forging a diversity of frightening beasts and demons.

Griffith shook his head. He gave superstition no quarter. Sleep played cruel tricks on the mind, none that had ever been realized upon waking. His crew, however, were notorious for indulging irrational fears, from multi-tentacled sea serpents to homicidal mermaids that spirited a man to the bottom of the sea and feasted on him whole, starting with his cock.

The familiar sound of feet pummeling the main deck seeped into the cabin. It was a soothing sound that told him everything was all right. The world had not ended while he slept. His ship had not been claimed by a fiery demon.

He stood from his chair and stretched with a great yawn. He didn't feel as rested as usual and his back ached from the uncomfortable angle at which he had settled into the chair. He rubbed his eyes for a good long while until he was certain the lids would remain parted.

He shuffled toward the bed. The plate of food on the bedside table remained untouched. The girl hadn't shifted an inch since the previous night. He checked to make sure her stomach was still moving. It was.

He went to his wardrobe and changed into a fresh pair of clothes. He had a difficult time removing his shirt, for it clung to his skin. When he turned the garment over he discovered that the entire backside was soaked with sweat.

For a larger man, the windingly narrow pathways between barrels and crates would have been impossible to navigate. The hold was the most expansive space below decks, but the cramped cargo made it seem claustrophobic.

It was an ugly place. A square beam of the sun's morning light seeped in via the open hatch; an impenetrable white glare untainted by the surrounding gloom of the shadowy wooden interior. The air was a putrid mélange of rotting wood, tarred hemp, gunpowder, spirits, and animals both living and dead. For Griffith, the smell signified achievement. He thought not of the hold's stench, but of the luscious aroma of vegetables on his future plantation; a future to be purchased with the treasures and goods he stacked here.

He continued along the slim path until he came to a brown chest that had been plundered from *Lady Katherine*. The chest was the length of a human body, resembling a coffin, and was carved with an intricate floral pattern. He hefted the lid. It arched with a *creak*. Several neatly folded London dresses were stacked within. He plucked the topmost dress and spread it out before him. The satin was colored a bright cherry pink that he imagined would match Katherine Lindsay's hair. He refolded the garb, though not as neatly as it had been folded when he had discovered it. He unfolded it and tried again, with less success. He sighed and gave it one last try, and was marginally satisfied with the results. He decided it would have to do and tucked the dress under his arm. He gathered a few more dresses from the stack, careful to keep them folded, and closed the chest's lid.

On his way out he saw a sack filled with kitchenware. He emptied the bag of its contents and stuffed the dresses inside, not wanting the crew to spy him bearing such potentially controversial items.

Griffith hurried back to his cabin. He knew very little of feminine ways, but he had heard that material possessions, such as expensive dresses, were chief among their priorities. The girl would delight in discovering that she had not been parted from her wardrobe.

It was commonly known to any pirate worth his salt that a woman married not for love of the man, but for love of his riches. Griffith was certain that Thomas Lindsay had made a respectable fortune from his business as a merchant shipper, but he doubted that Lindsay would have seen in a lifetime what *Harbinger* acquired from a month's plunder.

In the girl's mind, her husband's untimely death was undoubtedly a tragedy. She had probably developed a natural affection for the man out of sheer familiarity. This accounted for her irrational assault on Griffith. He was willing to forgive her for that; clearly she had been out of her mind at the time. Her five-day spell at the mainmast would cause her to think twice before she made any further attempts on his life.

It would take time to liberate the ties to her husband, but Griffith was confident that he was up to the task. *Harbinger* would do half of the job for him. It was a new environment and a new life. Thomas Lindsay was not a part of it. She would either concede to that fact or perish in her defiance. Griffith hoped for the former, but he would be forced to grant the latter if given no other option.

The choice was Katherine Lindsay's.

She was still sleeping like a baby when he arrived with the dresses. He was starting to wonder if she would ever rouse. Perhaps the cutlass's damage had run deeper than her thick skull. Griffith recalled an unfortunate accident involving one of his crewmen. The man had survived a harrowing plummet from a mast, suffering what appeared to be nothing more than a minor head injury, only to fall asleep that night and never open his eyes again. Yet still he breathed, lost in slumber. It was a month before the crew unanimously decided to put him out of his misery and give him to the sea.

Griffith turned the sack on its end and shook it, depositing the dresses onto the end of the bed by Katherine's feet. He spared her a final glance and hurried out of the cabin.

He found Thatcher curled over the gunwale, retching. The surgeon's massive belly contracted, and the pale contents of his stomach burst from his mouth. Griffith plugged his nose. The stench of Thatcher's vomit was infamously nauseating. The crew often jested that one whiff could kill a man faster than any poison. "You'll foul the ocean with all that sick," Griffith said.

"I can't help it," Thatcher replied, wiping his mouth and catching his breath. "It keeps happening."

"You're the doctor. Surprised you haven't figured it out on your own."

"I have figured it out," Thatcher declared. "I'm not meant to be on this ship!"

Griffith chuckled with a dismissive wave of his hand. "Belay that noise, Thatcher. If men were meant to be here, we wouldn't need to build ships."

"What a truly astonishing observation," Thatcher exclaimed sarcastically. "I feel better already."

"It's not my concern what you feel, so long as you're well enough to perform your duties. I've come to ask you to look on the girl. Do you think you can fit that betwixt your daily purging?"

Thatcher embellished a sigh. "What's ails her now?"

"A bout of sleep that's persisted since before noon yesterday, far as my knowledge."

The surgeon looked at him like he was crazy. "That's all?"

"That's not a long time?"

"All things considered? No."

Griffith brought his face close to Thatcher's, a mistake he instantly regretted when he glimpsed slimy chunks of half-digested meat stuck to those bulbous chins. He managed not to flinch. "You speak truth, Thatcher?"

The surgeon diverted his eyes, blinking copiously. "Why would I lie?"

"It escapes me," Griffith admitted. "But that doesn't mean you wouldn't. Sometimes men do things I don't understand. My lack of comprehension doesn't prevent these things from happening."

Thatcher smirked. "Do you comprehend even your own actions?"

"You refer to the girl."

"Very astute," Thatcher drawled.

Griffith let out a small breath of air that might have been a laugh. "I find myself . . . attached."

"That's not out of the ordinary, captain. She's a woman. And I'd wager that she was an attractive one before she was despoiled."

"She hasn't been despoiled."

"No?"

"No."

"Yet you worry for her health? Tell me, have you even shared words with this woman?"

Griffith feared he had revealed too much. He did not want Thatcher thinking him a romantic. "The girl is a possession. Like a monkey . . . or something of that sort."

"She's not a monkey," Thatcher stated flatly.

"I know that, of course," Griffith said, rolling his eyes. "Nevertheless, I would be most unhappy in the event of her untimely departure."

"When I was nine, my cat ran away."

Griffith withered. Thatcher was obviously not taking him seriously. It was time to spell it out for him. "It is no secret that you dislike your post here, Thatcher.

"My *post*?" Thatcher laughed bitterly. "Is that what you call this?"

"However," Griffith continued, unabated, "should my latest possession perish in her sleep, I may start to question your abilities."

Thatcher's face went a furious shade of red. He aimed a challenging glare at Griffith. "I still cherish the value of human life, if that's what you're getting at. Someone on this ship must."

"Good," Griffith said, impressed with the surgeon's sudden resolve.

Thatcher maintained his gaze a fraction of a second longer, before his eyes fluttered back to the sea. "Your pet won't die in her sleep, captain. Nor has she anywhere to run."

Katherine Lindsay woke three days later.

Griffith was leaning forward in his chair with a tattered chart spread across his desk. Over the past few years it had proven to be the most valuable of his charts, eluding the watery grave that several other charts had been sentenced to after proving less than useful. His left arm rested on the Atlantic and his right covered North America as he scanned the East Coast for a suitable place to moor *Harbinger* and gather food.

Before he could mark any prospective locations, the girl moaned. Griffith perked up like a cat becoming suddenly aware of a bird. It was the first sound he had heard from her since freeing her from the mainmast.

His farsighted vision was blurred due to staring at the chart for so long, and it took him a moment to focus on the bed. He vaguely made out her slender figure as she twisted beneath the sheets that she had pulled over herself at some point. She kicked the covers away, and with them tumbled the dresses that Griffith had set there. Her arm flopped out to one side, hand slapping down on the plate of food. She rolled over until she was flat on her belly. She slid the plate onto the bed and buried her face in it, gobbling the dried meat and hardtack. It was a repulsive display that Griffith might have expected from the likes of Thatcher. He assured himself that she was simply famished and that this was not the standard propriety of a British woman.

He slowly lifted to his feet, though he was uncertain how to proceed. She provided the answer for him when she sat up and hurled the plate across the cabin with near the velocity of a cannonball. He ducked. The whirling plate split the air inches above his head, bouncing off the door behind him and crashing to the deck with noisy fanfare.

"Bring me decent food, pirate!" she ordered in a husky voice. "Not this waterless muck!"

"Anything else, my dear?" he quipped.

"Yes! A sword that I might plunge into your stomach!"

"Should you find the means, you're welcome to try again."

"You've removed all means," she protested, indicatively flinging an arm toward the empty hooks below the painting of the brigantine.

"Surely you don't hold common sense against me," he laughed. "Self-preservation is chief among my priorities."

"That is the very least of which I hold against you," she said, her eyes glazing with tears. "Exactly how long do you intend to keep me on this ship?"

He could think of no reply that wouldn't be met with bile. He opted instead for a change of subject. "I put some dresses from your wardrobe on the bed, though you seem to have kicked them off. I hope they aren't terribly wrinkled."

"I don't want them!" she snapped.

He felt as if a fist had been driven into his gut. He had been certain that the dresses would ease her pain, yet she dismissed them with not even a glance. Was there no pleasing her? She was fortunate to be alive, let alone possess such splendorous garments. She should have been thanking him, not hurling plates and insults at him. And for what? A fool of a husband who had carried her into a lion's den?

He swallowed his disappointment and adopted a pleasant smile. "You look to have recovered nicely, Mrs. Lindsay."

A fleeting look of shock betrayed her. She immediately suppressed it and regained her composure. "You learned my surname from my husband before you murdered him!" She choked on the last three words, tears spilling over.

Griffith suddenly wanted to be anywhere on the ship other than his cabin. He needed an excuse to escape and collect his thoughts.

"I want to go home," she moaned, her voice failing her.

"You must be thirsty. I'll fetch some water." He made for the exit.

But he halted at the door, realizing that he had left his pistol on his desk, beside the chart. He hastily returned to the desk and picked up the weapon by the barrel. He flipped it once in the air and caught the grip, then stuck it in his sash.

As he started to leave, he realized he hadn't given his name. "I'm Captain Jonathan Griffith."

"I don't care what your name is," she sobbed. "I will not relinquish mine."

"I don't require it, Katherine."

This time she didn't bother to restrain her surprise. Her eyes widened into saucers and her lips quivered. Her defensive wall crumbled to pieces before him, and he knew then that this delicate creature was not the fiery demon of his nightmare. "How do you know my name?"

"Your husband provided it," Griffith said, and closed the door behind him.

The cool breeze that met him on the main deck coursed a bracing chill along his spine and straightened the hair on his arms. "Any problem can be fixed into a plan," he reminded himself.

8

NATHAN

From the forecastle deck, Nathan stretched his gaze past the bowsprit to the world he had once called home.

Harbinger was moored in a secluded estuary somewhere between Chesapeake Bay and Cape Hatteras, and boats were being readied for transport to the sandy shore. Nathan hadn't set foot on land in six months. He couldn't remember what standing on a motionless surface felt like. He worried that his ill-adjusted legs would falter and he would fall on his ass and all around him would share a laugh at his expense.

He remained emotionally sore from his humiliation at the mainmast, and the crew did nothing to ease his lament. He had endured a barrage of persecutions from their malevolent tongues. He opted to keep to his American brethren, who were far more understanding.

He spent much of his free time conjuring vindictive plots against the unappreciative girl. He wanted to make a fool of her in front of everyone, as she had done with him. But all his plots, from drenching her in pig's blood to stripping her naked, required that she be temporarily removed from Griffith. He doubted that he would ever manage to get her away from him. She hadn't been spotted outside of the captain's cabin since being released from the mainmast. Due to her residence there, the crew no longer frequented the cabin.

Even Captain Griffith seemed to be spending less time in the cabin. The crew's curiosity was irrevocably sparked. Nathan did not yet fancy himself the height of knowledge in piratical affairs, but common sense told him that a crew should not discuss their captain in hushed tones.

No good had come of this woman. Nathan's life as a pirate had been wholly uncomplicated before her arrival, and now he was as uncertain of himself as he was of the weather. Therefore, it was of little surprise that he took such immense pleasure from the incident that followed.

Katherine Lindsay, dressed in a cherry pink gown, burst from the cabin. Griffith was not far behind. She was putting up quite a fuss about being placed in a small boat with "brutish pirates."

Griffith slapped her in the face in an attempt to quiet her vociferous shrieking. This only made matters worse. She started slapping back, and he had to seize both of her arms to subdue her. He then dragged her to the bulwark, lifted her up, and shoved her over the edge. Nathan's perspective denied him view of her impact, but the sickening sound her body made when she hit the water confirmed that she had landed at an awkward angle, and brought an irrepressible grin of satisfaction to his young face.

Griffith turned to his crew and innocently shrugged his shoulders. "Well that's one way to get a woman off your ship."

"That's the *only* way," said Jack Billings.

"I thought five days at the mainmast dried the lass out,"

quipped Bald Ben. "Griff got her wet in five seconds!"

"Alright, alright," Griffith said, suppressing the ensuing laughter. "Get those floats in the water so I don't have to chase the wench too far up shore."

There was another bout of laughter, and then they resumed their duties. Nathan was the only one who saw Griffith cast an uneasy glance over the side to make sure he hadn't killed the girl.

The boat's keel slid into the soft sands of the beach. Griffith was up and over the rail before it stopped moving, snatching up one of the oars and bounding across the beach in pursuit of Lindsay, who hadn't made much headway. She had stripped off her cumbersome dress and was now wearing only a white underdress.

The swim had taken its toll on the girl. Griffith caught up to her with ease. He greeted her with the oar, bringing it down on her back with a sickening crack. Nathan clacked his teeth at the sound. He wanted her humiliated, but he didn't care to see a woman physically abused. She collapsed face-first into the sand and didn't move. Griffith took her by the arm and dragged her away from the tide and deposited her in a shady spot under a tree.

Nathan leapt into the water and immediately shivered from the icy chill that greeted his thin legs. Several of the men in the boat followed Nathan's lead and recoiled in much the same fashion. Livingston, on the other hand, was undaunted by the cold. He dunked his legs and pushed past the trembling crewmen, knocking one of them headfirst into the water on his way. "Has your cock never touched water?" he said, shaking his head in disgust.

Griffith returned to the boat, handed the oar to Livingston, and clapped sand from his hands, as though nothing had happened. He tossed the oar to one of the pirates and said, "Send the float back for another handful of men."

Two crewmen pushed the boat out into the water, hopped in, and started rowing for *Harbinger*. It returned with the ship's carpenter, a crusty seaman with a missing eye, poised with one foot on the rail and his arm splayed across a raised knee. He had instructed everyone in no uncertain terms to call him "One-Eyed Henry." The crew gleefully obliged his request.

"Oh Jesus," Livingston muttered under his breath, and spat on the beach for emphasis. The quartermaster despised any man whose inflated ego threatened to dwarf his own.

One-Eyed Henry leapt from his perch and landed with a tremendous splash. He then single-handedly hefted the boat, passengers and all, onto shore with a heave of his monstrous arms.

"That's a bloody beautiful display, mate," Livingston said to the carpenter.

"Aye," One-Eyed Henry replied. "Where be the food?"

"Haven't looked as yet."

"Well let's get to it then, eh?"

"We was figuring," Livingston said condescendingly, "we might set up camp and wait till the others make their way over 'fore we run off."

"That's not what I was figuring," One-Eyed Henry huffed. "Me belly's hungry now, isn't it?"

"I might help you with that," Livingston offered with a widespread grin and a light tap of his cutlass.

"You might try," One-Eyed Henry grinned.

Several months ago Nathan would have edged away from them, fully expecting a deadly brawl to ensue. But he knew that these two men often engaged in challenging displays of character that rarely served the benefit of either, and never gave to violence. Griffith was always on hand to step between them.

While violence was otherwise unlikely, Livingston and One-Eyed Henry were wasting precious time.

"Reassured that we all have balls, gents?" the captain quipped.

Livingston glanced indicatively at the unconscious girl in the shade. "Not so reassured, captain."

"Cap'n might agree," One-Eyed Henry chuckled, "if the fiercely lass hadn't fancied a taste o' his ear. I wager there's a bit o' man in her yet."

"Not till she's had a taste of me," Livingston declared.

Everyone laughed, even One-Eyed Henry, but Nathan wasn't convinced the quartermaster was joking. Livingston smirked, stubbornly refusing to yield his vicious gaze from the carpenter. For an instant, Nathan could have sworn he saw a hint of uncertainty in Henry's eye. For all his bravado, he feared Livingston, as did they all.

Griffith cleared his throat as nonchalantly as possible. "What say we get on about our business?"

Livingston broke his stare, ending the minor confrontation, and the men returned to their duties, which presently involved erecting tents.

Daylight was fading fast by the time the tents were up, and a strong wind glanced off the icy waters to sweep a wicked chill over the beach.

Three quarters of the crew stayed aboard the ship; the rest moved to the beach, where they would spend the night after a hunt. Their mouths watered at the prospect of a large dinner, and hunting parties were formed prematurely, instead of waiting until dawn as originally planned. Dozens of men gathered water into barrels from the river inlet while several groups went in search of food.

Nathan paired with Gregory, and Livingston led them. The

two young men followed blindly as the quartermaster plunged them deeper and deeper into the unfamiliar territory, using his cutlass to slice through wayward branches that threatened to slice their cheeks and prod their eyes.

Nathan arched his neck and glimpsed the darkening sky through the dense cover of trees. He wondered how they could possibly hunt in the night. It would have been better to wait on empty stomachs until morning. There was no sign of wildlife, other than birds that made their presence known through a wide variety of exotic calls.

The quartermaster remained quiet and, as a result, Nathan and Gregory were careful not to disturb him with conversation of their own. Finally, after what felt like an hour, Livingston said, "I've not seen a forest this thick since Annie Sutherland's cunny!"

"Who?" Nathan asked.

The young pirate instantly regretted his inquiry. Livingston was notorious for boasting about past sexual experiences to hapless crewmen who made the mistake of offering even a feeble interest. It was a testament to Nathan's poker face that he kept his eyes from rolling at what followed. "She be the last whore what I spoiled. A fine wench she were, but she's not seen another man since, I'll wager me life on that."

"Why's that?" Nathan pressed, knowing he had no choice now but to feign interest.

"Name a man bigger," Livingston proclaimed, seizing his crotch, "if you think you can find one, and I'll point him in her direction, so as she don't go lonely. I can't be retracing me steps on the likes of sentimentality, can I?"

"Of course not," Nathan replied easily, though he did not understand nor care to.

"Course not," Livingston nodded with wide-eyed sincerity. "That's a waste of everyone's time; worst of all mine! And wasting time is worse a crime than taking a woman to sea. What's your make of that?"

"The captain?" Gregory said suddenly, as though he'd been waiting for the opportunity to offer his feelings on the issue. Nathan shot him a sniping glare.

"Not the captain, boy!" Livingston shouted. "Plainly you're not listening to a word I'm saying. Better you should let your friend talk for you, as usual. What madness possesses you to bring up the captain?"

"No reason," Gregory shrugged innocuously.

Livingston halted, turned, and brought his face dauntingly close to young Gregory's. "That be a fucking lie if I ever heard one. Give us the true reason."

Gregory's bottom lip quivered.

"It's on everyone's mind, isn't it?" said Livingston. "Don't be afraid to unveil your woes, boy! We're all alone out here."

Nathan made his movements as natural as possible as he slowly drifted behind Livingston. He waited until Gregory looked at him and then put a hushing finger to his mouth. Livingston caught Gregory's glance and swiveled his head with near the agility and speed of a parrot. "What's that you're doing back there, young Nathan? Giving your friend some silent words? Well belay that! I'm only making certain he hasn't quarrel with our dear captain."

Gregory's face went pale.

"Of course that's not it," Nathan interjected, chuckling dismissively.

Livingston scowled at Gregory. "That true, boy?"

Gregory's reply was a silent, frenetic nod.

"Well that's good," Livingston sighed. "You had me worried I'd have to settle things meself out here in the middle of no-where whilst no one was watching."

"The crew might wonder why we came back with one less,"

Nathan offered. He instantly regretted saying it.

Livingston whirled on him. "I could say whatever I damn well fancied! I could say a big cat dragged him off, and they might gasp. I could say a flock of birds pecked him to death, and they might laugh. Or I could say I did him meself, with this cutlass. And mark me, no one would say a fucking word to that."

With that, Livingston turned and continued along the path. Nathan followed, moving ahead of Gregory so he wouldn't have to look at his fool of a friend. He hoped Gregory felt bad for having placed them both in a dangerous position, but he doubted he was smart enough to comprehend what he'd done. A man never spoke ill of his captain, pirate or no, unless he was prepared to back his words with the might of the crew.

As they trekked toward wherever the quartermaster was taking them, Nathan's anger at Gregory's idiocy subsided, and his perplexity with Livingston's sudden resolve heightened. He went over the conversation in his head again. He recalled Livingston's offhanded remark on the crime of bringing a woman aboard a ship. Livingston's choice of words seemed strange to Nathan now that he thought back on it. "Wasting time is worse a crime than taking a woman to sea," he had said. "What's your make of that?"

Nathan shook his head, quickly rejecting the silly notion. Nathan did not consider Livingston crafty enough to execute a deft segue as a means of uncovering gossip. His comment had simply been an offhanded reference to Thomas Lindsay.

"This looks pretty," Livingston said, interrupting Nathan's thoughts. Nathan looked up, and his breath caught in his throat.

They had arrived at an expansive clearing lined with wood fences. The clearing lifted at the center, atop which sat a marvelous white house, and beside it a less spectacular farmhouse. Horses and cows grazed freely about the plantation.

"Bloody cows," Livingston groaned. "Hope they've got something smaller. I'm not dragging one of those all the way back to the beach."

"Pigs and some birds maybe," Gregory suggested.

"I'll wager everything we need be inside that farmhouse. We'll take what we can and send another party back."

As Nathan looked up at the massive house, an inexplicable foreboding seeped into the pit of his stomach.

The black of night provided the only cover they needed as they climbed the hill toward the house, which was situated between them and the farmhouse. When they reached the house they ducked low to avoid the windows. There was only one light within, and Nathan couldn't resist a quick peak. A woman sat in the living room reading a book by candlelight. She wore a white nightgown that dipped low from the neck, and her skin was gorgeously accentuated by the soft orange glow. Her blonde hair, which was bound tightly to her head, was golden in the light. She looked more like a painting than a living, breathing person, but the slow heave of her bosom proved that she was indeed real.

Nathan only managed a glimpse of her, but that would be enough to sear the image in his mind for the rest of his days. She tilted her head slightly in his direction, her eyes lifting from the book to the window. Just then, Livingston grasped his collar and pulled him down.

"What did you see?" Livingston demanded in a high-pitched whisper.

"Only a woman."

"Did she see you?"

"No. I don't think so."

Livingston aimed a reproachful finger at his face. "Don't do that again."

"Aye."

They continued toward the farmhouse, slipping past the front door. Nathan's thoughts were lingering on the vision of the woman in the house when suddenly the door burst open and a man in his bedclothes emerged with a musket. Nathan and Gregory scattered in two separate directions.

Livingston thrust himself at the man, smashing into his stomach. The pair of them went tumbling into the house. Nathan struggled to his feet as the two men noisily thrashed about inside. The woman screamed.

Nathan glanced around. Gregory was cowering in a batch of flowers, proving no use to anyone. Nathan focused on the door, took a deep breath, and charged inside.

Before he made it in, a musket blast sounded, brightening the interior of the house like a contained bolt of lightning. Another glimpse, far shorter than the first, and a second image was forever seared in young Nathan's mind.

The three pirates returned to the beach dragging behind them sacks packed with the carcasses of pigs and chickens, and a single sack filled with vegetables and fruits. Wood was gathered and fires were struck. The pigs and chickens were tenderly roasted and the vegetables were boiled. The splendid aroma carried into the night along soft trails of orange-hued smoke.

Many of the pirates that remained aboard *Harbinger* boated to shore to partake of the merriment, bringing with them the two musicians (one talented with a fiddle and another not so talented with a recorder), a singer, and three blacks. The singer sang songs from a Dutch prayer book and the blacks danced around a central bonfire as the meat cooked. The beach came alive, and no one gazing on that celebration could have easily dismissed the men that took part in it as barbarous scoundrels.

However, Nathan Adams took no joy in the festivities. He had departed the beach with an empty stomach and returned with an abundance of food that he would not partake of. There was blood on the animals they had brought back, and not just the blood of the carcasses themselves.

He closed his eyes and saw a beautiful woman screaming as her husband's brains were splattered all over her white nightgown. The husband had yielded his life in a heartbeat, knowing nothing more of the world's troubles, but his wife would remain forever deprived of him. In the flurry of seconds that ended with his death, the man hadn't the time to consider his fate. She had a lifetime to contemplate hers.

Nathan blamed himself, suspecting that the woman had spied him at the window and alerted her husband. Livingston concurred with this speculation, allowing Nathan's guilt no relief, though Livingston was not nearly so distressed by the incident. He was more concerned that the bloodstains on his shirt were not likely to come out after a wash.

Nathan gathered his troubled thoughts and went for a stroll along the beach. As he walked, he passed the Seven, who were seated around their own personal barbecue, far removed from the celebration. They looked at Nathan. He nodded a greeting. They did not surrender their fierce glares, and he was forced to look away. He felt their eyes on his back as he continued along the beach.

It was not by intention that Nathan strolled to Katherine Lindsay's little camp. Far from the festivities he found her outside her tent by a small fire with a plate of chicken and potatoes, which he assumed Griffith had brought for her.

"If it's your captain you're looking for—" she started.

Nathan held up a hand. "No. It's not that."

"Well what then?" she demanded impatiently. Her raspy voice was wincingly unattractive. "I'm not what you would call a conversationalist."

"So you say," Nathan smiled, "yet you play at large words."

"All words are large words where pirates are concerned."

"I have a name, you know."

"On a flier somewhere, just above a reward for your capture."

He grinned, unfazed by the slight. "In very, very small print *below* the reward, mayhap. I'm not of much import, I'm afraid. A pirate only dreams of that kind of fame."

"So you enjoy all this plundering and murder?"

"I haven't murdered anybody," he protested.

"Tell me, pirate, what part of the ship do you maintain?"

He frowned. *What on Earth is this woman getting at?*

"I saw you," she explained, "very high up on a mast. Quite hazardously, I might add. You were fixing the sails."

He was getting impatient. "I was *mending* the sails, yes. What of it?"

"And mending the sails consequences a fast ship, does it not?"

"That is the general goal," he drawled.

"Which in turn leads said ship to its destination."

"That would follow."

"Which led you to the plunder of my ship and the murder of my husband!" Her face flushed red as tears welled in her eyes, but she did not surrender her hardened glare.

He looked away. "I did not kill your husband."

"No," she sighed. "You simply repair the sails that led murderous heathens to his ship. It doesn't really matter who killed him. He is dead just the same and nothing can change that."

He nodded solemnly. There was nothing to say that would make her feel better or make her words any less true.

"Did you, by chance, give your captain my name?" she asked suddenly.

"It hasn't come up."

Her watery eyes narrowed. "You are sure?"

"Absolutely certain," he said, though he honestly couldn't recall whether he had or not.

"I see," she said, and her head dipped low. "Please go. I do not relish the company of pirates."

Eager to oblige, Nathan nodded and started off, but stopped in his tracks when he saw three pirates staggering his way, passing a bottle of rum between them and giggling like little girls. They were mumbling things like, "Cap'n won't care if we have a go," and "Can't blame me, it be the rum," and so on.

Nathan glanced back at Katherine, who was wallowing in her tears and in no condition to notice anything beyond her own self-pity.

"Hello," said the tallest of the approaching pirates. He was lean and muscular, with long, stringy black hair, a square-jaw, a broad nose, and a protruding brow. His face was caked in dirt, lips badly chapped, and cheeks rosy with sunburn. He may have been twenty-five, but his lack of hygiene made it difficult to tell. Nathan did not know the man's name. "Be this your guard, boy?" His pronunciation of "boy" made it sound more like "bye." The pirates' accents were often a blend of various inflections, the final product being as muddled as their appearances.

Nathan swallowed. "Aye. Captain Griffith wanted me to watch over the lady for the duration of his absence."

The tall pirate raised an eyebrow, and the two shorter men snickered to each other. The tall pirate gave Nathan's shoulder a nudge. "What be your name, mate?"

"Nathan."

"Nayton!" the tall man announced and held out his massive arms for an embrace. Nathan kept his distance. The tall man waved the potential offense away with false modesty. "I be Magellan."

"Magellan?" Nathan stifled an urge to laugh and ask the man's real name.

Magellan's congeniality faded. "Right then, let's get right to it."

"And what exactly would you be getting right to?" Nathan wondered.

"We are all of us entitled to our shares of treasure, Nayton," Magellan proclaimed, and he pointed at Katherine. "Including that shiny piece of tail right there."

"Captain Griffith won't have that!" Nathan said, stepping closer. The shorter men repeated Nathan's protest in a mocking tone, and then burst into giggles. "You're drunk. You've misplaced your wits and I suggest you recover them."

"Thought we might find them here," Magellan said.

Nathan smiled. "I surely would have seen them. Be off."

Magellan screwed up his face. "I didn't hear that?"

"Have you misplaced your ears as well?"

"I don't think me boys be listenin' to their ears, if you take my meaning." Magellan snapped his fingers, and the shorter men flanked Nathan, seizing him by the shoulders and giggling uncontrollably. Magellan loomed over Katherine. She looked very small beneath him.

"What's this then?" said Griffith as he came sprinting up the beach.

The giggling men instantly released Nathan and backed away. Magellan turned, maintaining a smug expression where his companions had relinquished theirs. "Well hello, Cap'n."

"Is this what I think it is?" Griffith said, catching his breath.

"That depends on what you think it is, Cap'n."

Griffith's hand fell to his cutlass. "You've had too much to drink, mates. Let's return to the fires and I'll make certain you have plenty more."

"That's a fine gesture, Cap'n, but not what I be needing." Magellan smiled and tapped his cutlass. An agonizingly long and uncomfortable silence followed, during which the two men stared at each other with narrow eyes as Nathan, Katherine, and the other two pirates, who were no longer giggling, glanced anxiously from man to man.

The silence was finally broken when Livingston appeared. "Keep your hands from them cutlasses, the both of you. What be this? A quarrel and no one tells me?"

"Doesn't need to be a quarrel," Griffith said.

"Aye," Magellan agreed, smiling suggestively.

"Hold on!" Livingston interjected. "What the bloody hell are you talking about? Of course it needs to be a quarrel! Without quarrel, I'd question the necessity of me job. I'll have this done proper. We wait till morning so as everyone can see, per the usual rules."

"Not till we settle the terms," Magellan said.

Livingston threw his hands in the air. "Terms? A thousand hells! Name your bloody terms."

"I get a go with the girl after I kill the Cap'n."

Griffith shrugged. "If you kill me, she's all yours, though it's certain you'll be in for a few surprises once you have her. She bites."

The tall man grinned. "I'll cover me ears."

Griffith smirked. "That's not all she bites, I'm sure."

"At least I have the guts to find out."

"It's set then," Livingston happily decided, clapping his hands. "Tomorrow morning."

Magellan smiled politely at Griffith and started on his way back to the celebration. The shorter men followed after him, glancing over their shoulders. When they were a good distance away, they broke into another fit of giggles.

Griffith smiled reassuringly to Katherine. "He won't kill me."

She shrugged. "Shame."

Livingston spat in disgust. "You'll die for this bitch?"

"I won't die," Griffith replied. "You know that."

"Aye, I know that. I was talking to Nathan."

Nathan looked up. "Me?"

"Never come between a pirate and his prey," Livingston cautioned. "That man would have killed you."

Nathan looked at Katherine. Her eyes flickered toward him, and her lips vaguely curved into what might have been the hint of a smile.

"You did the right thing," Griffith said. He gave a nod of thanks before starting back up the beach. Livingston followed after him, sparing Nathan with a disapproving scowl.

"I hope he loses," Katherine muttered under her breath.

"It's in your best interests that he doesn't," Nathan replied.

She laughed bitterly. "My interests are no longer my own."

The next morning, the duel was the first order of business, and Nathan made certain that he had a place in the frontlines of the crowd.

Every pirate that had traveled to shore the night before now gathered round as Livingston informed the two participants of the regulations, though neither man needed any introduction. The quartermaster handed them their pistols and allowed them a moment to inspect their weapons. Magellan scrutinized his thoroughly, squeezing one eye shut and peering down the muzzle, checking the trigger and hammer, and finally nodding his approval.

Griffith didn't spare his weapon with as much as a glance. Livingston positioned the two men with their backs to one another and instructed each to walk ten paces, turn, and discharge his weapon. The quartermaster then took a step back and shouted, "Go!"

The crowd held a collective breath as the two men steadily paced away from each other, neither seeming the slightest bit nervous. At ten paces they spun and aimed. Griffith's gun discharged with an ear-shattering crack, billowing white smoke. Magellan's pistol exploded in his hand, snapping out of his grasp and spiraling away. He yelped pitifully.

Griffith drew his cutlass and lunged forward, growling like an animal. Magellan took notice and raised his damaged hand in protest. When that failed to stop Griffith's charge, he went for his cutlass. Before he could pry it free of the sheath, Griffith was on him with his sword raised high. Magellan's high-pitched shriek ended abruptly as the blade parted his head from his neck.

"I believe it's six hundred pieces of eight for a severed right arm," Griffith yelled to the crowd. "Shame we never figured compensation for the head." He kicked the decapitated head to the oncoming tide, blooding spurting from the neck in a morbid spiral.

The crowd's cheer was deafening.

9

KATHERINE

Katherine watched through a foggy window in the captain's cabin as the shore tapered to a thin line, barely distinguishable along the horizon. Her journey had brought her to America as promised, though not in the company she would have liked, and now she was being whisked away from the New World just as swiftly as she had arrived. The experience was far too ephemeral for her to derive any lasting impressions.

She left the window and moved to the bed, soreness echoing throughout her limbs. The ache wasn't entirely unpleasant. Her muscles felt taut, as though she had never used them to their full potential.

She propped herself upright on the mattress and crossed her legs under her petticoat, which spread out around her in a circle. She smoothed the ravaged skirt and plucked at loose strands of thread. Fancy dresses had no place on a pirate ship. If she continued at this rate, she would literally tear through her wardrobe in less than a month.

She examined her chest, noting that her skin had darkened to a fetching shade of copper, though there were still tinges of red here and there. She assumed that her face had taken on the same tone.

The wounds on her wrists were closing nicely, but they would leave scars. Her head no longer ached from the blow to her scalp, and the lesion seemed to be healing properly. She was thankful that the ghastly wound was cloaked by her thick hair.

The huskiness in her voice shocked her whenever she spoke, and she wasn't sure when, if ever, it would return to its original clarity. The water that the pirates had gathered from the estuary was a welcome change from rum, and it soothed her sore throat.

Her back throbbed where Griffith had stricken her with the oar, but that was a mere sting after hearing him utter her name. For the past several days her mind reeled over every conceivable possibility. The most horrible option she considered first and discarded swiftly thereafter; she would not entertain the notion that Thomas, her adoring husband, had surrendered her to this band of murderous thieves. Still, she had been puzzled from the beginning by Griffith's apparent knowledge of her hiding place prior to uncovering her. She recalled with a shudder the terrible moment he entered the cabin, and his deliberate footsteps toward the bed. Either this pirate was a remarkably deductive man, or he had been alerted to her hiding place beforehand. Neither accounted for him knowing her name. The ship was, of course, named *Lady Katherine*, but it had yet to be branded.

Inevitably, this process of thought led back to her beloved Thomas. She remembered him conversing reasonably with the pirate captain. Surely he would not have spoken of his wife, as there was no reason for him to do so.

Her mind raced forward, feverishly scrolling through the blur of events that had transpired since her capture. Prior to speaking with the captain, she had only talked with one man: Nathan Adams. She had foolishly exchanged names with him, and of this she questioned him on the beach, but he denied giving her name to the captain. She didn't believe him. He seemed a nice enough boy, but she reminded herself that he was a pirate, and lies came as naturally to a pirate as bad breath.

She sat in bed for a long while, wondering what she might do to distract these lingering contemplations. Based on the steep angle of the sun shining through the open windows, she guessed it was early afternoon. When her legs started to numb she crawled from the bed and paced round the cabin. Thanks to her time aboard *Lady Katherine*, she was no stranger to dawdling. She gradually made her way to the captain's desk and dropped into the chair.

A map of the West Indies was spread across the desk. She spent the remaining hours of daylight studying the map. She put her index finger to the east coast of Florida and slid it south, between Florida and the Bahamas. From there she curved westward and journeyed through the Straits of Florida. She trailed her finger over Havana and curved southward to hug the western corner of Cuba. She continued southeast along the Yucatan Channel and then passed beneath the Cayman Islands. She arrived on the southern side of Jamaica, halting to regard Port Royal.

She recalled a story she had heard in Lloyd's Coffee House on Lombard Street. She had accompanied Thomas there while he was on business. The proprietor of the coffeehouse, Edward Lloyd, published a shipping news for his patrons, and thus attracted many patrons of maritime interest. It was there that Katherine met a charismatic old-timer who told her a tale so biblical in proportion that she was inclined to disbelieve it, until Thomas confirmed it to be true. The old-timer claimed to have viewed the devastation firsthand, to which Thomas responded with a wry smirk, for it was unlikely. Port Royal, said the old-timer, was a bustling English colony that embraced piratical activity due to the profits it incurred. The governor wisely invited pirates to use the port as an unofficial base, thus sheltering the harbor with a fleet of dangerous ships that warded off Spanish and French attacks. Shopkeepers and merchants grew fat from the plunder that pirates brought them. In 1692 this errant prosperity came to a bloody end, seemingly by the hand of God Himself. A violent earthquake triggered a massive tidal wave that nearly swallowed the entire town, ending the lives of more than four thousand citizens.

Katherine presently paid her respects to the small blotch of ink that was Port Royal and started southeast. She set out across the expansively vacant Caribbean Sea, traveling what she approximated to be two hundred leagues before coming to Curacao. She curved her finger northeast from there, grazing the Windward Islands, and tilted sharply to the west to sail beneath Puerto Rico. She passed under Hispaniola and neared Port Royal once again as she rode the Jamaica Channel into the northeastern slant of the Windward Passage. At the exit of the passage she turned northwest and continued until she reached the island of New Providence in the Bahamas.

Nassau was the second name she recognized from memory. She'd heard many of the pirates speak this name with bated breath, and she guessed it was *Harbinger's* ultimate destination. However, unlike Port Royal, she knew little of Nassau.

She would have continued studying the map if not for the dimming light. Nevertheless, by time she was done, she had fashioned a near flawless mental picture of each island's name, location, and port. When finally she looked across the cabin, anything beyond three feet was blurred by her closely-focused vision. She blinked until it cleared.

The door swung open. Griffith entered with a candle that flooded the cabin with its dusky orange radiance. Katherine suppressed an urge to spring from the chair. She forced a nonchalant expression.

"Appointed yourself captain already, have you?" he said. When she didn't laugh, he gestured to the chart. "It's the Caribbean."

"I can read," she replied flatly. She had her elbows on the chart, chin resting atop interlocked fingers.

"Naturally." He lit candles around the cabin and moved to the liquor cabinet. "I thought we might share some wine."

"Thinking doesn't become you."

"Really? And what *does* become me?"

"Murder."

He opened the cabinet and produced a bottle of red wine. "I approach with great anticipation the day we end these pointless banters."

She started to her feet. He motioned for her to stay in the chair. He uncorked the bottle of wine and tilted its long neck her way. She curtly shook her head. He shrugged and threw back his neck for a hefty swig. She glanced at the polished cutlass dangling from his belt. When he finished, he offered her the bottle a second time.

"Perhaps just a sip."

He grinned and handed her the bottle. She arched her neck and pursed her lips to prevent any wine from seeping through, but the taste was so sweet on her lips that she couldn't help but part them just a little. The wine was delicious, but she allowed no more than a few droplets to spill onto her tongue.

An hour later, she was engaged in rapturous mirth with the pirate captain. They passed the bottle back and forth, and she lost count of how many intended sips had become mammoth gulps.

"You weren't meaning to take any," Griffith said between swigs.

"Not at all!" she shouted, thinking for no particular reason that she couldn't be heard unless she pitched her voice at deafening decibels. "In fact, I was meaning to get you perfectly drunk before stealing away your cutlass and," she burst into cackling laughter, "and impaling you right through your heart. Assuming you have one."

The spasms in his stomach nearly knocked Griffith from the desk.

"I'm serious!" she said, feigning offense.

"I believe you," he replied, indicating his mauled ear.

Her chest heaved as she broke into a fresh set of giggles. "I can't believe I did that."

"Well, the evidence is plain for all to see, save for me. And what I cannot see must not exist so long as I ignore all evidence to the contrary."

"I should have done worse."

"And you may yet get the chance."

She frowned vacantly. The cabin contorted. She felt as though she was moving in slow motion. The bobbing of the ship and all the creaks and groans that came with it took on a sluggish, somber quality. Rising clearly amidst this slow chaos, a single question formed. "Why?"

"Why what?"

"Why am I on this ship?"

He shrugged. "You're beautiful."

"So I've been told," she whispered, with a distant, cynical smile.

"You don't believe it?"

"If there's one thing that has been made abundantly clear

over the course of my life, it's that it doesn't matter what I believe."

"Katherine," he said, "you must be delirious not to see it."

"Perhaps it's the world that suffers delirium."

"No doubt it does," he conceded. "But I know beauty when I see it."

She stood up too quickly. Her head felt like a dead weight on her shoulders. She swayed dumbly, struggling to gather her solemnity. "And you steal whatever catches your fancy?"

"I would make a very poor pirate if I did not."

"Your plunder must not include people!" she protested, and nearly toppled in the process. She thrust out a foot to regain her balance.

"Where else might I have found my crew? Those blacks you see on deck, they were slaves, Katherine. Now they live free lives."

"How lovely for them," she scoffed. "What of my life? What of my husband's life? You murdered him!"

He stood and circled the desk, moving uncomfortably close. "Your husband betrayed you."

"Never!"

"The coward surrendered his wife to me to save his own skin. He disgusted me and I killed him for it."

"You lie!" she said, tears spilling over.

His drunken gaze narrowed. "I enjoyed killing him."

"I don't believe you."

He touched her cheek. "Then why do you cry?" She pulled away and faced the opposite direction. "You know it's true, Katherine. Tell me, how else would I know your name unless your husband provided it?"

She faced him, eyes red and watery but no less fierce. "I gave my name to one of your crew and *he* told you, not my husband. Please end this charade."

He blinked. "I knew nothing of this. With whom did you speak?"

"What does it matter?" she sneered. "Your senses are impaired. You won't remember any of this come sunrise."

"Likewise," he grinned. He turned to retrieve the bottle of wine. "We pirates sustain our spirits better than we let on."

She pounced while his back was to her. She grasped the hilt of his cutlass and slid it free of the sheath. He turned a disbelieving gaze on her. She pointed the tip of the blade to his throat and cocked her head with a jubilant grin. "I wonder how well you will sustain your spirits as they drain from your neck."

He regained his composure and managed a smile. "You're welcome to kill me, but what then?"

"That really doesn't concern you."

"I think you're bluffing. Kill me and you'll incur the wrath of one-hundred vengeful pirates."

She pressed the point into his neck, a tiny bubble of blood forming on the tip of the blade. "You think highly of yourself. Perhaps they'll appoint me captain."

"Maybe." He elevated his chin. "Perhaps they'll fuck you to death."

"You think that scares me now?"

"Yes," he said.

She knew he was right, but she wouldn't let him see it. She would throw herself over the side before allowing the crew to get at her.

"I think you're bluffing," he said.

"Perhaps I am. Perhaps I won't kill you. Perhaps I'll just take another piece of you as I did your ear. Perhaps I'll remove that piece that worries me most."

Flickering candlelight glimmered in the tiny beads of sweat clinging to his forehead. "You've nothing to fear."

"No?" She glanced indicatively at his crotch. "Why not?

Does it not work?"

"It works, last I looked," he replied tersely.

"Then why shouldn't I be afraid? I am so very beautiful, remember?" She gave the hilt a slight nudge, and the bubble of blood popped, trickling down his neck. "That wasn't a lie, was it?"

He lowered his chin and looked into her eyes. The sword faltered a notch. He pulled back suddenly and slapped the blade away from his throat, barreling into her and pinning her against the bulkhead. He seized the hand that held the cutlass and smashed it against the bulkhead until her knuckles bled and her fingers opened. The weapon fell. He hissed hot breath onto her cheeks through clenched teeth. "What must I do to end this hostility?"

"It will take more than wine."

"Clearly," he nodded. He released his hold on her and went to retrieve the cutlass. He wiped the blade clean of his blood and returned it to the sheath. He looked at Katherine, his face lost behind a mesh of raven black hair. "Damn your fiery blood, girl. You know nothing of the world and even less of the sea. How is it that your poor dead rich husband came to so fine a business? On the backs of the poor, under the cover of law! No such law fosters me, and so I must be a villain. I cared naught for merchant squabs whose sails I mended without so much as a nod of gratitude. Instead they offered me the heels of their boots dug firmly into my spine, and they did worse to the others. What was I to do? Let them kill me and the boys who served alongside me? No! I fought back, and the crew fought at my side. They needed only the inclination. We took their swords and with those swords we took their lives. I felt nary a weight on my conscious, for they were naught but dogs."

His eyes drifted past the wooden barriers of the cabin to

glimpse some distant, dreadful memory. "Alas, it was not enough that we give their bodies to the sea. Undeserving were they of so rich a burial."

Katherine released the breath she didn't realize she'd been holding in. She pressed her back against the bulkhead, silently praying that the boundaries of reality would give way and that she would be thrust magically through the hull, away from this nightmare and into the sea. "You ate them?" she said, not bothering to subdue the trembling in her voice.

"We're not animals, Katherine. We cooked them first."

10

LIVINGSTON

Livingston closed his eyes and permitted himself a smile as the warm breeze caressed his face and washed over his scalp. When he reopened them, he knew he was not dreaming.

It seemed an eternity since the last time he looked on New Providence. The sun's shimmering reflection danced on the crystalline waters from a cloudless sapphire sky. Nassau harbor brimmed with over four hundred pirate ships that altogether formed a floating brown city. Livingston took pride in the fact that *Harbinger* stood out as one of the larger, more attractive vessels. The majority were rundown sloops and schooners with torn sails and sloppy decks. Several ships were careened near the shore, tilted at sharp angles with the crew scattered along the exposed sides of the hulls, scrubbing away.

The long, natural harbor carved between New Providence and Hog Island allowed for two possible entry points and doubled the escape routes. It was unlikely that a warship large enough to pose a threat could enter the shallow harbor without her keel running aground.

A thin contour of blinding white sand separated the shoal waters from the infinitely lush island. The grand settlement that lined the harbor denoted a merging of ships and land. The taverns and the stores and the homes were little more than dirty shacks wrought of wayward planks and roofed with palm fronds, in addition to tents erected with spars shabbily covered by old sails. The colony gave off a natural kind of amphibious beauty.

The jungle that shrouded the island paradise encased the odd, makeshift structures that otherwise might have appeared unsightly. Many of the buildings assimilated the jungle into their architecture, with palm trees cutting through their roofs.

The only unnatural blemish of industrialization was a run-down fort that stood on a hill outside of town. Livingston chuckled to himself as he recalled a persistent rumor about a hermit named Sawney who was squatting at the fort. He had yet to see the old man for himself.

Livingston sensed the crew gathering behind him. Most of them had been to Nassau the year prior, but the colony had expanded dramatically since that time, both in structures on land and ships in the harbor.

Harbinger's voyage had been uneventful since her departure from America, consisting of nothing more than lollygagging and nightly celebrations on the main deck. The provisions they had acquired on the mainland had been greedily consumed to near exhaustion. Their bloated bellies did little to ease the communal depression that swept the deck. It was Livingston's job to read the thoughts of his crew. He knew that the recent surge in celebration was the result of unquenchable boredom.

Harbinger satisfied their every desire except one, and the fierce Katherine Lindsay was not an option. The last man to make an attempt on her had lost his head, and deservedly so.

The crew happily obliged Griffith's murderous action. As long as he brought them good luck, he could kill or fuck whomever he pleased. As far as they were concerned, Katherine Lindsay was off limits. Not a thread of gossip escaped Livingston's ears, yet he had heard no complaints directed at Griffith. So long as *Harbinger* continued her victorious streak, Griffith would remain their entrusted captain.

Still, their loins had been aching with the promise of New Providence and the pleasures they would find in the taverns and brothels. They'd been at sea for far too long. They had packed the hold to the brim, and they were eager to spend everything they had earned. As Livingston looked on the bustling community, he knew that the crew's desires would be well met and their pockets completely emptied by the end of the vacation. They would return to sea happier and poorer than when they left, and so the cycle would continue until their luck ran out.

There was no sign of Nathan Adams. Livingston had glimpsed very little of the boy since leaving the East Coast. He hadn't seen him socializing with his American brethren or climbing aloft, as he so loved to do.

He couldn't help but feel partially responsible for the boy. Livingston was not a social man, and he did not consider Nathan a friend. There was only one man aboard *Harbinger* that he allotted that honor, and that was Jonathan Griffith. However, Nathan was different. Livingston had no sons that he knew of, but he liked to think he had infected the West Indies with at least a few dozen bastards. He liked to think that his offspring would resemble Nathan in spirit, graced with insurmountable ambition.

But Nathan's ambition was stably faltering. He knew the boy was lamenting the events that had taken place on the mainland. Nathan had seen his share of violence in his time aboard *Harbinger* and had seemingly brushed it off like water from a duck's back. So why was the lattermost event so disturbing? Perhaps this boy wasn't the pirate Livingston had hoped he was. There was no place for loners on a ship, where every man depended on the other. Livingston prayed that Nathan would end this selfish phase as soon as the leisurely pace concluded.

Livingston shook his head, aggravated that his brooding prevented him from enjoying the full splendor of the island before him. Normally, this sight would be enough to steal all his worries, on those rare occasions when he actually worried.

When he realized that his nerves would afford him little comfort, he pulled himself away from the glorious view and descended below decks, where he found Nathan between two crates, playing with a chicken.

"The ship's in no peril, I trust?" Nathan said curtly, as if to indicate that his duties were not required.

Livingston shook his head.

"Then what's your business?"

"The resolve of every man on this ship be my business."

"I'm fine," Nathan replied halfheartedly. He ran his fingers through his mop of sandy hair.

"A fine liar," Livingston scoffed.

Nathan blinked.

Livingston kicked the chicken out of his way and kneeled beside the lad. "I know what you're about, boy. I weren't always an old coat, and I had my share of fury to sort through. My hair was just as full as yours, 'fore it slid off me noggin."

Nathan's involuntary smile brought Livingston immense satisfaction. He swallowed the perplexing emotion almost as swiftly as Nathan censored his smile. An uncomfortable silence followed, and it might have sustained an eternity if not for a diplomatic squawk from the chicken.

Livingston grunted as he rose to his feet. "Are you really too stubborn to partake of Nassau's many pleasures?"

Nathan's head perked up involuntarily. He attempted to mask his excitement, but Livingston was already grinning, knowing he had the boy's undivided attention.

"Stick by me, lad," said the quartermaster, "and you'll know the finer points of the finest port merging sea and land."

11

GRIFFITH

Griffith strolled through the jungle bazaar as pirates auctioned their plundered goods to voracious traders. The street, if the sandy pathway could be called that, was packed with pirates of every shape, size, and color. Sordid merchants offered every manner of outlandish goods, and the roar of their haggling was deafening. Blacksmiths sold swords and axes, some of them fine, others shoddy, depending on the dealer. Several women dotted the crowd, examining dresses that varied greatly in cultural fashion.

Griffith had but one item in mind as he perused the bazaar: a pet for Katherine Lindsay. She had insisted on accompanying him to the colony, and he might have granted her request had he not spied a certain desperation in her eyes. He assured her of the futility of an escape attempt. This was a pirate colony, and there were worse sorts she might fall in with. Her only hope for a steady income would be through prostitution. She was quick to retract her request.

She had been uncharacteristically submissive since Griffith claimed that he and his crew had resorted to cannibalism in overthrowing their former superiors. It was sheer nonsense, of course, and he'd shared a good laugh with Livingston about it. He could not deny that he had thoroughly enjoyed the little ruse. He would reveal the truth in time, but he needed her to remain submissive, locked safely away in his cabin.

Wearing away at Lindsay was a delicate process that would take time. A gift was in order, but what to get her? Eventually he came to a tattered advertisement posted to a palm tree, flapping in the wind:

Parrot from Vera Cruz

Very pretty and yellow and red
Biggest bird of the West Indies
Well educated and good humoured
Talks English, French, and Spanish
Visit Sams shop for more
Don't fancy birds? Buy a monkey for cheap

Griffith didn't care for parrots and monkeys. Loudmouthed birds were as cantankerous as the worst of any pirate crew, and rarely did they offer true companionship. And his one experience with a monkey didn't end well; he doubted an animal that used its own feces as a projectile would win the girl's affections.

Before he could find a local pet shop and resolve the matter, he happened upon a tavern that he did not recognize from his previous trip. It was one of the larger and more organized structures of the colony, two stories tall. The sign outside said SASSY SALLY'S. A marvelous whiff of turtle meat was enough to divert Griffith's intended course.

He cut across the street, pushing through a crowd of pirates, and ducked through the low entrance into the tavern. Despite the bright midday sun, the tavern was dark inside. Thin traces of light seeped in through hemp-draped windows and creases in the less-than-competently-fitted planks that made the walls. Decorations were mishmashes of whatever useless trinkets the owners had acquired in their travels, ranging from shark jaws to exotic bottles to rusty cutlasses.

The ambience was restricted to low banter between pirates, most of them seated in pairs, some of them keeping to themselves, all of them drinking. Homely whores were diligently pawing at the loners, who offered barely audible protests.

Griffith made his way through the clutter of long tables to the bar and snapped his fingers to get the attention of a portly cook. "Is that green turtle soup I smell?" The cook grunted a reply and disappeared into the kitchen. He returned with a large bowl of soup and grudgingly thrust it at Griffith, nearly spilling the precious green contents. "And a bottle of brandy, if you'd be so kind," Griffith added with a smile.

With his meal and drink in hand, Griffith very carefully stepped up the perilous circular staircase to the second floor, which had rooms on one side and a balcony on the other, open to the sunlight. Griffith walked out onto the balcony and took a seat at a small table near the railing, where he was provided an unobscured view of the colony and harbor.

Along the beach several well-tanned children ran and played, oblivious to their seedy surroundings. Two of them pursued a scruffy dog that was more than happy to retreat into the water. The children were the consequences of reckless nights between pirates and whores, and they rarely knew their fathers. Griffith wondered if any of these brats were spawned of his crew.

He absentmindedly took a sip of soup as he watched the children, thinking on his own future offspring. The glorious flavor of the sherry-laced broth was enough to distract his brooding. It was the finest green turtle soup he'd ever tasted, and he savored every sip, nearly forgetting the brandy. When he remembered his thirst, he grabbed the bottle and attempted to pry off the cork. It didn't budge, so he placed the bottle's neck at the edge of the balcony railing, drew his cutlass and struck off the top, which spun into the air and arced downward to strike a hapless pirate on the crown his head. The pirates occupying the balcony broke into tumultuous fits of laughter. The hapless pirate glared upward, but could not discern the culprit amid so many laughing men. He grumbled a curse and continued on his path. Griffith tipped the bottle in a toast to the laughing pirates and threw back his head for a hefty gulp.

A heavy hand slapped his shoulder. "Jonathan Griffith, is it?" said a deep voice.

Griffith grasped the pommel of his cutlass. "Who's that?" he said, tilting his head.

Jack Cunningham grinned down at him. "Already causing a ruckus, I see," the larger man quipped.

"Damn your blood, Cunningham! I had half a mind to slice you in two!" Griffith stood. The two men shook hands and gave each other hearty pats on the back.

"It's lucky I'm still standing," Cunningham taunted, "seeing as you never had more than half." And then he frowned. "And your ear isn't in much fairer shape. What a bloody mess!"

"An accident. Take a seat." Griffith kicked out a chair.

Cunningham was a tall fellow with massive bone structure. He was not the sort of pirate with whom anyone picked a fight. He had a scraggly blonde beard and curly blonde hair, all of which enshrouded his red face. He wore only black, with pistols painted the same color.

Griffith had first made Cunningham's acquaintance at the wayward port of Tortuga, and the two became fast friends after bemoaning the woes of civilized society and the contrasting joys of piracy. Shortly thereafter, they joined forces and pillaged the Spanish Main for many successful plunders, until they went their separate ways. Their parting had not been either man's desire. They were bound by the democracies of their respective crews. Cunningham's crew voted to travel south, while Griffith's voted to travel north, to the Atlantic.

"I trust you've seen more success than me," Cunningham said, glancing at the harbor.

Griffith smiled. "I don't wish to provoke your jealousy."

Cunningham shook his head in disgust. "Fools! Did I not tell them that the Atlantic was the proper route?"

"Indeed you did," Griffith nodded.

"I need a new crew," Cunningham sighed. "They'll damn me to the depths if I don't quit myself of them. They're a gay lot, but not a brain among them. Forged as a whole, perhaps a quarter of a brain, if that's not too generous an estimate."

Griffith nodded to the harbor with his chin. "I don't see Jennings' ship, though I might have missed it amid all the others."

"He's gone on the account. I've little doubt he'll return with wealth beyond my wildest dreams."

Griffith offered his brandy. Cunningham shook his head. Griffith nudged the bottle closer and jiggled it. Cunningham broke into a smile and accepted the drink. He took a big swallow.

"This place has become huge," Griffith said, looking over the colony.

"It won't last."

"How's that?"

"Word has it England is growing tired of constant reports. Providence is set betwixt two major shipping lanes, eastward and westward, hence its import. How long do you think they'll allow us to persist in our occupation?"

Griffith laughed. "Let's see them fit one of their warships in that harbor without her keel grinding her to a halt."

"What makes you think they'll only send one?"

"They won't spare two warships on a ruddy little island in the Bahamas. They've got better things to do, and far greater worries, mark my words."

Cunningham took another gulp of brandy. He wiped his mouth on his sleeve and handed the bottle back to Griffith. "I wonder if someone once said the same of Port Royal."

Griffith stirred his spoon in what remained of his turtle soup. "A different situation, what with the earthquake. Bad luck, it was."

"Aye," nodded Cunningham. "Everyone has their share of luck to contend with. Most of it bad. Rumor has it they're sending us a governor."

"Then I place great pity upon that man, whoever he may be."

"Woodes Rogers is the name on everyone's tongues."

Griffith allowed himself a small chuckle. "I've read his book. You know the one? Found it on a British merchantman. The man is little more than a glorified pirate, and not much of a writer."

"Never happened across the book," Cunningham said. "Wouldn't read it even if I did. We've already got a governor, you know. Ol' Sawney in his fort."

"I'm amazed he's not dead," Griffith said, happy for a change in subject. Sawney was always good for a laugh.

"Very much alive, in fact."

"Where's he find his food?"

"A couple of Porter's men saw him fishing a while back. They took note of his fishing pole, which I'm told is finely crafted, and ran after him to steal it. Old man ran off on his skinny legs faster than any rabbit and they never caught up to him. He climbed a boulder and yelled his triumph down at them. They're calling him Governor Sawney now. Crazy old coat mistook their sarcasm for sincerity and now he fancies himself the true governor. Imagine that! He came out of his fort last week and took to the streets, proclaiming new laws to banish pirates. Called us an infestation. Never struck the old man who he was preaching to. I sent some of my boys after him, but he's so damned fast that they couldn't catch him either. Not so sure anyone would kill him if they ever managed to catch him. I think everyone likes him, in a way." A shadow passed over Cunningham's face. "Well, maybe not Thatch. Or Teach. Whatever his name is. Not sure he likes anybody, not even his own mother."

Griffith straightened his back. "Edward Teach?"

"Aye," Cunningham nodded slowly. "I met the man once. He made attempt to impress me by drinking rum spiced with gunpowder, after setting it ablaze. Shame he didn't blow himself up. He's a repulsive man, and his beard is indeed very black."

"I've heard he sets it on fire," Griffith said.

"I've heard that as well. Hard to believe. If true, it must scare the living hell out of his victims."

"I'd imagine so."

"I don't usually give to gossip," Cunningham said, inclining his head, "but he might have sliced up one of the whores at a brothel not far down the street. One of my crew saw him there. Teach accompanied the lass upstairs and came down shortly after. They found the girl in her room. They say the floor was flooded with two inches of her blood." Cunningham shook his head, staring off into the ocean. "It's the sea that does these things to men. No other explanation for it. Happened to one of my boys. He went off one day and took his cutlass to my boatswain, Harkins. You remember Harkins?"

"Aye," Griffith said. "He's dead?"

"The dog cut him to ribbons. Just hacked away until you wouldn't know what Harkins looked like if you were judging by his face. Never seen anything like it, and I don't care to ever see anything like it again. We marooned the dog on an island and didn't bother to give him a pistol to do himself in with. Figured the best revenge was to let the elements take him. Normally I wouldn't do something so vicious, but it was the crew's will. I can't say I didn't take a small bit of pleasure in it, ashamed as I am to admit it."

"No sense feeling bad for that." Griffith lifted the bottle for another sip of brandy and was surprised by its lightness. He peered inside to find it empty. He frowned and set the bottle aside.

He looked to the beach. A single child remained, making a sand castle. The boy seemed perfectly content by himself, without the company of his friends.

"So simple for them," Cunningham said, his gaze fixed on the same boy. "Not a worry in the world."

"I'm close, Jack," Griffith heard himself say.

"Close to death, maybe."

"Could be," Griffith shrugged. "It's worth the risk."

"I'm not so sure," Cunningham replied, still watching the boy.

"I feel it on the horizon."

"Of course you feel it, Jon. We've all felt it. That's why we're out here slaughtering innocents, and not just them, but ourselves. How many of your crew have died? I can't recall, personally. Can you?"

"Men die," Griffith said, keeping his frustration in check. Cunningham had always lacked vision. "Whether it be by my hand or another, men will always die. There are no innocents at sea."

"Does that make you feel better?"

"I feel nothing. It's not a justification, only a simple truth."

"Your truths conveniently relieve your guilt."

"I have no guilt," Griffith said. "You mistake me for you."

"I mistake you for a human being."

Griffith stood abruptly and adjusted his shirt. He had grown weary of this conversation. "I *am* close, Jack. Closer than I've ever been. When next we meet, I will have that which is mine."

Cunningham offered an infuriating smirk. "Then go, Jon, and take that which is not yet yours."

12

KATHERINE

It was late in the afternoon when Griffith returned. He opened the door just long enough to drop a kitten inside, and without another word he slammed the door closed. A moment later, a timid pirate entered carrying a little wooden box of sand. She instructed him to put it in the corner.

The gift might have touched her heart had it been presented by any other man, and with any degree of ceremony. The animal proved an immediate aggravation when it squatted in the wrong corner and did its business. The rancid stench was unbearable, and the kitten spent a long time scratching around the mess. "You little idiot," Katherine scolded. She pointed to the sandbox. "The sand is over there."

The kitten was a tortoise shell; a trio of colors that belongs only to females, dominated by black fur and mottled with orange and creamy highlights. Her massive round eyes were stretched wide at the lids. She meowed incessantly as she scampered about the cabin with her head tucked low to the ground. She would occasionally glance up at Katherine and sniff the air with a bobbing nose, and then continue to explore.

When Katherine grew tired of the little animal's pointless yet methodical trekking, she said, "I'm not giving you any food, if that's what you're searching for."

The kitten looked at her with those stupid round eyes and screeched a reply.

"What?"

Another meow, this one louder and longer.

"I don't have any food for you."

The kitten darted forward. Katherine backed away as the furry thing bounded toward her with startling velocity. She instinctively thrust out her foot and kicked the kitten sharply in the ribs. The animal went somersaulting halfway across the cabin.

Katherine instantly suffered a pang of guilt. She rushed over and dropped to her knees. The kitten sprang to its feet and started to bolt, but Katherine seized it by the waist. The kitten warbled a protest as Katherine lifted it into her lap. "I'm so sorry, little one," she said.

The kitten put up a large fuss for so tiny a thing, with surprisingly powerful little muscles beneath her furry exterior. Katherine inferred from the animal's fierce struggle that it was not badly injured. After a while, the kitten stopped fighting her embrace and settled into her lap. It started to purr.

The door opened and Thatcher stepped in. "Hello, Miss," he said with an awkward smile.

She smiled back. "How can I help you, Douglas?"

He seemed astonished that she hadn't forgotten his name, and it seemed to take him a moment to remember his purpose for entering. "The captain wishes me to look on the beast. Seeing as I'm no veterinarian, I protested loudly. To no avail, as always." He gestured to the kitten. "I see you're acquainted."

"Feisty little creature," she said, smiling faintly. "I acted dreadfully toward her and I'm making amends."

"She doesn't appear to be holding a grudge," he remarked. "Have you thought of a name?"

Katherine frowned. "Far too early for that. I'm not entirely certain I'll be keeping her."

Thatcher chuckled. "Whatever you say."

He kneeled beside her and took a closer look. He was sweating terribly, even at this late hour, and his stench dwarfed the kitten's droppings in the corner. Nevertheless, Katherine was grateful for his company. She took Thatcher for a kinder, gentler pirate, and thus far he'd given her no reason to think otherwise. In fact, the portly surgeon didn't seem much of a pirate at all. All of the pirates aboard *Harbinger* were lean and chiseled, and Thatcher was neither.

"Right," Thatcher said, "let's have a look at her."

Katherine hesitated. The kitten was fast asleep in her arms and she was afraid to wake her.

"Something amiss?" Thatcher asked.

Katherine giggled at her capricious emotions and shoved the kitten into the surgeon's arms. The animal woke up as Thatcher examined it. He set the kitten on the deck and watched as she wobbled around on clumsy paws.

"Yes," Thatcher nodded conclusively. "This is indeed a cat."

For the first time since before her capture, she bubbled with laughter. Thatcher must have thought her insane. "I'm sorry," she said, wiping water out of her eyes.

"It's quite alright," he replied. "Actually, it's a nice sound."

The kitten rubbed up against her leg. Katherine scooped her up and clutched her to her breast. She looked at Thatcher, who was watching her intently. His eyes fluttered nervously away. "Why aren't you on shore with the others?" she wondered.

He let out a puff of air that sounded like the popping of a balloon. "They fear I'd attempt an escape and deprive them of their surgeon. I haven't a clue where I might go on a pirate island. In fact, that's the one place I can think of that's worse than this ship."

"You're here against your will?"

He hesitated. "No."

She sensed that he didn't want to talk about it. She fought an urge to persist. "I've been in this cabin for too long," she sighed. "I would love to get outside."

"Then now's your chance," he said as he stood. "Captain Griffith has left for shore, and there are naught but a few men in the decks below, last I looked."

It wasn't until well after nightfall that she mustered the nerve to venture outside. She peeked through a crease in the door to make sure no pirates roamed the deck. When she was satisfied the coast was clear, she carefully opened the door, so that it wouldn't creak, and stepped out into the warm Bahaman night air.

She shuffled warily past the mainmast, regarding it with a respectful eye. The anguish of the days she had spent there returned to her, the memory manifesting physically throughout her body. She shuddered and forced herself to turn away.

As she looked at the pirate colony, she forgot the ordeal at the mainmast as swiftly as she had recalled it. The view from the main deck was breathtakingly panoramic, as opposed to the blurry impression she had derived through the foggy windows of the cabin. The colony was bathed in an amber glow, contrasting the dark sky above. She heard the distant chatter of taverns and commotion in the streets. The beach was speckled with bonfires and resounded with bouts of laughter and the occasional gunshot. Despite the colony's beauty, she was happy to be separated from the sinful pleasures that the pirates were indulging at this late hour.

Her ears picked up a muffled, high-pitched yowl from the cabin. The little kitten was already pining for her affections, and her yowling, however faint, might have stirred the men below. Katherine felt a rush of panic.

She spared one last look at the island, and then retreated to the sanctuary of the cabin.

13

NATHAN

Nathan's heart pounded as Livingston ushered him toward the hellishly beautiful building. The Strapped Bodice had been constructed around two palm trees that jutted through the center of a spired roof, which was made of tattered sails that were illuminated by the orange glow of the candles within. Livingston shoved Nathan up the uneven stairs and through the small entrance. The door slammed shut behind them, and Nathan knew nothing more of the outside world.

The interior was simply a large open space with stairs in the back that led to a second floor. Candles had been set in small circular patterns on the floor, and within each lounged a beckoning female, some loosely dressed, others bare as the day they were born.

Nathan's heart threatened to rupture. He desperately looked to Livingston for refuge, but the quartermaster had already fallen into the arms of one of the whores, burrowing his nose into her ample bosom.

Nathan briefly considered fleeing, but quickly dismissed the notion; Livingston would announce his cowardice to the entire ship, and he would be a laughing stock yet again.

All of the women called to him, whistling and smiling flirtatiously.

"Come here, boy!"

"He's a young one."

"Hard as an ox, I'll wager."

"Fancy a suck?"

Despite his trepidation, his breeches suddenly felt snug at the crotch. There were blondes, brunettes, and redheads. Some were skinny, others were more exotically built, and some, like Livingston's, were plump.

Nathan, however, had no interest in the large strumpets. He eliminated the plump whores first, and the emaciated whores second. Left with only five choices, he decided to narrow them down by breast size. He dismissed the small-breasted whores immediately. Two remained.

He chose a girl whose eyes brilliantly ensnared the candlelight. She was Spanish, with thick black hair, copper skin, and full lips. She wore a loose-fitting bodice and petticoat, and he knew she would look splendid without them. He managed to keep his hand from shaking as he held it out to her. With a deceptively shy grin she took his hand and pulled him toward her with surprising strength, until his chest was pressed against her breasts. She seized his lower lip with her teeth. When she allowed him to catch his breath, he asked her name.

"Annabelle," she replied sweetly.

"Nathan." He smiled, the muscles around his mouth and chin twitching nervously. He wasn't sure what he was supposed to do now. She slid her hands around his waist.

"Would you like to come upstairs with me, Nathan?"

He swallowed. "I would. Very much."

"Good," she said. She leaned forward and whispered into his ear, "Because I would very much like you to come upstairs with me." She took his hand and guided him toward the stairs. Nathan glanced around for Livingston, but didn't see him or his plump whore anywhere.

He followed Annabelle, hypnotized by the swishing of her hips as she moved up the stairs. She glanced back to make sure he was still following, and curved a smile at him.

The second floor was much like the first; a large room without walls. However, this room was separated into partitions of draped hemp that displayed silhouetted bodies, masculine and feminine, cast from candlelight in endless motion.

Annabelle took Nathan to an empty partition with a bed of thick, raggedy blankets. She closed a drape behind her, turned to him and started unlacing her bodice. The edges of the garment pushed outward with every loosened lace. Unable to contain himself any longer, Nathan reached out and grasped her bodice by the strings, ripping them apart and freeing her breasts. He gathered them into his hands and squeezed, licking one of her nipples. It hardened on the tip of his tongue.

She pulled away. He watched from the bed as she finished undressing. His eyes drifted to the curly black hair between her legs. She dropped to her knees and unlaced his breeches, sliding them to the floor. She eagerly took him into her mouth. He clutched her hair and climaxed far too quickly. She rose up and pressed against him, breasts mashing his chest. Her raven hair shrouded his face as she kissed him. Her tongue tasted salty. "I'm sorry," Nathan gasped between kisses, embarrassed.

"It's fine," she shrugged. "We have all night."

He woke in the early grey hours of dawn to a breeze that swept through the window and riddled his bare skin with goose bumps. Annabelle was fast asleep, her body fitted into the curve of his, with her back to his chest. He brushed strands of hair away from her cheek, and she stirred in her sleep. He moved his hand to her hip and let it rest there. In the dim morning light he could see how glaringly white his skin was compared to hers.

He put his hand beneath the sheets and slipped his fingers between her legs. Her inner thighs were hot and damp. He slid a finger in and out of her. She moaned softly and tilted her head. "Good morning," she whispered.

"How long were you awake?" he asked sheepishly.

"That depends," she replied. "How long were you doing that?"

"Not long enough." He gently bit her neck.

Beside the bed sat his cutlass and pistol. She reached out and ran her finger along the shiny blade. "What's it like?" she asked wistfully.

"What?"

"Being a pirate?"

He shrugged. "The coin is nice."

She grinned suggestively. "And the women?"

"The women are unmatched," he declared.

She turned to him and sat up, distracting him with her breasts. "I'll wager you've matched with many."

He shook his head matter-of-factly. "You're the first."

Her jaw dropped open. "You lie!"

"Never."

"You're far too experienced."

Now he was certain she was being facetious. "Not at all."

She lifted a skeptical eyebrow. "Am I to trust the word of a pirate?"

"Probably no more than I should trust the compliments of a strumpet."

She clutched her left breast, feigning injury to her heart, and collapsed onto the bed. He chuckled and fell on top of her.

After a leisurely morning, she accompanied him to Sassy Sally's, where they shared a plate of turtle eggs. The eggs looked slimy and milky. Nathan summoned all his courage and popped one in his mouth. His apprehension was instantly forgotten. The flavor was superb, and soon he was shoving turtle eggs down his throat without a care.

Annabelle, who had more familiarity with turtle delicacies, was genuinely amused by his initial reluctance. "Never saw a pirate with a fear of turtle eggs," she laughed.

"I fear nothing, Miss . . . what is your surname anyway?"

"Don't know."

"No last name?"

"Don't know," she repeated with an innocent shrug. "Is it important?"

Nathan frowned. "I suppose not."

When they finished the eggs, they sat back and regarded the harbor. It was a beautiful day, as always, and the cool breeze that washed off the water helped keep the temperature down. There were more children playing on the beach than the day before, many with their mothers nearby. A dozen men were sprawled out in hammocks stretched between the trunks of palm trees.

The harbor was still packed with ships, some of them sailing away, several more sailing in. Two of the ships that had been careened yesterday were gone, and a few others were now turned on their opposite sides and being cleaned. Not far off, another ship was running aground in preparation for the same procedure. Like the majority of the ships in the harbor, these ships were small and easily careened.

In the distance, *Harbinger's* great hull and reaching masts stood apart from the crowd. When Annabelle asked Nathan which ship he belonged to, he had no difficulty pointing it out for her. She threw him the same skeptical look she had earlier that morning.

"I tell you true," he insisted.

"She's a fine ship, that's certain," Annabelle said with a smirk. "She even stole the eye of many townsfolk as she was mooring to, especially with her dreadful black flag, big as can be. No doubt she stole your eye as well. Now, stop putting me on and tell me which sloop is yours."

"I'm generously paying you just to break your fast with me," he said. "Is it so hard to believe I'd belong to so fine a ship?"

"All men pay me well," she replied, "and with far queerer notions than breakfast in mind."

He felt a stab of jealousy, and it must have shown on his face because she recoiled indignantly. "I see," he said.

"Nathan, please don't start that already."

He smiled, feeling instantly silly. "Apologies."

"Don't be sorry, either. You're not the first man to lie about the size of his ship."

Her cheerfully dubious nature left him debating whether he might strangle her to death or smother her with a kiss. It was an alien emotion, and he wasn't certain if he enjoyed it or despised it.

She sighed luxuriantly, oblivious to his quarrel. "What shall we do now? Has your coin given out yet? Or does that hole in your pocket have no end."

"Does yours?"

"No," she said with a lick of her lips.

Nathan peered over the railing and scanned the bazaar, which was busy with pirates and women. "I should like to take you shopping," he said.

"Really?" She seemed genuinely impressed. "And what would we buy?"

Nathan spotted a merchant offering brightly colored dresses, with many women gathered round. "A dress."

The gown Annabelle fancied was made of green brocaded satin, which Nathan thought an appropriate match for the island milieu. It didn't take her long to pick out the garment; she spent most of her time making sure Nathan was content with buying something so expensive for a girl he barely knew. He insisted. The garment was so lovely that she eventually gave in.

They left the bazaar and headed back to Sassy Sally's, where Nathan rented a room for the two of them.

The fitting of the gown perplexed her. Nathan offered his help, but the workings of the garment were more complicated than anything he had encountered at a mast. When he seemed to be doing more bad than good, Annabelle slapped his hands away and insisted that she be allowed to figure it out on her own. She told him she wanted him to see her wearing the dress, not putting it on, as that would spoil the effect. He relented and faced a window as she continued to tussle with the gown.

It seemed an hour before she finally allowed him to face her again. He turned and gasped. The shiny green gown worked beautifully with her copper skin and dark hair. The gown barely clung to her shoulders, plunging into her heightened cleavage.

She gave a slight curtsy and grinned. He reached out, took her hand, and drew her near. He slid a hand around her waist and placed the other on her chest, just below her neck. He shook his head in disbelief.

"What?" she asked, face turning red.

"You're beautiful."

Her lips twisted into a mock scowl. "Because of the dress?"

"A dress won't work without something beautiful to fill it," he said.

She rolled her eyes, but her frown had faded.

Dusk along the beach beheld a far greater beauty than day, the dark blues of both sky and ocean accented by glowing lanterns from the hundreds of pirate ships floating in the harbor. The orange radiance danced off the calm water in shimmering streaks. The star-filled sky, which appeared so brilliant when seen from the open sea, paled in comparison.

The beach was deserted, aside from a few pirates snoring in their hammocks. Nathan and Annabelle had walked nearly to Sawney's Fort by the time their legs grew tired. They rested on a small mound of smooth rocks that faced the harbor.

"You've told me nothing of yourself," he said. "How did you come to this island? You're Spanish, yes?"

"I'd much rather talk about you."

"What more is there to say? I'm a pirate. That's really all there is to it."

"I'm a strumpet," she smiled. "That's really all there is to it. I suppose we're not all that interesting, you and I."

"That would explain the match." He nudged her shoulder playfully.

"When do you leave?" Her tone was less than cheery.

"Not for a while," he said, putting his arm around her.

"But you'll leave just the same." She rested her head on his shoulder.

"Can't stay forever, of course. The coin is good now, but it will run out."

"Will you come back?"

He looked at her and found that she was staring at him and not the view. "There's no better place for pirates, or so I'm told."

"None better," she agreed. "But that doesn't mean Nassau will remain this way forever."

"What do you mean?"

"I'm a whore, Nathan. I hear every gossip that touches this island. Folks are saying that the British want to do away with the pirates. Word is they're sending a governor."

Nathan smiled reassuringly. "It's just talk. Why would the British want to stop pirates? The island officials are perfectly happy to accept our plunder."

"They are," she nodded, "but the British are greedy. That's no secret."

"The Bahamas rightly belong to pirates, if you ask me. The British have lost these islands fair and square." He indicated the hundreds of ships in the harbor. "Stay your worries. I'd like to see their warships meet a fleet as that one."

Her silence made it clear that she was not convinced. For a long while, the only sound was that of the gentle waves washing over the sands of the beach. Finally, she brushed her nose against his cheek. His lips found hers and passion took them both. They made love on the rocks, looking into each other's eyes the entire time.

When they finished, they used their clothes as blankets and gazed up at the stars. Their naked bodies were saturated with a blend of sweat and salt from the briny ocean air. He rested his hand atop her belly and she held it in place with both of hers.

Nathan now knew that however long *Harbinger* remained in the harbor would not be long enough. He had once realized how small *Harbinger* was in comparison to the world; he was now aware of how small his piratical ambitions were in comparison to falling in love.

A more qualified man, such as Edward Livingston, might have dismissed his prompt declaration of love as premature, but Nathan could not deny the glorious ache in his heart.

As he lay on the rocks with Annabelle, he wished that the moment would last forever. However, he had never accepted God and therefore had no one to pray too, and there were no stars falling from the sky that night. He doubted that a sudden acknowledgement of religion or whimsy would fulfill his desires.

He remembered a story he'd read as a child that took place in medieval times and centered on an old sorcerer whose name he could not recall. One of the sorcerer's more powerful spells magicked time to a halt. A young knight in love with a princess who was set to marry a prince she did not love begged the magician to use the spell on him and the girl, so they might extend one night into a lifetime. Nathan couldn't remember how the tale ended, only that it ended in ironic tragedy. Nevertheless, he wished he knew a sorcerer.

Frustration consumed him. Captain Griffith was sheltering a woman aboard *Harbinger* without hazarding the consent of his crew. It was becoming obvious that Griffith did not intend to ransom her, as he originally promised. Any other man would have been marooned for so blatant a crime. Nathan didn't wish this on Griffith, and he doubted the crew would turn on their overly fortuitous captain, but he thought it profoundly unfair that Griffith should be permitted such privileges while others were strictly forbade them.

He looked to the sea. There was a time when one glimpse was all he needed to bring him contentment. A single day had changed that. Now he viewed the sea as an insurmountable adversary that would ultimately steal him from the harmony he had discovered on an island in the Bahamas.

14

ANNABELLE

The pirates would have made her rich, if not for Charles Martel, the owner of the Strapped Bodice, who took a fair portion of every night's wages. Still, she profited well enough to eat, buy suitable clothes, shiny trinkets, and even save a bit, which was more than most women could hope for.

Her troubles were seldom, and her occupation was far more comfortable than stories alleged. She was well known among the strumpets of the Strapped Bodice, which was the most renowned brothel in the colony. She had no qualms taking pirates into her bed, so long as they paid well enough. It was a job and it paid better than any other that was available to her, and there were so very few jobs available to a woman on a pirate island.

Her career was not nearly as hazardous as gossips that spread with the fervor of a plague would have you believe. She knew for a fact that the rumor of Edward Teach murdering a whore in her brothel was false. Yes, a whore had indeed perished, but she had taken her own life by slicing her wrists. The rumors no doubt started because the strumpet's suicide took place on the night of Teach's visit. Purely coincidental, though not unlikely, given that Teach frequented the brothel whenever he was in Nassau.

Annabelle could think of any number of reasons for a strumpet to off herself. Maybe the dead woman had gotten herself pregnant. They had all heard tales of botched abortions. Pregnancy was the worst mistake a whore could make, and one of the most frequent. Annabelle was meticulous in her precautions. Her life was not a complicated one, and she had no desire to make it so with a child.

She was thankful, however, that her mother had made that very mistake. Her mother had been seized from a Spanish ship by pirates and, after finding herself stranded on Tortuga, turned to the brothels in order to earn a decent living. Her father was a random pirate who she would probably never meet, or simply would not recognize if she did. She had nightmares about unknowingly bedding her own father.

She had been born and raised in a brothel and introduced into the profession at the age of twelve. Shortly thereafter, her mother contracted an inexplicable malady that claimed her life all too swiftly. Annabelle hadn't shed a single tear for her mother, whose affection blossomed for men with deep pockets but rarely for her own daughter.

When Martel moved his business to Nassau, where it was guaranteed to rake in a tremendous profit, he took the best of his whores with him, and Annabelle had swiftly proven his most prized strumpet. "Her skin outshines your best gold," Martel would tell his clients on rare occasions when they attempted frugality. "It's a fair exchange as far as you should concern yourself. As for my views, I must have lost a piece of my mind to give her priceless pleasures away and entreat so scant a sum in return. Take advantage of this fine tender while I'm still inclined to madness."

And never did the pitch fail. Annabelle took to bed every manner of pirate that came to her. After a time, none of their sordid eccentricities surprised her. In addition to her physical talents, she was gifted in making each man believe that he was different than the one before. In truth, she forgot each as quickly as she took on the next.

Apart from his clothes, there was little about Nathan Adams that resembled the pirates she was used to; he possessed virtues that his kind were notoriously absent of. Nathan was attractive, intelligent, and a romantic.

"You're a terrible pirate," she told him. It was the highest compliment she had ever paid.

He was too good to be true, and she often wondered if his wide-eyed innocence was a ploy. As time progressed, she came to realize that he was interested in no other part of Providence. He had eyes only for her. She could not deny that his affections instilled her with an uncharacteristic bashfulness. Instead of masking her timidity, she used it to her advantage.

In the month they spent together, he treated her like a princess, showering her with extravagant dresses and jewelry. He allowed her to take no other man to bed while he courted her, and overpaid her in exchange for her temporary fidelity. Martel offered no objections once he saw the wages she was collecting from Nathan alone.

By the end of that month, she suspected that the boy had exhausted his earnings. That night, in the privacy of their room, while she was washing her clothes, she spoke her mind. "I'll have no more of it," she said sternly. "You've wasted on me what I reckon most men spend in a lifetime."

"I've wasted nothing," he shot back curtly. "It was coin well spent."

He'd been distant all day; chuckling faintly at her jests, as though he hadn't really heard anything she'd been saying, but wanted to remain polite.

"What's wrong, Nathan?"

"Nothing."

She tilted her head and smirked, like a knowing wife. She knew he fancied the prospect of marriage, as foolish a notion as that was, so she acted the part. "You're lying."

"Fine," he sighed. "I suppose it's unfair to keep it to myself any longer. Won't make it any less true, will it?"

"What?"

"I leave on the morrow."

This did not hit her as hard as she pretended. Nathan was a pirate, and a pirate was bound to his ship. A pirate ship never remained in one port for long, not even the best of ports. Nor was it usual for a whore to stay with one pirate for a month, but that is exactly what had happened.

"Oh," was all she said. She knew men hated an emotionless reaction. She briskly turned away and went back to scrubbing a fancy dress against a rippled washboard. Her disappointment was not an act, though it was hardly for the reasons Nathan probably expected; she doubted the next pirate would be as generous with his purse.

"Annabelle . . . " he started.

"I'm not angry," she said too readily, too cheerfully.

"No, of course you wouldn't be," he conceded crossly.

"And when will you return?" she asked as innocuously as possible.

"I don't know," he replied. There was a long silence. And then she felt his hands on her waist and his breath on her ear. *This is how husbands hold their wives,* she thought. "But I will return," he whispered.

She didn't look at him just yet. She knew exactly what he

was thinking. He was thinking that if she looked at him, the balance of her emotions would be tipped too far and she would burst into tears.

She stifled a giggle. Men were such simple creatures. Boys were even simpler.

She woke in the middle of the night to find him wide-awake, sitting up and staring pensively through the open window. The candles in the room were extinguished and the only light was that of the moon, which cast their naked bodies in a ghostly white radiance.

The rustling of palm trees mingled with the endless crashing of waves as each washed over the beach and then retreated to the sea, one after another.

Annabelle put her hand on Nathan's stomach, brushing the tips of her fingers over his rough abdominal muscles. His belly shuddered in reaction to her touch. She had discovered that he was ticklish and she exploited it at every opportunity.

"Have you slept at all?" she asked.

He shook his head.

"What were you looking at?"

"My ship."

"Show me."

"I've shown you a hundred times."

"And I never once believed you." She sat up and snuggled close to him. "Perhaps a hundred and *one* will do the trick."

He sighed and pointed to the harbor. She followed the line of his finger to the same ship he had indicated before. "Still that one, eh?"

"The very same. Her name is *Harbinger*. Watch me on the boat tomorrow and see which ship I row to, and you'll know I've not steered you false."

"I believe you," she said, patting his stomach. And that was true. She had already spied him boating back and forth on a number of occasions, but she enjoyed teasing him. "I'll watch you on the boat, but not to see which ship you board." She realized that part of her truly meant this, because she would likely never see him again.

"I would bring you to sea with me," he told her, "if it weren't against the code."

She cackled. "I always get a laugh when I hear a pirate speak of codes."

"I was serious."

She chewed her lip penitently. "I know." *Stupid boy,* she thought. *You really do mean it.*

"Would you go along if I invited you?"

She shook her head. "No." It was the most honest answer she had ever given him. For all the coin he had emptied into her pockets, she figured she owed him that much.

"Not even if it was fair to take a woman aboard?"

She rolled her eyes. "A woman trapped on a ship full of sweaty pirates? It's nice of you to offer, but I think I'll save my tortures for the fires of Hell, thank you."

15

LIVINGSTON

"I'm not going."

Livingston furrowed his brow. He was beginning to wonder if young Nathan Adams was more trouble than he was worth. "That's just like your sort," he growled. "You fall on your ass for the first whore what gives your spar a lick."

"I'll not be swayed," Nathan shot back with infuriating conviction and a high-held chin that reminded Livingston of all the dead men who had refused to cooperate with him.

"Plainly you wish me to convince you otherwise, or you wouldn't have put me to task."

"I wanted to tell you myself. I figured I owed you that much." Nathan's tone implied that nothing else was owed. He turned away and set his hands on the rail, facing the colony.

"Good of you to ask," Livingston shrugged. "The answer's still no."

Nathan spun round on him, his cheeks flushing red. "I was not asking permission!"

"Nor were I permissing!" Livingston shot back, swiping a hand through the air, past Nathan's face. Mistaking the gesture as an intent to strike, Nathan flinched away and primed a retaliatory fist. Livingston shook his head in disbelief. "Simmer down, boy. I weren't about to hit you." In truth, he would have hit him if he thought it would make any difference. But the boy had already been struck by something worse.

Nathan's shoulders sagged. He nodded somberly. "Sorry," he sighed. "Of course you weren't."

"Gods!" Livingston cried, reaching for the sky. "What could this woman have done to put such a murderous fury in you? Swallow your milk, did she? A rare find that be, and sure to put a craze in any man's head, even one with a skull so thick as yours."

"She's a fine woman," Nathan insisted.

"And a fine pirate. She's plundered your senses."

"I gave them willingly."

Livingston mashed a fist into his palm before it could fly of its own accord. Fire swelled in his breast, but he sucked it in and proceeded calmly. "I reckon her dresses got fancier the longer she stayed at your side. She couldn't have run you cheap."

A flickering uncertainty registered in Nathan's eyes. The quartermaster had found his niche. He moved closer. "Ah," he grinned, "not a cheaply lass, were she?"

Nathan clenched his jaw.

"But certainly worth your wages, eh?" Livingston added with a wink.

"Every piece."

It was clear that the boy had developed a potent affection for his strumpet, and while Livingston didn't quite understand it, it was worth exploiting if it meant preventing a promising young man from throwing away his career. "Let's say you remain at your whore's side. You don't want her putting to bed with swabs while you're sweeping a tavern floor for bits and pieces, do ya? Not a pleasing notion of romance by any man's eyes, least of all a young pirate with fortune calling."

Livingston set a hand on the boy's shoulder and tossed a conspiratorial glance about the deck, as though what he was about to say was of the utmost importance. "Now, have you told your girlie your feelings on the matter 'fore I talked sense into you?"

Nathan hesitated. "I didn't want to get her hopes up."

"Ahhh," Livingston grinned, "No wonder you came to me! You needed persuasion against wayward notions."

Nathan withered before him.

"Don't be shamed, boy, for it only proves you have some sense in you yet. More so than I was like to grant you a few minutes ago, but we'll put that sad affair behind us where it rightly belongs. It's well and good she thinks you're going to sea, because that's exactly what you'll do, and you'll return a richer man and buy your bonnie a home. She'll love you for the rest of your days, and you'll love her back, if she's lucky. And maybe you'll love other whores too, as your reformed whore will surely know that the wants of a husband extend well beyond a single strumpet. The beauty about whores, I should think, is they aren't a picky lot. Not anything like the sort in the captain's cabin, with her nose in the clouds. Stay away from that sort, if you wish to keep coin in your pocket."

"I would share myself with no other," Nathan proclaimed, regaining his conviction.

Livingston curled his lips into a scowl of disgust. If he had eaten recently, he might have retched all over the deck right then and there. "That's the daftliest thing I ever heard, boy. Talk like that again and I might be less inclined to sway your foolish notions."

137

Nathan smirked lopsidedly.

Livingston nodded to Nassau Port. "You know what waits for you here, boy." He turned and pointed to the gap between New Providence and Hog Island that would lead *Harbinger* out to the open sea. "Out there, you've yet to discover!"

"Which one is Annabelle?" Livingston asked, looking over the whores lounging about the Strapped Bodice.

The leathery skin of Charles Martel's cheeks bulged as his tongue worked from one side to the other. He looked like a creature born of the sea that had sprouted legs and ventured on land. He had small, black eyes seemingly devoid of irises in the low light, and he was mostly bald on top, with scattered strings of curly black hair that glistened like wet seaweed running from one ear to the other. His overly sunburnt skin resembled a dry lakebed, with flaky cracks running along his arms and legs. Livingston wondered if he had some sort of skin affliction.

"Who be asking?" Martel spat through teeth stained black.

Livingston seized the little man by his scrawny neck and drew him near. "I be asking."

Martel's tongue slithered out to moisten his cracked lips, like an eel emerging from a crevice. "I mean no offense. She's a popular girl, is all. Sees a lot of men with heavy coin."

"One in particular, and hardly a man. Only a boy, this one. You know the lad?"

"Aye," said Martel. "Pays well, he does."

"I have coin," Livingston growled, not missing Martel's meaning.

"Then she's yours for the night, she is."

"I won't need so long." Livingston released the repulsive man and gave him a shove. A skinny whore sprung from her circle of candles before Martel collapsed gracelessly onto them. He brushed at his clothes to make sure he hadn't caught fire.

"How much?" Livingston growled.

"Payment won't be necessary till you're through," Martel said, lips twitching into what might have been a smile, though there was nothing but fear behind it. Sweat trickled down his brow, flickering in the dim candlelight.

"Where is she?"

"Upstairs, she be."

Livingston started toward the stairs, then stopped, spun on his heels, and aimed a steady finger at Martel, who had been in the process of rising from the floor. He halted in place, legs bent and wobbling. "Do not disturb me, little man."

Martel gave a fervent shake of his head. "I'll leave you to her, I will."

Livingston ascended the stairs and checked each room until he found her. She was lying in bed with a book and a candle, the sheets pulled over her breasts. Her eyes rose above the page, and she smiled welcomingly. Livingston had no trouble seeing what Nathan saw in her. She was indeed beautiful. A little *too* beautiful.

"I'm enjoying a break, handsome," she said.

"My purse says otherwise," Livingston replied.

"Your purse talks, does it?"

Livingston grinned. "It sings. Fancy a tune?"

She regarded him narrowly for a moment, and then closed the book and set it on the small bedside table, next to the candle. She stretched, one hand rising above her head while the other slid the sheet away from her body. She was completely naked. Her thick black hair spilled over her shoulders to touch her nipples. Despite her curves, she was still much too skinny for Livingston's tastes. Nevertheless, he was instantly aroused.

"Should I bother to get up?" she asked, smirking.

"No," Livingston said.

"Prefer to be on top?" She giggled wickedly and opened her legs, giving him full view of everything in-between. Livingston wondered if she had adopted such a naughty persona with Nathan Adams. He doubted it.

"Never give a woman the high ground," he said.

"You're a smart man."

"Not really," he sighed. "Just smarter than a woman."

"Doesn't take much," she grinned. She was telling him what he wanted to hear. She was far more intelligent than most of her ilk, he had to give her that. She even knew how to read, which was uncommon. "Then again," she admitted, "I don't keep the smartest of company."

He sat on the edge of the bed and set a hand on one of her feet. She flinched ever-so-slightly. "Sorry," she laughed, her voice rattling. "Your hands are cold."

"No they're not," he replied flatly. Nothing was cold on this island, least of all his hands, which were presently damp with sweat. This woman was afraid of him, and rightfully so. He squeezed her foot and yanked her a few inches closer. Her eyes betrayed an unmistakable flash of fear. She composed herself instantly and retrieved a smile. She lifted her other foot and set it in his lap, massaging his crotch. He stared between her legs.

"Do you know who I am?" he asked.

She shook her head. "Should I?"

"Just curious if young Nathan spoke of me," he answered.

Her foot stopped massaging him for less than a second. "Nathan? You're one of his crew?"

"He be one of *my* crew," he grated irritably. "Has he named hisself 'captain' already?"

"Hardly," she said, maintaining her false smile. "He rarely speaks of his crew."

"It's likely he didn't want to frighten you," Livingston grinned.

She waved a dismissive hand. "Pirates hold no surprises for me."

He took hold of both her ankles and yanked her toward him. She let out a pitiful yelp as he twisted her onto her belly and crawled on top of her. He grasped a handful of her hair and jerked her head back. She gasped. He licked her cheek and then thrust her face into a pillow, holding her in place. She squirmed in vain beneath him, hands slapping at his thighs.

"You're undeserving of the lad," he whispered into her ear.

With his free hand, he fumbled to get his trousers open. She lifted her head just long enough to release a truncated scream that did little more than pain his ears, before he shoved her face back down into the pillow.

He returned to *Harbinger* late that night, glimpsing a figure atop the quarterdeck, near the helm. He knew it was Griffith, thinking on the journey ahead.

Livingston was unable to suppress a sly smile as he ascended the slim stairway to join his friend. Griffith glanced at the quartermaster, looked away, and swung his head back around for a second look. "What affords you so much glee?"

Livingston quickly traded his smile for a less jovial scowl. "The passing memory of a moistened cunt," he answered.

"There's blood on your shirt," Griffith observed.

Livingston searched his shirt until he discovered a few tiny spatters on the left breast. He licked his finger and rubbed at them, but succeeded only in smudging the stains. "Could be anyone's," he said with a shrug.

"Looks fresh," Griffith replied in a nonchalant tone.

"Is it a problem?" Livingston asked, perhaps too defensively. He didn't like being questioned, no matter how casual the interrogation.

Griffith raised his hands harmlessly. "Meant no offense."

"How I spend my coin is my business," Livingston growled.

"It's no consequence to me what men do with their wages. Better that they lose their riches before they return, thus their wants never cease."

"Aye," Livingston agreed, and they spoke no more of it.

Harbinger's hold had been lightened of its precious cargo in exchange for far less than the total worth, but far more than the crew could spend in a night. They had vacationed in Nassau Port for a month before exhausting their fortunes. The hold was now packed with provisions, supplies, and livestock. The winter season was just beginning, and they would have to patrol the waters of the West Indies for fresh plunder.

"The Windward Passage," Griffith said. "It feels lucky. I'm confident the crew will agree."

Livingston nodded his assurance. "They will. Warm waters is always welcome."

16

KATHERINE

The kitten was good company, but Katherine's boredom was insatiable. As the months progressed, she came to realize that she would rather die than spend another day in the cabin. And so, on the morn of an early February day, she swung open the door and stepped on deck.

It was not as it had been in Nassau. Pirates were everywhere, and all of them tilted their heads to stare at her as she emerged from her den. She leveled her chin and continued on her way, pretending she was oblivious to their ogling. It was as if they had forgotten her since her time at the mainmast and suddenly discovered that she still lived. After a while they returned to their duties and seemed to forget her all over again.

She ran her fingers along the bulwark while admiring the vibrant sea. The rippled sand was visible through the shallow water, yet there wasn't a single spot of green on the horizon to mark land.

She remained at the bulwark for the better part of an hour,

until Griffith and Livingston passed by. She received a tentative glance from Griffith and an evil eye from Livingston. Both men then started whispering conspiratorially to one another.

That night, Griffith said nothing of the day's events. He merely collapsed into his chair and fell asleep.

Katherine stayed awake for a while, playing with the kitten. As she rapped her fingers along the deck and the kitten lunged to nip at them, she considered venturing on deck again on the morrow.

On the second day, she remained outside for an hour.

On the third, two hours.

And so this cycle continued until it was common for her to remain on deck for the better part of the day. Her excursions were hell on her dresses, and soon not a single garment was left unspoiled.

Apart from her initial few ventures, the pirates paid her no heed. If she was in their way, they hastily brushed past her. She amused herself by stepping in their paths and watching them stumble to avoid her.

As much as she disliked Captain Griffith, she was grateful that he had engaged in the duel with the tall, funny-accented man. She wagered that there wasn't a pirate aboard *Harbinger* who would make such an attempt after *that* deadly incident.

For many weeks Thatcher was the only one to hazard a conversation with her, but he hurried off whenever anyone took notice. Coated in a glistening sheen of sweat, his stench was all the more repugnant outside. Katherine wondered if there was any water left in his body, for it seemed to be escaping through his pores at an alarming rate.

One morning she found Nathan Adams and one of his American friends loitering around her usual spot at the bulwark. She made no attempt to amend her course, not wanting to appear put off by their presence. Nathan stood and greeted her with a smile and a small bow that nearly gave her a laugh.

"It's good to see you about," he said.

"It's good to be about," she replied with a smile. "Though I doubt your fellows share such sentiments."

At that, Nathan's comrade rose awkwardly from his seat. "Not at all," he exclaimed. "It's always nice to see a woman about."

Nathan rolled his eyes. "Sit down, Gregory, before you frighten her back to the cabin."

"It would take far worse than your friend's compliments to prompt my retreat," she joked.

"She talks funny," Gregory whispered to his friend. "Long words and such."

"Introduce yourself, Gregory," Nathan prompted, nudging him in the ribs.

"Gregory Norrington," Gregory murmured timidly.

"Pleased to meet you, Gregory," Katherine said, offering her hand. Gregory seemed unsure what he should do with her hand, so he did nothing except stare at it dumbly.

She spent the remainder of the day with Nathan and his friend, talking at great length of England and then listening to their tales of America. She worried that their duties were not being attended to and frequently asked them if her company was a burden. They insisted the ship was in perfect working order. Still, wayward glances from Griffith and Livingston made her nervous.

Her fears were confirmed when she returned to the cabin that night and found Griffith waiting for her in his chair. "I must say, parading yourself about my deck like a whore is a drastic shift in character."

"I am no whore, captain. Much to your disappointment, I'm sure."

He stood up, the chair falling away behind him. "Mind that sharp tongue! I've already lost one ear to it, and I don't mean to forfeit another."

"Why am I here?" she demanded. "I serve no purpose!"

"Convincing me of that wouldn't be in your best interests."

"Then convince me otherwise," she replied stubbornly.

He set his jaw. "I owe you no explanations."

"Only lies, it seems."

"That's enough!"

"Hardly!" she shouted, stepping closer. "If death is all I have to fear then take my life. This cabin suffocates me! You've taken the only thing that mattered to me and substituted it with a cat. A bloody cat!"

"By the powers, woman," he shouted, throwing up his hands. "You drone on and on about that foolish husband of yours. I'd be less maddened if his ghost came back to haunt me."

"Am I to forget him?" she asked, eyes lining with tears.

"Frankly, I haven't a single care what you do with his memory, so long as it fades from mine."

"I see," she smirked. "The pirate doesn't want to be reminded of his victims, yet he's content to steal their wives."

"I'm hardly content, Katherine. You make certain of that."

"Then allow me to go outside! It's all I ask. I'll surrender the bed if I must. That chair must be murder on your back."

He held up a finger. "The only reason you enjoy that bed every night is because I permit it."

"And I'm grateful for that," she said, managing her best smile, though it was spoiled by her watery eyes and reddening cheeks. "The crew does not hate me. They barely notice me. I'm not a burden, I swear."

"You know nothing of their feelings or desires." He ran his fingers through his raven-black hair in a gesture of frustration.

"I'll not have them lay a finger on you."

"They won't," she insisted. "You made certain of that on the beach. They hardly look at me for fear of losing their heads."

"Do you intend to remind me of every man I've killed?"

"Only the men you've killed for me. I could scarcely bear the burden of all the rest."

He relinquished with a sigh. "I suppose you'll venture outside whether you have my blessing or not. You are a woefully stubborn girl, Katherine Lindsay."

With that, he strolled across the cabin and plopped down on his bed with a luxuriant sigh. "I'd almost forgotten how inviting this mattress was."

He was asleep and lightly snoring within five minutes.

Katherine settled into the chair and spent a long time trying to tilt it just right, nearly falling over in the process. Eventually she gave up and opted for the deck.

She didn't get a wink of sleep. Later that night, with the first hints of dawn, she quietly tiptoed to the bed. She watched him as he slept and, for the first time since her capture, allowed herself to consider his looks. The surreal quality of the early morning light allowed her temporary reprieve of the baggage that she had weighted upon this otherwise attractive man. She wondered if she would have stolen a glimpse in passing under other circumstances, not knowing him for the monster he was. His thick black hair, strong jaw, and soothing voice hindered her resolve, though she had never admitted this to herself until now.

The awful possibility of Thomas's betrayal festered in her mind. She simply could not account for Griffith's knowledge of her name, as she was now uncertain that Nathan Adams had revealed it.

She stowed these thoughts away, but did not permit herself to forget them.

The next morning she found Nathan and Gregory waiting for her in the same spot. "Hello, Katherine," they greeted in unison.

"Good morning, gentlemen," she replied, offering a small curtsy by lifting her petticoat slightly.

"That gown is a disaster," Nathan remarked.

"And your clothes look no worse for wear than the day we met. I should like something more practical."

"You want to dress like a man?" said a wide-eyed Gregory, and he received Nathan's elbow in his ribs.

"Well," she blushed, "it sounds indecent when you put it that way."

"But no less true," replied Nathan with a grin.

"The truth is these dresses won't survive another week."

"Follow me," Nathan said.

She had never descended below decks. She still wasn't sure that she trusted this Nathan Adams, though he had always seemed a nice enough boy. Despite her wariness, the promise of new clothes got the better of her, and she cautiously trailed Nathan and Gregory into the dark depths.

She could've sworn she'd stumbled into a barn, for there were animals everywhere. The place stunk of cattle dung and God knew what else. She had to kick away several squawking chickens that haplessly brushed against her legs.

Nathan led her to a small partition that was sectioned off from the hold by crudely positioned planks. He opened a large, rusty chest and took a step back.

"Have at it," he said. "Take whatever strikes your fancy. I reckon those clothes will fare better than your poor gowns have done."

Nathan and Gregory left her to her privacy. She shuffled

through the heaps of clothes until she had gathered a white shirt, brown trousers, and a red silk sash. She stripped off her gown and slipped into the trousers. They were overly baggy, so she fastened the sash around her waist to keep them from sliding off. She put on the white shirt and buttoned it halfway, leaving it open in the shape of a V at her cleavage.

When she ascended to the main deck, she was almost a perfect fit for her surroundings.

She wasn't on deck long before Griffith caught glimpse of her. He halted dead in his tracks and stared in disbelief. He opened his mouth, as if to say something, and then seemed to think better of it. He continued on his way.

Katherine returned to the bulwark, enjoying the ease of movement that the trousers provided. The dip in her shirt exposed a good deal of her chest, and if she were to bend over, a pirate would be treated to a view of her breasts. She found that amusing, though she had no idea why.

As the months passed, Katherine's skin took on a comely hue of rich mahogany. The sun bleached her hair with streaks of fiery orange. Her appetite strengthened, and by spring she had gained ten pounds.

Anyone who hadn't known Katherine Lindsay prior to this metamorphosis would have mistaken her for a native of one of the countless West Indian isles. Never would they have guessed who she really was.

Nathan constantly likened Katherine's appearance to a woman named Annabelle. He seemed genuinely happy when he spoke of Annabelle, so Katherine obliged his stories, no matter how often he repeated the same tales over and over. The magnificent sparkle in his eyes delighted her as she listened.

"I'm in love with her," Nathan unabashedly announced one

night, after drinking too heavily. "It's the finest feeling I've ever felt."

"I know," Katherine nodded. "And nothing shall surpass it."

Through Nathan and Gregory, Katherine made fast friends with One-Eyed Henry. She looked past his relentless come-ons and, to her surprise, discovered a gentle-hearted man trapped within the gritty shell of a pirate. It didn't hurt that they shared a profound dislike of Livingston.

Nathan taught her to unwind the endings of ropes with a wooden fid and then splice two separate ropes together. She became so good at it that she was from then on allowed the privilege of splicing all of the ropes that needed adjoining. She took pride in this newfound talent, even though it was one of the simplest tasks to be performed on a ship. She earned the respect of several of the crew. Katherine became "the splicer lass," and while there were many that still frowned upon her and cursed her as bad luck, they were now a swiftly dwindling minority.

She was convinced that one man, however, would never warm to her. "So she splices ropes," Livingston sneered. "One day someone will find her *real* talents, should they think to look between her legs."

He always referred to Katherine as "her" or "she," even when he was speaking directly to her. "She looks nice," he told her. "When she takes on a little more weight, even I might fancy a go, if she's lucky."

She wished a thousand violent deaths upon him, but one would be enough.

Nathan mocked her in a far friendlier manner, though no less disturbing in its insinuations. "Splicing the ropes, eh?" he remarked cheerfully. "Tell me, would that not consequence a fast ship, and thus promote our piracy?"

She threw him a fierce glare, and he repentantly waved his

hands and insisted, "It was only a jest!"

17

GRIFFITH

When spring ended, the crew elected to remain in the West Indies rather than return to the East Coast of North America, for they were fond of these waters and saw no immediate need to replenish their fortunes. They spent most of their days on islands gathering water and catching turtles and sunbathing. They had careened *Harbinger* on three occasions, scraping the hull of the seaweed and barnacles that thrived in the warm waters.

The ill crewmen who had been confined to an isolated spot in the hold had all perished. Otherwise, the crew remained relativity healthy, their bellies gladdened by fresh water and the wholesome meat of turtles.

Griffith was inclined to agree with the crew's decision to stay, though logic told him it was a bad idea. The North Atlantic was far more lucrative, and each year the Caribbean had seen fewer merchant vessels treading her perilous, pirate-infested waters. It was a fine place to spend the winter, but

Griffith had found very little profit over pleasure.

He had watched Katherine Lindsay blossom. The constant sun had darkened her skin. She was eating heartily now, and her bony angles had filled to pleasing curves. She allowed her wild mane to flow freely. He was finding her increasingly hard to resist, and he could have sworn that her eyes beckoned him with every glance.

Still, dignity preserved him.

It was an early morning in July when *Harbinger* happened upon a ship in the Florida Straits after months of aimless sailing. She was a three-masted galleon, with a square-rigged foremast and mainmast, a lateen-rigged mizzenmast, and Spanish colors running above all three. She was graced with an elaborately ornamented stern and a red trim along her bulwark that was emblazoned with golden patterns.

"This is the stuff of dreams," Griffith muttered to himself.

After viewing her through his spyglass, he descended the forecastle to the main deck and made his way to the cabin. He opened the door and peered inside. Katherine was sprawled out on the deck, yawning as she woke.

"Stay inside," he instructed. "You're not to leave until the battle has ended."

"Battle?" she asked, suddenly very much awake.

He abruptly closed the door and ascended the stairs to the quarterdeck. The helmsman grinned eagerly when Griffith approached.

"What colors?" said the helmsman.

"Fucking Spaniards," was Griffith's grim reply. "They fight like devils."

"Aye," the helmsman replied. "What course?"

"Give chase."

Griffith turned and set his hands on the rail. Much of the

crew gazed up at him. "Man the fore chase! Make ready the starboard guns and small arms! And hoist our colors!"

The decks came alive as men rushed to their stations in waves. The black flag was ascended to the top of the mainmast, and the bloody crimson heart and bone-white cutlass that impaled it shined brilliantly against the broad of daylight.

It was an hour before *Harbinger* was close enough to fire a chase gun. Though elegant in appearance, the galleon was large and cumbersome, and *Harbinger* had little trouble gaining on her.

The blast of the forecastle chase gun, which sent up a plume of water near the galleon's port side, did little to slow her. Spaniard sailors rushed frenetically about her decks and scaled the rigging to make adjustments to her sails.

"She doesn't relent," said Livingston as he joined Griffith on the quarterdeck.

"Where the bloody hell is Robertson?" Griffith wondered, scanning the main deck for the crewman in question.

"Right here," came a reply, and Livingston moved out of the way as Louis Robertson ascended the stairway with his musket at the ready. "Who needs a shot through the skull?" the marksman asked, dispensing with formalities.

"Take out their helmsman," Griffith instructed, "as well as any man fool enough to replace him. Let's make them fear their own helm."

A musket ball whizzed past Griffith's cheek. Louis's eyes went wide. Griffith turned to see the helmsman clutching his face, blood spurting from between his fingers. He collapsed onto his back, trembling violently. The spasms descended into sporadic twitches before ceasing entirely. His hands fell away to reveal the ruin of his face. The shot had punched a fair chunk of his nose into his skull. A dark pool of blood widened about his head.

Griffith, Livingston, and Louis dropped to their bellies.

"Looks like they had the same notion," said Livingston.

"Aye," Griffith warily replied.

Louis started to crawl toward the helmsman, but Griffith stopped him. "You're of no use to him. He's dead. Get yourself out of sight and discover their marksman! After you've killed him, take out their helmsman."

"Aye, captain!"

Louis crawled to the rail and stuck the barrel of his musket through an opening. He squeezed one eye shut and swiveled the barrel as he searched for his prey.

A second shot whizzed overhead and struck the helm, splintering one of the spokes. Griffith clenched his jaw. The enemy marksman was taunting them, daring another man to take the helm and be shot down for his trouble.

"A thousand hells!" shouted Livingston.

"He's crafty, this one," muttered Louis.

Griffith reached out and seized Louis's ankle, squeezing hard. "Find him quick and blow his 'craft' straight out the back of his head!"

Louis shook his head. "Haven't found him as yet."

"Don't waste a shot till you have!"

A third shot chewed into the deck a foot from Griffith's face. He pulled back instinctively.

"That was close," Livingston remarked.

Griffith frowned. "Too close for a marksman on level with our deck."

"The hell's that mean?"

Griffith inserted his forefinger into the hole, confirming that the projectile had entered at a slant. He looked to Louis. "Either this marksman's shots carry the weight of a cannonball, or he's fixed himself aloft. Search their masts! I'll bet my share of that ship's booty that you'll find him there."

"Aye," said Louis. He angled his musket upward. After a moment, he said, "Got him!" and fired.

Griffith and Livingston popped up their heads in time to see a man plummeting from mizzen topmast shrouds. He hit a yard on his way down, which instantly silenced his scream, and tumbled to the deck.

Louis turned to Griffith and grinned.

"That's it, boy!" Livingston shouted. "Now for the helm!"

The three of them started to their feet. Griffith heard a thunderous report and the subsequent howl of a cannonball. The bulwark shattered in a hail of splinters and Louis's body exploded at the midsection. His upper torso spiraled aloft and tumbled over the edge; his lower torso splashed blood and guts all over the quarterdeck. Griffith and Livingston fell backwards, showered in the spray of Louis's insides. As Griffith struggled to his feet, he was dimly aware of shouting on the main deck.

One-Eyed Henry peeked over the top of the stairs and said, "Who's dead?"

"Sadly for you," Livingston replied, "I'm breathing."

"Jesus," Henry exclaimed when he saw what remained of the marksman. He covered his mouth. "Was that Louis?"

Griffith felt a murderous rage rising inside him, and one glance at Livingston revealed a similar emotion made plain on the quartermaster's blood-covered face.

"Not a single Spaniard on that ship will survive this day," Griffith proclaimed. "Get down there, the both of you, and tell any man with a musket to aim for their helmsman, and any man who takes his place. Stop that ship dead, and then she's ours to broadside. White flag or no, she's scuttled by the end of this, and the waters will forever run red where she rests."

Livingston and One-Eyed Henry nodded firmly and started to their duties.

"And get another bloody helmsman up here!" Griffith barked.

He grasped the railing and made for the stairs. His heels nearly skidded out from under him in the gore that had pooled from the bodies of the marksman and the helmsman. As he descended the narrow stairs, he glanced down and saw blood trickling down the steps.

When he set foot on the main deck, a few of the crew stared at him with horrified expressions, faces pale. Griffith had to remind himself that he was covered in blood. "Let us show these Spaniards that the only thing worse than a white flag is a fucking black one!"

They raised their cutlasses and cheered.

A second helmsman passed Griffith and fearlessly proceeded up the blood-streaked stairway. Griffith turned around to call after the man, and he felt like he was moving in slow motion while everyone else was a step ahead of him. "Fine on the starboard bow!" he ordered the new helmsman. "Steer us as close as possible for a broadside. And when you hear a report, be sure to duck!"

"Aye!" said the second helmsman, and he continued to the quarterdeck.

Griffith returned his attention to the main deck. The four Musketmen moved to the starboard bulwark and each fell to one knee, setting their musket barrels on the gunwale. Four shots rang out simultaneously, and one of them stole the life of the galleon's helmsman. The spray of blood was visible even from afar. Later, the Musketmen would argue with equal conviction over which of them made the killing shot.

Griffith watched as the Spaniards scattered frantically about their deck in a peculiar pattern. They would drop to their knees for a moment, fall back into a circle, and then repeat the process. One by one they would fall out of sight, until there were roughly a dozen of them left on the deck.

The Spaniards didn't bother to replace their helmsman, and the ship tilted to her port, which slowed her considerably. *Harbinger* was gaining on her at an alarming velocity.

Griffith looked to his newly appointed helmsman and screamed, "Hard to port!"

The helmsman spun the wheel and *Harbinger* started to turn, but the evasion was too late. The elevated bowsprit plunged into the galleon's forecastle bulwark and raked across the deck as *Harbinger* turned. One of the Spaniards found himself caught between the sweeping bowsprit and a hulking cannon. He tried to duck, unwittingly placing his head within the bowsprit's path. His skull burst like a watermelon as it was smashed between the bowsprit and the cannon. A mangled body with nothing but a lower jaw for a head tumbled through the shattered bulwark and into the water below. The cannon rolled along the deck, catching yet another unlucky crewman. Pieces of his insides exploded from his mouth as the cannon pulverized his torso.

Griffith had never seen anything so beautiful, with the lone exception of the woman in his cabin.

The blood-soaked bowsprit tore free as the ship turned, and *Harbinger's* starboard side crashed into the galleon's port. Men on the opposite ship had to brace themselves to keep from falling over. Three of them were less successful than the others. The first two plummeted headfirst into the abyss, and the ships pulled apart just long enough to swallow them up and crush two of them, dashing the third man in his companions' blood as he slipped downward, clawing at the hull of his ship and shrieking like newborn baby. He managed to grasp a jutted bit of planking, but his legs had gone too far, and the ships' hulls ground together a second time. His body rolled like a greased ball bearing while the ships moved in two separate directions.

Splintered bones jutted from his skin, and chunks of his face smeared across the wood. His warbled shrieks faded.

Livingston bellowed, "FIRE!!!"

Cannons boomed and small arms cracked from both ships. The galleon's deck was higher than *Harbinger's*, which gave the galleon's heavy cannons the advantage. Many pirates were pulverized as cannonballs tore across the deck in sweeping grey blurs that arced into the sea.

Harbinger's shots blasted gaping cavities in the galleon's hull, but Griffith couldn't be sure of the death toll, since most of the galleon's crew had mysteriously vanished. Why would they retreat below deck in the middle of a fight? Were they cowards?

The pirates on the forecastle lit the fuses of their granado shells and tossed them onto the galleon's decks. The small bombs exploded a few seconds later, sending two Spaniards hurtling over the bulwark. In an attempt to avoid shrapnel, another unfortunate Spaniard made the mistake of leaping between the two ships, having learned nothing from the three that had gone before.

Several pirates tossed grapples while others were content to scale the galleon's hull, using their axes and cutlasses for leverage. Three Spaniards appeared at the bulwark and aimed their pistols down to fire upon the climbing pirates. Two of them were instantly taken apart by guns from Griffith's crew; the third got a shot off before the hook of a misguided grapple came down on the back of his head and exploded from his cheek. He dangled there for the rest of the battle, mouth gaping as his jaw gradually came unhinged.

One of the Jamaicans caught a musket ball in the throat and made gurgling noises before he lost his grip on the hull and plunged into the crevice. He clawed at the galleon's hull to avoid the same fate as the smashed Spaniards, but succeeded only in prolonging the inevitable.

Two Spaniards finished loading a cannon just as one of the pirates climbed onto the channel below their gunport. The pirate set a slow match to the fuse of a granado shell. He reached for the opening of the barrel with his granado, intending to toss it in, but the Spaniards fired the cannon and the granado exploded in the pirate's hand. When the smoke cleared there was a smoldering, sticky black stump where the man's arm had been, and he screamed and toppled from the channel, disappearing into the gap between the ships.

The cannonball responsible for the pirate's grisly death barely missed *Harbinger's* mainmast, and Griffith let out a breath of relief as it continued into the ocean.

Livingston unsheathed his cutlass and charged, and he promptly slipped in blood and fell on his rear. One-Eyed Henry ran past him, taking up the charge along with a mob of pirates, attaching himself to the galleon's hull before Livingston could get back on his feet. "Fucking hell," Livingston growled, glancing angrily about to see if anyone had noticed.

"Don't worry," said Griffith as he moved past with cutlass in hand. "They've got other cares."

Livingston followed, taking his steps cautiously. "Where do you think you're going?"

"To kill some Spaniards," Griffith announced. "A fight like this one means they've got something worth fighting for, wouldn't you say?"

18

NATHAN

Nathan didn't know how he had survived the battle thus far, but he suspected that luck was largely a factor.

As he scaled the side of the galleon, he glanced up and saw One-Eyed Henry and Gregory climbing over the top of the bulwark. Gregory halted in place and glanced down at Nathan, his face ghostly pale. Whatever he glimpsed on the other side of that bulwark had mortified him.

Nathan looked down, risking dizziness, and saw Griffith and Livingston making their way up the hull below. The sight of his captain so eager to engage in battle filled his heart with a powerful urge to press on. He summoned all his energy and hauled himself upward, and he didn't stop climbing until he reached a gunport.

Gregory lingered just below the bulwark to the left of the gunport, clinging to the side. Nathan glanced at his friend as he came alongside him, but Gregory's face was pressed against the hull, his lips moving with no words emerging.

"Gregory?" Nathan said, freeing one hand just long enough to grasp his friend's shoulder. Gregory jerked away and nearly fell. Nathan shook his head and continued on. He reached through the gunport and sunk his cutlass into the deck for leverage. He squeezed through the slim wedge between the cannon and the opening.

A blanket of sparkling shards littered the deck, scattered like stars across an inverted night's sky. Dozens of pirates had fallen and were clutching their sliced feet while cursing and moaning. Rolling around on the deck made matters worse, and their hips and legs were bleeding as well. The Spaniards, who all wore boots, were moving about with ease and thrusting their blades into wounded pirates.

One of the Jamaicans stepped on a particularly jagged shard and started hopping about and yelping. He slipped in a puddle of blood and collapsed onto his belly. He looked up with a face full of glass, carved beyond recognition, and shrieked at the heavens.

Nathan was frozen in terror. There was no way he could traverse that deck, unless some unlucky Spaniard died near enough for him to steal a pair of shiny boots. No wonder Gregory was petrified.

All was not lost, however, since One-Eyed Henry was wearing boots. It was not normal for him to do so, and Nathan guessed that he had adorned them just before the battle, expecting such a tactic. *Nice of him to warn us,* he thought while grinding his teeth.

Henry sliced a Spaniard from behind, placed his heel on the man's back, shoved him to the ground, and slid his body forward. When he realized what Henry was up to, Nathan slid back out of the gunport and punched Gregory's shoulder. "Get up here, you coward!"

"Too much glass," Gregory muttered.

"I think Henry's solved that problem," Nathan said.

"How'd he do that?"

"Come up and see."

Nathan crawled back through the gunport and stood, for the first time, on a Spanish galleon's deck. Gregory wasn't far behind, glancing around timidly as he got to his feet. When he realized what Henry was doing, he grinned. Nathan and Gregory flanked Henry and added their heels to the body, sweeping a path through the glass with the corpse. They howled their cries of war.

A Spaniard charged Nathan, screaming like a demon driven from Hell. Nathan staggered backwards, collapsed against a cannon, and instinctively thrust his cutlass forward. The Spaniard impaled himself with his own momentum, though Nathan did not see it; his eyes were squeezed shut. He felt a warm splatter of blood on his arms and face, and the dead man collapsed against him, sliding along the blade. Nathan spent several precious seconds trying to get out from under the corpse, and finally he was able to push the body to one side and wrench his cutlass free.

When he stood he was treated to the battle in its full scope.

One-Eyed Henry was taking on two Spaniards at once. He quickly impaled one and was then stuck in the leg by the second. He cried out, reared back, and raked his blade across the second Spaniard's chest. Henry limped away and fell to a safe spot near the mainmast, and from there he would watch the remainder of the battle.

Gregory readily took the carpenter's place. He was wielding his cutlass with the grace of a crazed monkey, and the wild strategy, if one could call it that, seemed to be working for him. That is, until he wedged himself between two bars of the capstan and was unable to swing his cutlass without his elbow hitting one of the bars. A Spaniard seized the opportunity, slashing Gregory's belly and spilling his guts. He dropped to his knees and frantically attempted to put each slimy tendril back in its place. A second blade entered his chest, pinning him to the capstan. His hands fell limp at his sides, and his intestines christened the deck.

The battle afforded Nathan no time to comprehend what he had seen. Spaniards were crawling out of the square opening of the hold like spiders to replace those that had fallen. The two that had killed Gregory started for Nathan, and the sight of them nearly stopped his heart. Fortunately, one of them was tripped up by a gleaming rope of intestine and fell into the mess.

Livingston and Griffith finally hefted themselves over the bulwark and raised their cutlasses. Nathan fell between them, exchanged a nod with each, and joined them in a charge. The second of Gregory's killers moved to intercept. The first got to his feet and, doused in Gregory's blood, aimed for Nathan with determined eyes. Strangely, Nathan lost his fear. Perhaps the presence of Griffith and Livingston calmed him. He held his cutlass high above his head and bellowed a war cry at the top of his lungs. The Spaniard skidded to a halt, but his feet were too far ahead of his body and he fell flat on his ass. Nathan got on top of him, placed a foot on his belly, and plunged his cutlass into the man's left eye socket.

Livingston spun about the deck like a tornado, his cutlass whipping this way and that, impaling the chest of one man, slicing the throat of another. He wedged his blade so deep in one Spaniard's skull that it refused to come loose no matter how fiercely he tugged at it. Seeing a chance to bring this monster down, another Spaniard raised his sword and charged. Livingston released the grip of his sword, letting the body fall away, drew a pistol from his sash, and blew a hole through the charging man's head.

Griffith was a different story altogether. He picked his victims one at a time and took them apart with several precise jabs of his blade. His efforts seemed lazy in contrast to Livingston's, but he was no less efficient, and he was exerting far less energy. Every stroke of his cutlass was met with the flesh of an enemy.

Four of the Seven came over the bulwark, led by the tallest, who was gritting a cutlass between his teeth. The Spaniards nearest them were unable to suppress their fear. They ran, and the blacks pursued like giant shadows. The tallest caught his prey first, hacking away at his skull.

"Toss a granado in the hold!" One-Eyed Henry shouted to anyone listening. "There be a whole nest of the bastards in there!"

With Livingston and Griffith presently engaged, Nathan grimly concluded that he alone was the man for the job. But it was Gregory who had carried the granado shells. Nathan shuffled around a group of clashing pirates and Spaniards and found Gregory's body at the capstan, carefully stepping around his guts. He rummaged through his dead friend's pockets and produced two iron granado shells and a small slow match, the cord of which was still sizzling. He sparked the fuses of the granados.

He stood and glanced about for the hold. His eyes found Henry, who was pointing frantically, and he followed the carpenter's gesture until he rediscovered the hold. "Get rid of those before they blow!"

The hold was just beyond Griffith, who was dueling the Spaniards as they came out of the hatch one at a time. Nathan glanced at the granados. Their fuses were burning down too quickly and there was no way he'd have enough time to move around Griffith. He reared his arm for a swing and hurled both granados in a perfect arc over the captain's head. He turned and covered his ears, trusting that the bombs would find their target.

"Get down, mates!" Henry shouted.

The explosion rocked the deck. A shrill ringing sound pierced Nathan's ears, and for a long while he heard nothing else. He looked around and saw many men with their bellies pressed to the ground. A black cloud of smoke blossomed from within the hold, expanding and roiling as it engulfed the sails above.

Griffith and Livingston were the first to their feet. They cut down many of the Spaniards before they could get back up. The pirate crew followed suit. No mercy was given. Several Spaniards offered their surrenders, flailing their arms pitifully. They met their makers instead.

Six of the Seven were now accounted for. Nathan assumed the seventh man, who was not present, had died back on *Harbinger*. The tallest of the Seven managed to get behind one of the Spaniards and twist the man's head very slowly, until it made a horrible snapping sound. Unfortunately, another of the Seven met his death on the edge of a blade before the battle was done, and now they were five.

When only one Spaniard remained alive on the deck, with the pirates closing around him in a circle, Livingston marched right up to him, drew the last of his pistols, and shot the man between the eyes, dashing his brains along the deck.

Griffith looked to the smoking hold and then to One-Eyed Henry. Henry indicated Nathan with a nod. Griffith stared at Nathan, aghast. Nathan could only read the movement of Griffith's lips, as his ears were still ringing, but he was certain Griffith said, "Good boy."

Griffith's eyes focused just over Nathan's shoulder. Nathan turned in time to see the Spaniard captain emerging from his cabin with a sword in one hand and a pistol in the other.

Nathan fell out of the way as the Spaniard captain charged. Griffith raised his sword and rushed to meet the Spaniard's charge, his mouth open in an apparent scream, though Nathan still heard nothing.

No one moved a muscle. Not even Livingston.

The Spaniard aimed his pistol, but Griffith was already close enough to knock the weapon away with a quick swipe of his cutlass. The Spaniard resorted to his sword. The duel lasted only a few seconds, but it felt to Nathan as though seconds were minutes. Finally, Griffith swung his sword from above in a one-handed, overhead arc, forcing the Spaniard to raise his sword in defense. With his enemy's abdomen unprotected, Griffith drew his pistol, buried the muzzle into the Spaniard's stomach and squeezed the trigger. The Spaniard's body lurched as the shot passed through him. He stood there for a moment in shock, a thin stream of smoke wafting from of his back. He collapsed to his knees, bloodshot eyes burning furiously.

Griffith knelt beside the captain and leaned close. "Was it worth it?"

The Spaniard was dead before he could reply.

The hold was a mess of smoldering bodies and charred crates. The smell was horrific, and it was difficult to see through the swirling mist. Closer inspection revealed the shattered remnants of several barrels at the heart of the explosion, and One-Eyed Henry muttered, "Gunpowder." He tapped Nathan's arm and said, "Your granados must've set the barrels alight, as they couldn't do all this damage by their lonesomes."

Nathan's hearing had returned to him, though the ringing had not entirely faded. He wondered if it ever would.

As the pirates passed through the smoke, they happened across a moaning Spaniard whose skin had been sheared from the right side of his face. A hole had burned so deeply into his cheek that his teeth could be seen. One-Eyed Henry grasped the man by his hair and slit his throat.

"Should've let nature do its slow work," said Livingston.

"Nature did not toss those granados," Henry said.

Nathan felt an infuriating swell of regret. All of this was his fault. He had helped conclude the battle, but had stolen so many lives in the process. He shook his head. *It was them or us.*

Livingston let out a great sigh. "Dammit, Nathan. You've blown up all our treasure."

Nathan had to clench his jaw to keep from spinning on his heels and giving the quartermaster a piece of his mind. He had probably saved every man on the deck from the Spaniards. What was the point of treasure if they weren't alive to spend it?

The smoke prevented them from seeing what waited at the aft section of the hold until they were within close proximity:

Thirteen blackened chests.

Livingston eagerly tried to open the foremost chest, but the heat of the metal latch stung his hand and he jerked away and hissed through his teeth. "Bloody hell!"

Someone behind Nathan barked a short laugh.

Livingston spun on the pirates. "The next dog who laughs at my misfortune won't have a throat to laugh with!"

"Easy," said Griffith as he walked past. He unwound the sash at his waist and wrapped it around his hand. When he opened the chest, the pirates were bathed in an unearthly glow.

Nathan did not offer a helping hand when the chests were one-by-one transferred from the deck of the galleon to *Harbinger*. He spent the entire time at the capstan, beside the corpse of his best friend, who would never gaze upon the treasure for which he had perished. All of the blood had left Gregory's face, leaving nothing but a pale face with sunken cheekbones and dark hollows around wide eyes that sightlessly reflected a cloudless sapphire sky. His fingers were gnarled about his gaping stomach, hands and arms lined with spidery rivulets that trailed from the wound.

Somehow, Nathan managed to keep from retching. The image of Gregory's corpse was yet another permanent addition to a grotesque gallery, hanging alongside that of a blonde woman cradling her murdered husband.

The main deck was littered with the corpses of Spaniards and pirates, but Nathan could not discern the bodies of the enemy from those of his comrades. They were a soulless mass of sprawling carcasses, distinct only for the various positions in which each had fallen. The manner of their deaths, brave or cowardly, was unimportant, for the survivors would recall only the treasure they had gained. They would forget those they had slaughtered and lost in gaining it.

Nathan looked to the sky. He damned his peripheral vision for not blinding him to the galleon's morbid surroundings. He would have welcomed a batch of tears, but they did not come.

"Lost many good men," said a familiar voice. Nathan looked up and saw Livingston standing over him, gazing across to *Harbinger*. His leathery pate was stained in blood. "And more are sure to join them."

Nathan opened his mouth to reply, but could think of nothing to say.

"It's rough about your friend," Livingston sighed. "Our toll, she's high, but let me bring you a piece of ease, boy. The Spaniards? They lost it all. *Harbinger*? She took it all, and lost but a few. Those be hard truths. The results be plain for all to see."

"My friend is dead," Nathan said. His voice sounded distant even to him. "No words will soften that truth."

Livingston looked down at Gregory and smiled faintly.

"Not the brightest lad you'd ever meet, I'll say that much. But I'll also say he weren't a quitter. Not a whim of coward in that one. I wish I'd known it sooner."

"You would have, if you'd bothered to look."

Livingston's perpetual scowl softened. His face shadowed over with a foreign solemnity, and for a perplexing moment, Nathan thought him a kinder man.

The moment swiftly passed, and he was Livingston again. "Mourn for as long as you need, boy. But when you set foot on your rightful ship, know that you're rich as a king. As for your friend Gregory . . . we should all die so brilliantly."

19

THATCHER

More attention was paid to the black chests that were being hauled onto *Harbinger's* deck by way of block and tackle than to the twenty-two dead and the eight wounded that were scattered about the main deck, awash in swaying pools of blood and seawater. When one of the pulleys snapped and a chest came crashing to the deck, the pirates showed no concern for the man it crushed. Instead they scrambled to scoop up the jewels and coins that had spilled when the lid came undone. Just another dead pirate, and a slightly larger share for each of them.

Thatcher held the collar of his shirt over his nose and mouth as he traversed the deck. He wasn't sure where to begin. The ship's best marksman and helmsman were dead. The Musketmen were now four. The Seven were now five.

Cannonballs had inflicted most of the damage upon both ship and crew. The more fortunate victims, Thatcher concluded, were those who had been killed instantly. Only two men had survived cannon wounds. One man's arm had been ripped from the socket when a cannonball hurtled past. Another had lost a leg. The remaining injuries were gunshot wounds and cuts of various shapes and sizes.

Thatcher opted to help the one-armed man, for the one-legged man had lost too much blood to be saved. He set his canvas case down and knelt beside the injured pirate, while the one-legged man shrieked for his attention.

"I'll get to you next," he assured him.

"There won't be no blood left in me!" the one-legged man protested.

Unfortunately, Thatcher realized, *you're quite correct.*

"Oh Jesus," the dying man wailed. "It's all draining out of me now!"

Thatcher ripped off his shirt and tossed it to him. "Then plug it with that."

"I'd rather die than see your fat naked belly!"

"Then see yourself dead!" Thatcher spat back.

The one-legged man grunted a laugh and then bunched up the shirt and pressed it against his stump. "I suppose it'll do."

No, it won't do. You'll be dead in a few minutes.

Why he was inclined to save the lives of maimed pirates was a mystery to him. In the end, he knew that they would hold a grudge against him for what they had lost, rather than thanking him for prolonging the eternal fires they were sure to suffer.

Thatcher was hotter than ever, and the salty red water that continuously splashed over his legs did nothing to cool him. He reached for his canvas bag and found that it had been swept a few feet away. He leaned over to retrieve it and collapsed face-first into the red water.

The one-legged man laughed at Thatcher's clumsiness, and then gave to a fit of violent, convulsive coughs. He rolled over in the water and didn't move again. Thatcher spared a moment to watch the man's stomach, and he quickly determined that he was no longer breathing.

"Just as well," said the one-armed man through clenched teeth. He was an Englishman named Norton, and he maintained a paradoxically chipper expression. "Was tired of his braying."

Thatcher retrieved his canvas bag and set it on his patient's lap. "As was I."

"He was of no use minus a leg anyhow," the one-armed man continued.

Thatcher rolled his eyes. "And what use are you minus an arm?"

"I'm a lefty is what I am."

It was twilight by the time Thatcher was attending to the last wounded pirate. It was a minor gunshot wound to the leg, but this one had a penchant for the melodramatic. "Oh, I won't last!" he cried as Thatcher dug a surgical spoon into his leg. "Better I should strangle at the gallows than suffer another minute of this! Find me some rum! Let me die as I lived! Drunk!"

Thatcher easily fished out the steel ball. He dropped the bloody shot in the man's shaky hands and told him it was a "souvenir."

"I won't have it!" the man wailed, and he tossed the ball to the sea. "I'm sure to ne'er walk again!"

"You'll walk," Thatcher assured him as he slipped the spoon back into its slot in his bag. "You might have a slight limp on that leg, but you'll walk."

"A limp, you say! Why not cut the thing off and have done with it!"

Thatcher rolled up the canvas bag and tucked it under one arm as he stood. He gave a slight start when he saw Griffith standing before him. The man was stained as red as *Harbinger's* decks. "You've done a fine job here, Thatcher," Griffith said.

"The cannons fared better. You've lost a fourth of your crew."

"It's true," Griffith nodded. "And fine men they were. Their lives afforded us this victory."

"Victory!" He spat the word. "Is that what you call this?"

"You will receive your honest portion, Thatcher. We're all of us rich men now."

Griffith smiled reassuringly and started for his cabin. The man strolled across the ravaged deck as though he had nary a care in the world.

Thatcher ground his teeth. His share of the treasure did not interest him unless it would buy his freedom, and he was convinced that only death would part him from Jonathan Griffith. As he approached the shattered port bulwark, he found himself wishing that he had been caught in the path of the cannonball responsible.

20

KATHERINE

The sounds of battle had long since faded, but only in the last hour had Katherine mustered the courage to emerge from her hiding place within the hollow of the desk. The first shot to pierce the hull had sent her scrambling for cover, and she immediately felt rather silly cowering while the crew fought outside, but when a second shot zipped past her ear, she easily abandoned her pride and ducked beneath the desk. When she was certain the battle had concluded, she crawled out on all fours and peered through one of the fresh holes. After she was satisfied that *Harbinger's* pirates were the victors, she lit a single candle on the bedside table.

She wondered what would have become of her if the enemy had won the battle. Would the Spanish have returned her to her family? Or would they prove even worse than the pirates, and send her below decks for the crew to have their way with? Perhaps she was safer here. Griffith hadn't so much as touched her.

The murky hues of twilight were yielding to the black of night by the time Griffith returned. He looked affright, caked in dried blood from head to toe, black hair matted to his head, and his clothes utterly despoiled. At first she thought the blood was his, but then she realized that there was no way he would still be standing if that were so. "You look horrible," she couldn't help but say.

He set his cutlass on the desk and started to take off his shirt. She turned away and listened to the rustle of cloth. "Any stray shots get at you?" he asked.

"No."

"You've got wounds on you."

She glanced at the scratches on her arms and remembered that she had been cradling the cat when the battle commenced. The animal had gone ballistic, tearing away from her like a small, furry hurricane, taking pieces of her skin in the process. "The cat," she replied dismissively. "The first shot put her in a frenzy, and I suffered the worst of it. She's cowering under the bed. I don't think she'll ever . . ."

Absentmindedly, she turned round to face him while she was explaining. Her words trailed away. He had cleaned much of the blood from his face with the crumpled mess of his shirt, and now he was scrubbing his arms. She gaped at the lean muscles that had been concealed by the loose-fitting shirts he usually wore.

"I'm sorry," she said, and started to turn away.

"For what?"

Her cheeks filled with warmth. She swallowed the girlish emotion and twisted her face. "For nothing, if you want the truth. It was merely a courtesy. Something this vessel is severely lacking. I don't begrudge you for not recognizing it."

"You are fierce with words," he said, his eyes gleaming.

"I have no other means," she replied, leveling her chin. She

176

decided she would not shy from him again. She was sick of it. "Should I be silent, like a good slave?"

"I don't expect that."

"How very thoughtful of you," she chuckled.

"Nor do I expect you to forget what I've done." There was no trace of remorse in his tone. He was merely stating a fact.

"Tell me, what sort of pirate needs to justify his crimes to his victims?"

"I justify nothing. But I don't expect you to forget."

"What *do* you expect of me, captain? I've often wondered. I linger here, in this dark cabin, waiting for your expectations to rise."

"And you grow impatient?"

"Is that what you think?" Scathing laughter bubbled out of her.

His face flushed red. "Then what is it?"

She sighed, considering the question. The answer came slowly from her lips, each word under careful scrutiny. "I grow weary of waiting for the inevitable."

He arched an eyebrow, studying her narrowly. "You would get it over with?"

Yes, she realized.

"I have no stamina for games, Katherine. I've just killed a ship full of Spaniards."

She took a step closer. "Is that your problem? Stamina?"

"That's not what I—"

"When you leave this cabin, do you tell your men that you ravished me? That I screamed your name? Surely you don't tell them that you've not so much as removed your boots! That would be embarrassing."

"What's gotten into you?" he wondered, blinking in sudden frustration.

"Not you, that's for a certainty."

His brow creased, revealing lines she hadn't known were there. "This is not the woman I took aboard my ship. You're talking like a whore."

Her pulse quickened. "Isn't that what you wish me to be?"

"No," he said, firmly shaking his head. "Whores are not hard to come by."

"But I am a rare gem, yes?"

He tossed his shirt away and aimed a threatening finger squarely at her face. "Stop this."

She held his gaze. The air was thick with humidity, and she fancied she could see swirls in the moisture dancing between them. She felt a trickle of sweat run down her back beneath her shirt. "I will not. What story will you tell your men when you leave tonight?"

He glared hungrily at her, eyes scaling her body. "The truth."

"And what is the truth?"

He edged toward her. His face was still littered with tiny specks of blood, which became more apparent as he drew near.

I should be frightened.

His breath grew heavier with every step. She prepared herself, abolishing the bloodthirsty murderer from her thoughts and welcoming a handsome rogue, albeit a rogue with blood on his face. She purged the battered remnants of Thomas's memory, which she had struggled so diligently to preserve after these many months. It was not as difficult as she had guessed it would be. She told herself she could barely recall his face, and that he hadn't been so great a husband. What kind of husband took a woman to sea, anyway?

You begged him, an irritating little voice reminded her.

He should have known better, she reminded the other voice. *It's his fault I'm here now, forced to placate this savage who knew my name before I had the chance to give it. Thomas, what have you done to me?*

Griffith lifted her by the waist and flung her to the bed. He crawled on top of her and straddled her with powerful legs. He held one of her arms in place as though he feared she might squirm loose, though she had no intention of escaping.

Why am I not frightened?

He ripped her shirt open and buried his face in her breasts. His warm, wet lips encircled a nipple, and for a moment she was nervous that he might bite down. He was surprisingly gentle. The nipple hardened as he caressed it with his tongue. The bristle of his chin, which he had not shaved in days, tickled her skin as his mouth moved toward her neck. She tilted her head to one side, dodging his lips.

He slipped a hand into her trousers and massaged her. A palpitating torrent washed through her, prompting her to moan things like "no" and "stop it," though she meant none of it. Secretly she wished it would never end, even as the glint of the cutlass on the desk across the cabin ensnared her eye. *Too far.* Even if she could squirm out from under him, he would be on her before she could reach the sword.

He undid her trousers and slid them to the deck, following them down. She started to get up, knowing she should not allow herself to enjoy another second of this. He drew her legs out from under her, and she collapsed feebly onto the bed. He opened her legs and delved between her thighs. Her fingers spread into his hair, moving of their own accord. She gathered tufts of hair into each hand, balling them into fists. *Now this might work,* she thought. A sharp twist of his head and perhaps his neck would snap. And if his neck didn't break, perhaps the pain would daze him, and perhaps that would buy her enough time to sprint over and take up the cutlass.

And then . . . what then? Would she have the courage to do what she must? Would she have the strength to plunge the blade into his heart? *Of course you will. Your rage will fuel you. And you will smile down at him as the life flows from his chest. And when you emerge from the cabin, shrouded in his blood, they will look on you in horror.*

She arched her back as his tongue worked diligently.

Your rage will fuel you.

A hand reached up to grasp one of her breasts.

Your rage will fuel you.

The atrocities he had committed were irrelevant in contrast to the overwhelming gratification he delivered her now. She found herself quivering uncontrollably as some piece of her screamed in protest, lost in a fog of pleasure.

Your rage will fuel you . . . if only she could recall where she mislaid it.

Over nine months she had learned to accept despair as a way of life, never to be amended. It was only fitting that the man who had caused her so much grief should now take that pain away. It was the very least he could do.

When he was finished between her legs, he came up searching for a kiss with glistening lips. She seized his neck and bit down gently, holding him there with one hand, and reaching down to guide him into her with the other. He was heavier than Thomas ever was, and he leaned into her with every thrust; Thomas had always seemed afraid of injuring her. The muscles of his neck strained, but she held him firmly in place, keeping his lips away from hers. His breath was hot on her shoulder. He stank of sweat and salt and death.

As she nibbled at his neck, she fleetingly wondered if it was possible to murder a man by gnawing through to his jugular. How long would it take him to die? Would she be doused in a gush of his blood? Would his life fade swiftly, or would he prove resilient even in the throes of death, and use his final moments to strangle the life out of her?

He twisted free of her grasp, his mouth opening, descending toward hers. She summoned all of her strength and shoved him to one side, rolling on top without letting him slide out of her. She wrapped her sinewy legs around him and set her hands on his pectoral muscles. She thrust against him, writhing on the perspiration between them. Her fingers curled as she raked his chest, leaving jagged red trails. His eyes flashed with excitement. He clutched her breasts and gritted his teeth.

If she had concealed a blade beneath the bed, she might have used it now. She wondered if he would remain hard after she plunged it into his chest. She realized, with some alarm, that she was smiling.

It was not long before he climaxed, and the moment showed plain on his face. She thought he looked a bit absurd, as though he had suddenly been struck dumb and could not salvage the scattered pieces of his mind. She held him there for a moment, grinding ferociously against him until he softened inside her. As she pulled away, his manhood fell limply to one side, looking much less impressive now.

She sat upright in the bed, facing the opposite direction. His fluids trickled out of her to dampen sheets, and she stared impassively at the translucent stain. A hollow ache echoed into her stomach from between her legs. Her entire body was soaked in sweat, her saturated hair matted to her face. She stared at her legs, which were no longer the bony twigs she had always known. The candlelight played strikingly upon her mahogany-tinted skin, which she favored over the ghostly shade she remembered.

She had never enjoyed being naked. It revealed to her all of the awkward angles that were conveniently cloaked beneath heavy dresses. However, as she looked over herself now, she was in awe. It was her first opportunity to thoroughly examine herself. Since her capture she had always changed her clothes in speedy fashion in order to avoid spying eyes. She had never wanted Griffith to glimpse her naked, though she had always known it would come to this eventually.

Something twitched in her peripheral vision. She was drawn to the clothes that had been hastily discarded beside the bed. Her trousers were moving. She recoiled with a gasp.

"What's the matter?" Griffith asked.

She leaned over the edge of the bed and reached out to pluck her trousers away. The cat perked her little head up and offered a curious meow. Katherine sighed and lifted the cat into the bed. "Poor thing," she said. "She's still shaking from all those loud guns."

"Amongst other loud noises," Griffith chuckled as he sat up. He looked down and frowned. "Your cat soiled itself on my shirt."

Katherine had a look for herself. The kitten had indeed left little black droppings all over Griffith's shirt. "She must be making a statement," she giggled.

"A statement written in shit," he grumbled.

"I'll clean it later."

"Speaking of cleaning up messes, I should check on the crew."

"I'll be here," she said. *Where else would I be?*

He moved in for a kiss, but she tilted her head away with a coy smile. He halted apprehensively. "No?"

"You got what you came for," she answered bracingly. The kitten bounded off to play with a speck of dust.

"More than you realize," he replied. "The Spaniards surrendered wealth beyond our wildest dreams, Katherine."

"What makes you think I share your dreams of wealth?"

"Is that not why you married a wealthy man?"

"There are many reasons why I married him," she said, though she was having trouble recalling a single one. She stared into the flame of the candle flickering on the bedside table. When she finally looked away, a bright spot had burned into her vision, obscuring anything she stared directly at. She looked at Griffith and saw only raven hair and the outlines of a strong jaw. His features were lost in the flame. "None of them for wealth," she said. It wasn't true, but he hardly deserved truth.

"What of security?" She saw his jaw moving, but his face remained veiled in light.

"Any woman dreams of security," she replied distantly. "It is a base survival instinct."

"I must confess," Griffith sighed, "I have no idea what you dream of. Maybe one day you'll tell me."

She allowed herself a light giggle, one that she knew he would misinterpret as a nicety.

And he didn't disappoint. "That's a pleasant sound," he said. "Before tonight, I don't believe I've heard it."

His features gradually came into view through the white blot of ghostly flame. She saw a pair of eyes and a mouth, indistinguishable from any other. "You didn't eat those men on your former ship," she blurted suddenly. It was not a question, merely a declaration of obvious fact. She would have bet her life that there was not a cannibal alive who whispered sweet nothings in the ear of a woman.

"Of course not," he conceded, lowering his head. "When did you figure that?"

The blot dulled into a dark haze, and his face was once again obscured. She shifted her gaze, and out of the corner of her eye she saw a man far younger than Griffith, grinning boyishly. "When fear subsided and common sense took hold."

A crease in his brow returned him to his true age. "Is it so hard to believe a pirate would consume his victims?"

She blinked until her vision fully returned to normal. "No.

Not at first. You were very convincing. But then I realized that, despite your crew's belligerence, you're only men, molded of the same inclinations as every other."

He frowned. "I think I should be insulted."

"It was intended as such."

He reached out to pinch one of her nipples. She glanced down and saw that he was already growing hard. She mounted him and leaned forward, teasing him with her lips before pulling away. He undoubtedly mistook her mischievous grin for flirtation, though it was actually the result of an inward muse.

Your lips will never touch mine.

21

LIVINGSTON

The galleon's great cabin was extravagant. The red sheets and pillows of the bed were lined with swirling gold accents that shimmered in the thin rays of morning sunlight slipping through drapes of brilliant red linen that hung from absurdly tall windows. The large round table in the center of the cabin was bedecked with burnished goblets and spotless silverware. The table's legs ended in four massive lion's paws, carved of mahogany and polished to a smooth shine. The paws were set upon a fine crimson tapestry woven with a detailed map of Spain.

Livingston saw jealousy made plain on Griffith's face as he entered the cabin. The captain swiftly withdrew his scowl and, with a great intake of air, adopted a smirk. "Trinkets, he had them all," said Griffith, "but the most precious he lost in battle."

"That would be?"

"His life," Griffith answered, withering.

"Right," Livingston replied. He never understood why men felt the need to wax poetic after a fierce battle. Perhaps it made them feel better about killing. Personally, he required no incentive. Death was as natural as life.

"She's a fine ship," Griffith went on.

"Do we take her for ourselves?" Livingston had been asking himself this question for the past hour, and he hoped Griffith would say no. The ship was grand, but she was also far less maneuverable than *Harbinger*. And her absence was not likely to go unnoticed by the Spanish. The galleon may have been part of a treasure fleet and had fallen behind or, worse yet, sailed ahead. It was possible there were more on the way.

"No," Griffith said, answering Livingston's prayers. "We've taken the best of her. The worst will return to find her, and waste no time exacting vengeance. Best we're not around when they arrive. We've dawdled long enough."

"Aye," said Livingston, "and she took some of our best." He let out a protracted sigh, for his mind had been lingering on the many deaths that had brought such a victory.

Griffith nodded broodingly. "Thatcher thinks cold of us."

Livingston's regrets escaped him in a sudden puff of air. "Fuck Thatcher and his bellyaching. My conscience bites at me enough, and still it smells better than that fat beast! I'll see to it that he burns before I do. We're all of us bad men out here. I'll wager the Spaniards came to this treasure with less reputability than we, and less quarrel!"

"No doubt," nodded Griffith. "It's the loss of the men that twists my gut."

"Aye, the men," Livingston said. "There's Louis, of course. A good lad with unmatched aim."

"We'll need a replacement."

"Nathan Adams." The name came too easily to Livingston's lips, and Griffith seemed pleasantly surprised by the swiftness of his response. Livingston immediately withdrew. He didn't want Griffith thinking that he had attachments to any particular crewman, so he laughed and said, "And Katherine Lindsay be a perfect fit for Henry's apprentice."

Griffith's face twisted. "Henry's apprentice?"

"No offense," said Livingston with a shrug, "but I dislike the woman, and she shares my feelings, or so I would wager by her cruel looks. I don't blame her for those, as mine be far uglier. But I see her uses, and those aren't with the lines. I'm told she's fine with the knots and better still at splicing. A perfect pair, Henry and she, as I like neither one of them. Or would you rather keep her in your cabin for all of eternity?"

"Is her being in my cabin a problem?" Griffith's tone was flat and inscrutable, as one who is attempting to keep his emotions in check, but Livingston knew the man well enough to know when he was roiling to the brim.

Livingston maintained a strategically innocuous manner, though his words were anything but. It was a tactic worse than outright accusation, as there was no defense against a man who so innocently made his claims. "The men don't always voice their woes," he said as he massaged his chin with his knuckles.

Griffith stared at him for a long time. "Is it a problem for the men, or a problem for *you*?"

"If it were, I'd have solved it."

"You'd stroll into my cabin and kill her yourself?"

"I shouldn't need to remind you that the cabin belongs to us all. Or have you forgotten?"

"Of course," Griffith relinquished immediately, blinking rapidly. "Any of the crew is welcome to my cabin. And though it's certainly not as rich in furniture or space as this one, I've never locked my door to them, and certainly never to you."

"True that be," Livingston said. And now that Griffith had considered and refuted every point, only one tactic remained to Livingston. "When I said the crew don't talk about you and the woman, I might've held back a piece."

"Eh?" said Griffith with a raised eyebrow. "What? What have they said? And which ones? I'll have words with them myself."

"Now, now," Livingston replied in a calming voice, "it's not fair I should speak gossips of the dead."

"They're dead?"

"Yes," he sighed. "So I guess, in that regard, there's little concern to you."

"Who were they?"

Livingston gave another sigh, and he had trouble avoiding a grin for his slyness. He thought it profoundly clever to use the dead as sources of gossip; they wouldn't have the chance to deny these words, so there was no better scapegoat.

"If the gossipers are dead," said Griffith when Livingston didn't answer immediately, "it won't hurt to know their names."

"Gregory Norrington, largely," Livingston replied. He saw no deception in revealing this name. Gregory was utterly dead.

Griffith shook his head. "That boy had not a brain in his skull large enough for thoughts of his own. This must have come from another. I never saw Gregory parted from Nathan Adams. And Nathan has more smarts than he lets on."

Livingston realized his mistake too late. He hadn't meant to place Nathan under scrutiny. "The words came from Gregory, not Nathan."

"The smart one whispers," Griffith drawled, "the stupid one talks. You know this."

"Everyone talks eventually."

"Indeed," Griffith replied with a thin smile that lacked its usual affability. "I hope they don't talk through the dead." He embellished a shiver. "That would be most unsettling."

Livingston saw that his ruse was failing. Frustration flushed in his cheeks, and his next words were too loud and too forceful. "What is it you plan to do with your share, eh? It's no secret that you hoard your earnings!"

Griffith recoiled, but he would not give to anger, no matter how badly Livingston wanted him to. "I take no more than my fair share of plunder. What I do with it is my business, as is true of any member of this crew."

Livingston didn't like that one little bit. "When the elected captain deserts his ship for a whore, it becomes *my* business."

Griffith appeared too stunned for retort. There they stood in awkward silence for what seemed a minute or more. For a brief moment, Livingston wondered if he had been too hasty. He clenched his teeth and cursed his faltering resolve where his friend was concerned. He was not a man of apologies and doubts.

"Anything else you wish to say?" Griffith finally asked.

"Yes," Livingston growled. "What kept you in your cabin all night? Surely not the loving arms of Katherine Lindsay? You reek of murder and sex."

"I would think the aromas complimentary."

"Then your nose is plugged."

"A man is immune to his own scent," Griffith replied, and abruptly swiveled and made for the exit.

Livingston spread his arms, perplexed. "What the fuck does that mean?"

22

GRIFFITH

His skin sizzled as the flames lapped at his arms and legs, and he wobbled about the bed in a frantic attempt to roll away, but his back seemed weighted to the mattress by some unseen force. The wall of fire parted at his feet, and there he expected to find his escape route, but *she* blocked it.

Her hair spewed flame from the roots, and her obsidian claws lengthened as she reached for him. She arched her back and heaved her chest in a great, guttural laugh that was somehow even worse than the fire upon his skin. Her laughter died abruptly and she fixed her terrible gaze on him. She bent over and crawled onto the bed, shoulder blades slinking up and down in a rhythmic motion, one after the other, like a stalking cat.

Her skin was no longer colored ivory, as it had been in the previous incarnation of the nightmare; it was now a deep red. She loosed a set of skittering giggles as she crawled on top of him. The fires chewed at his skin, but that searing pain was second to the horror of her looking down on him, and the infinite blackness in her eyes, which now reflected nothing. Though he was lying on his back, it felt as though he was dangling at the edge of a great precipice. She closed on him until there was nothing but the empty void of her eyes, and the fire about him was whisked away by an icy wind that struck the warmth from him as swiftly as diving into North Atlantic waters on a winter day. The ice struck bone first and spread throughout every muscle and vein until finally it assailed his heart. He longed for the fires that only seconds ago threatened to devour his flesh.

He plummeted into nothingness, and in that impenetrable, infinite blackness he eventually came to the alleviating realization that he was dreaming. He had fallen for too long, and fear gradually gave to reason. He attempted to jar himself awake, slapping at his face and pinching his arms, but he kept falling and falling. When it seemed he would never stop plummeting, a thin blurry line parted the blackness and opened into a massive oval that revealed a dark brown world carved with dozens of indistinct lines. He blinked until the lines formed the woodwork of the cabin overhead.

He was awake.

He felt his skin. It was neither cold nor hot. He felt the sheets at his waist. They were not on fire. He tilted his head and found Katherine Lindsay naked in the bed next to him. She was no longer a terrible host of fire, but beautiful and peaceful in her slumber, with a faint smile etched into the creases of her lips, induced of fairer dreams than his. She lay flat on her back with her breasts pointed upward, steadily rising and falling with each shallow breath. He placed a hand atop her chest. She rolled against him and groaned happily. Her eyes were narrow slits that barely saw. Her hand wandered beneath the sheets and felt between his legs. She pressed herself against him. He was instantly aroused.

She was lazy in her movements. He saw the opportunity to make a play for her lips, which she had stubbornly denied him so far. He kissed her forehead and then her cheek and then started for her lips. She swiveled her head just in time, so that his mouth found her neck instead. Even half-awake she denied him fulfillment of this simple yet oddly enticing desire, which had become all the more attractive as he gradually realized he was being deprived of it.

And then she was on top of him, grinding furiously, her hair spilling about his face, lips just out of reach. He clutched her swaying hips, digging his fingernails in until she winced. As he neared climax, she suddenly rolled off him and seized his manhood, holding it firmly in place without further motion. The orgasm was virtually nonexistent, with only a few drops of his seed dribbling down her hand. He choked back rage.

She fell asleep before he could regain himself and chastise her. He wondered if she had ever really been awake. He turned over and desperately tried to finish what she had started, but it was no good. He remained flaccid and frustrated.

For the remainder of the night he was unable to sleep, for their lovemaking had been too disappointing to expunge the memory of his nightmare.

He dressed early that morning, but decided to leave his boots. He wanted to feel the air on his toes. When he ventured on deck the sky was dark purple and the air possessed a fresh chill that would not persist beyond sunrise. Bright stars dotted the sky, but they faded as they neared the eastern horizon where the purple surrendered to a bluish radiance. There he saw the pointed sail of a small, single-masted ship, fine on the starboard bow. The few crewmen who were awake gathered round as Griffith took out his spyglass and viewed the distant ship.

"She's closing fast," he said to no one in particular. "A sloop, I think. No other would be capable of such speed."

"Pirates," said one of the crew. A sloop in these waters was a sure indication.

"Bound from Nassau," wagered another.

"Should we tell 'em that we already took the treasure?"

The ensuing laughter stirred the pirates that had been sleeping on the deck. "What's all that noise?" one of them grumbled as he sat up.

"Who cares?" replied another. "Unless it's another galleon bursting with treasure, stow it and let me sleep."

When the sloop drew near enough, she hailed *Harbinger* under a tattered black flag with a white skull and crossed cutlasses. It was not long before she was passing on *Harbinger's* starboard side, with her short and lowly captain stretched over the bulwark, yelling, "Reverse course or yield your careers! Better you should make for Tortuga!"

When Griffith implored an explanation, the man tossed over a rolled parchment. The sloop's stern passed before the captains could exchange further words.

"What ship be that?" said Livingston as he ascended to the quarterdeck.

"Didn't get the name," Griffith muttered as he unrolled the parchment. "They were in a hurry."

Livingston and a few others stared over his shoulder. It was the last thing he expected to see:

A royal proclamation from King George himself.

Griffith had difficulty understanding the true implications beneath the long, tricky words. At great length he came to its meaning.

"Damn the idiot King George!" exclaimed one of the pirates who apparently knew how to read and had also just figured out what the parchment meant.

"When the sun comes up," Griffith said grimly, "the light won't render this nonsense any less impossible to read. From what I gather, Nassau is in British hands."

The pirates muttered various curses.

"According to this proclamation," Griffith announced as he turned to the gathering crowd, "King George will grant us pardon if we surrender ourselves willingly to the new governor in Nassau."

"Old Sawney?" laughed a pirate.

"I'm afraid we're not so fortunate," said Griffith. "This new governor is very real, and likely a good deal saner than Old Sawney."

"Sawney's real! Saw him, I did!"

"Shuttup!" Livingston spat. Of anyone, he seemed the most disturbed by this news. "They'll take our plunder. That's the price of our surrender."

"There's time to decide," Griffith said. "But for now I'd suggest we alter present course. Should this parchment have found us a month ago or more, I might have been inclined to accept its terms. As it stands, the offer is sound, but not with the fortune that rests in our hold."

"We make for an island," suggested Livingston, "and stow our booty there."

Griffith was nodding his agreement before Livingston had finished his sentence; he already knew what the quartermaster intended. "And then we return to Nassau," he added, "and gladly accept this fool governor's pardon."

"And when things is finally settled," said Livingston with a growing smile, "we return for our treasure."

About an hour after the sun rose, Griffith and Livingston briefed the crew on the situation and informed them of their plan. A vote was called and the response was unanimous, though not without minor reluctance from several men who were not yet clear on the issue.

Griffith returned to his cabin.

Upon stepping within, his bare heel slid into something wet and clumpy. He raised his foot and found it smeared in cat shit. He shook his head and scanned the cabin for the beast. "Shits everywhere but its litter," he growled.

While Katherine slept, he cleaned his foot and looked over charts of the area. He found an island marked by a small blotch of ink. *Harbinger* had happened across the island a few years prior and Griffith had dotted its coordinates on the chart in case he might someday use it as a cache.

He sat back in his chair and regarded Katherine Lindsay, who remained asleep in the bed with the morning light glowing on her soft skin. He closed his eyes and imagined that the two of them were not in a cabin on a ship, but in a large house on an expansive hill that overlooked the sea. And outside, instead of the coarse banter of pirates, he heard the festive laughter of children.

Exhausted from a restless night, he fell asleep in his chair with a smile on his face, and his imaginings carried into his dreams. And for that long and rejuvenating rest he knew nothing of fire-haired demons or British governors and their treacherous pardons.

23

THATCHER

The Englishman named Norton, who had accepted the loss of his arm without a trace of fuss, was dying from an infection. Thatcher found him in a secluded partition of the hold talking to a pig. The pig never responded with anything more than an oink, but Norton reacted as though his every remark was being countered. "Is that so, Mr. Pig?" he said. "Well, how about we see what Mr. Thatcher has to say about that, shall we?" He extended a bottle of rum with the one arm he had. "What do you have to say about that, Mr. Thatcher? Eh? I say, 'one more drink, vicar!'" He took a hefty swig, but more rum spilled down his shirt than into his mouth.

"I might be of more help," said Thatcher, "if I knew what the discussion was about."

"Of course," Norton replied. "Mr. Pig here insists I have every reason to live, however I'm more than certain my death is at hand. You must know the terrible pain I'm in, you being a doctor and all."

The pig gave another oink.

"Of course he is!" Norton bellowed at the animal. "Are you daft or what are you? Anyways, it's rude to interrupt. Not everything I say I'm saying at you, you know." And then he fixed a stern eye on the pig until he was convinced that it would offer no further opposition. "Aye, that's right," he said. "Anyways, what was I saying? The pain is awful, it is. It goes forever on and it won't stop short of my death, so I figure I'll end it right off. But that's not so easily accomplished as it is spoken, you know."

"I know," said Thatcher.

The pirate started to cry. "Truly I wish I could do it. I've tried and failed every time, as you can guess, seeing as I'm not dead. I've asked Mr. Pig to help me with it, and though he thinks ill of killing, he agreed. Only problem being his stumpy hands can't handle a pistol. I think he knew all along it would never work, and that's the only reason he agreed to do me in."

"Smart pig," said Thatcher.

Norton's shoulders started to shudder and his chest started to heave. He lowered his head and lost himself in tears. "Oh God," he moaned. "Oh God, oh God." The tears etched white trails through the dirt on his cheeks. His eyes widened as they met Thatcher's. "Seeing your face now, I know it's hopeless. You look on me as one who stands over a grave. Oh God."

Norton dropped the bottle of rum and frantically felt about his waist with shaky fingers until he found his pistol. "Here she is!" he exclaimed with a grin that contrasted his tears. And then he thrust the weapon at Thatcher. "You do it! Mr. Pig can't. He doesn't have opposable thumbs."

Thatcher held up his hands and shook his head. "You put that down," he insisted. "I will do no such thing. Not while there's life still in you."

"You call this life?!" the man screamed, throwing the gun.

The pistol smacked Thatcher painfully in the head. "You're no different than Mr. Pig! I can hardly tell the two of you apart! Get away from me, fat man!"

Thatcher sat up and plucked the pistol from the ground. He held it at an awkward angle. "I've never touched one of these."

Norton turned over, putting his stump to the bulkhead, and curled into a ball. "Hooray for you," he said.

Thatcher looked from the pistol to Norton. He knew that this man had only a week left in him at most, and it would be the most painful week his miserable life. The request made perfect sense, unfortunately.

The gun was a simple contraption, and it required no loading; Norton had already taken care of that. Thatcher cocked the hammer back, as he had seen the men do, but he did so with far greater care, for his palms were sweaty. The hammer clicked into place. He clenched the handle with two hands and aimed the weapon at Norton's stomach.

The dying pirate perked up hopefully, but he frowned when he saw the direction Thatcher was aiming. "Not the belly, you fool! You'll blow my guts out, and I reckon that's the only pain worse than the one I feel now. The head. Aim for my head, if you please."

Thatcher's hands trembled as he raised the barrel. He touched a finger to the cold metal trigger. He struggled to pull it, but it wouldn't budge. He wasn't sure whether his finger was stubborn or the trigger. After a moment, when Thatcher did not fire, a dismal look fell over Norton's face. "You're not going to fucking do it, are y—"

It was then that the trigger relinquished, snapping back suddenly. The hammer jerked forth. The flint sparked the frizzen and ignited the powder in the priming pan. The shot cracked so loudly in Thatcher's ears that his eyes squeezed shut involuntarily. He felt something large and hefty brush against his thigh. When he opened his eyes, he saw the pig running to the opposite end of the hold. He turned to look at Norton, but couldn't see through the rising cloud of smoke. He inhaled, taking smoke into his lungs, and started coughing. The gun fell from his grasp.

And then, as he was recovering, a hand tightened on his shoulder. He looked up into the fierce, unblinking eyes of Edward Livingston. Thatcher expected the man to pounce on him right then and there.

But Livingston didn't pounce.

Instead, the quartermaster said, "By the powers, Thatcher, you've had it." It was the calmness in Livingston's tone that filled Thatcher with dread.

"The man was dying," Thatcher attempted to explain.

Livingston only smiled. "You might've saved that shot for yourself, as I can guarantee you far worse a death."

Thatcher was relieved when he saw Griffith make his way into the hold along with several others. The captain was a far more reasonable man than Livingston, and the quartermaster would not murder him in front of the captain.

"Someone heard a shot," Griffith said. And then he saw Norton's corpse and frowned. "What's all this?"

"Thatcher saw fit to murder one of our crew," Livingston answered.

Thatcher laughed nervously. "Murder? He was dying. He asked me to do it. He *begged* me, in point of fact!"

Griffith took on a disconsolate expression that was perhaps worse than Livingston's. "You might've come to me first, Thatcher."

"The pistol went off! I didn't mean to do it!"

"I've had it with your stench," Livingston said. "Count your days. The first island we come to will be the end of you."

"No!" Thatcher screamed. He looked past Livingston and

pleaded to Griffith with outstretched hands. "Don't desert me!"

"Desert you?" Livingston laughed, stepping in front of the captain. "Your quarrel be with me now, Thatcher. You've killed one of the crew, and I'll see you dead for that."

Thatcher felt dizzy. The confines of the hold seemed to stretch away from him, and Livingston seemed to grow as tall as *Harbinger's* mainmast. Hot beads of sweat streamed down his temples and cheeks.

Griffith's voice was distant, small and unhelpful. "He's our surgeon, Edward."

Livingston's voice was thunderous. "He's a murderer! I see no use for a surgeon who kills his patients!"

Griffith stepped around Livingston and fixed Thatcher with a piteous gaze that reminded him of Norton's woeful words not moments earlier: "You look on me as one who stands over a grave."

After Griffith and Livingston left the hold, Thatcher sat in seclusion, attempting to regain control of his body, which was trembling so violently that he thought it might fall apart. His mind spun endlessly with dreadful images, each more gruesome than the last. It wasn't until he looked on the corpse of Norton that his shivering ceased. The tranquility of Norton's lifeless face cleansed Thatcher's mind of its reeling. It was a face he had seen on many corpses, and until now it had meant nothing to him.

The shot had carved a clean hole in the center of Norton's forehead. His hair rested in a sticky mass of blood and brain matter, where his skull had ruptured. Thatcher closed Norton's eyes and did not look at him again. Shortly thereafter, several pirates descended into the hold and carried Norton's body aloft.

They did not spare a glance at Thatcher. As far as they were concerned, he was dead already.

Thatcher wandered the deck for six days, as would a man who strolls about a dream, with not a care or fear in the world. And whenever his thoughts were of death, he recalled the tranquil face of Norton, and a smile came to his lips. His time on Earth was nearing its end, he knew, and he looked often to the sky and lost himself in its cerulean brilliance as he pondered what waited for him beyond.

However, on the sixth day his bliss fled from him as he gazed on the lush green island that bore his fate. He crumpled to the deck and was overcome with a dread more terrible than any he had ever endured. The face of Norton and the sky above brought him no comfort; he feared he would remember neither.

There is nothing beyond this, he realized. *As horrible as this life is, it's all I have.*

Somewhere behind him, he heard the discordant laughter of Livingston.

24

KATHERINE

A white beach bordered the island, and its hilly center was densely packed with dark trees. The late afternoon sun cast a serrated pyramidal shadow over the eastern beach where the pirates boated to shore.

Katherine had insisted on going, but Griffith was strangely hesitant. She pressed on, and finally he admitted, "There will be a duel." To that she offered only a shrug. She had seen these pirate duels before, and though they were bloody she wouldn't let anything prevent her from escaping the confines of the ship, if only for a day.

As the boat was rowed toward the beach, she peered over the edge until she glimpsed shallow sands through the lucent waters. When the keel slid ashore, she hopped out ahead of the others and set her feet in the cool water. She smiled as the soft sand slid between her toes.

Griffith leaped into the water behind her, along with several others. He left a man aboard and ordered him to return the boat to *Harbinger* to retrieve another group. He then took Katherine's arm in his and they started onto the beach.

A group of crewmen that had arrived earlier had settled on the beach with a pile of supplies. Griffith took blankets, poles, and a sheet of hemp. Katherine followed him to a secluded area beneath a cluster of palms, where he deposited the materials. "I wager you won't have any trouble pitching a tent," he told her, and he abruptly left to meet the next arriving group.

She spent the better part of two hours pitching the tent, and in the end she was suspicious of its fortitude against a strong wind. Still, it looked as good as most of the other tents that had sprung up along the beach during that time. She found a log and dragged it to the front of the tent for a makeshift seat. She didn't realize how exhausted she was until she sat down.

The blue sky deepened. The island foliage flushed red at the edges and splintered the rays of the declining sun. The tip of a coned shadow fell from the highest point of the island and stretched far into the sea. It wasn't long before the shadow faded entirely and the island was blanketed in the dusky afterglow of twilight.

Katherine watched as the pirates gathered firewood and prepared birds, pigs, and turtles for dinner. Fires burned late into the night, soft pillars of smoke reaching high into a boundless sea of twinkling stars.

Katherine's stomach started to growl. She ignored it at first, and then it growled all the louder. She wasn't in a very sociable mood, and she had hoped that Griffith would bring her a plate of food, but his present whereabouts was a mystery. As she forced herself to her feet she became aware of the soreness in her legs from kneeling for so long.

She slowly made for the barbecues. Many pirates nodded to her as she passed by. She had become something of a celebrity due to her talent with ropes. They did not expect much of women, and were easily impressed by one who accomplished even the simplest of their many tasks.

Several of them beckoned her to their various circles to try their meals, and she politely declined. Most of the meat was charred black from lingering in the fire for too long.

A whiff of something sweet drove her along a trail, and she followed it all the way to One-Eyed Henry's camp. The carpenter was pouring a steaming concoction of rum and coconut juice on turtle meat. He handed Katherine a pewter plate and said, "Take what you can handle, but don't go stingy in your portions, thinly lass." Katherine heaped as much meat onto her plate as would fit. Her eyes proved larger than her stomach, and she finished only half of the delectable meal, which was as fine on the tongue as it was to the nostrils. She thanked Henry profusely and headed back to her camp.

She crawled into her tent and collapsed in the blankets, her belly bloated and her lips smacking of coconut and rum. The soothing sound of waves spilling gently over the beach quickly sang her to sleep.

She was stirred early that morning when Griffith returned. He carefully fit himself into the blankets, trying not to wake her, and she made no sign to let him know that he had done just that. He wrapped an arm around her and was lightly snoring within minutes. She had a difficult time getting back to sleep, for he stunk of sweat and soil, and he lacked the usual brackish fragrance that she had grown fond of. Briefly she wondered what he might have been doing so early in the morning, but sleep claimed her before she could further contemplate.

When she woke, Griffith was gone. She sat up and rubbed her droopy eyes for a long time. She thought she heard a voice, but it was obscured by a wave breaking over the shore. She listened until she heard another. And then she heard two voices, and then three, and then came a roaring volley.

She crawled from her tent and stood up and stretched. On the beach a ways off there was a huge gathering of pirates. It looked as if the entire crew was there. They were shouting and cheering.

Someone said, "Might as well put the gun to your own head, Thatcher!"

"Will he stink so fierce when he's rotting?"

"Can't be worse!"

Katherine's breath caught in her throat. She forgot her drowsiness and dashed forward. She pushed through the sweaty crowd of pirates until she came to the forefront, where she bumped shoulders with Nathan Adams. He had a grim look on his face, and she tapped him twice before he noticed her.

"Oh," he said. "Hello, Miss Katherine."

She squinted against the glare of the bright white sands and saw Livingston, Thatcher, and Griffith. Griffith had his hand on Thatcher's shoulder and was quietly saying something to him. Livingston was inspecting his pistol. Griffith handed Thatcher a pistol. Thatcher accepted it with a miserable nod.

"Oh no!" Katherine exclaimed. "They can't do this!"

"It's done," Nathan glumly replied.

"But that awful brute will kill him!"

Nathan fixed her with a stern glare. "And you'll be next if you don't keep quiet. Livingston's mad, I tell you. He's lost it. Even Griffith isn't for this."

"Then why does he allow it? He's the captain, isn't he? He can stop this."

"Quartermaster's got more say than captain."

She shook her head, fighting tears. "What could Thatcher possibly have done?"

"Killed a pirate is what he did."

"Not Thatcher!"

"Yes Thatcher. Put the poor fellow out of his misery. It was the right thing, but Livingston wouldn't have it."

Before anything more could be said, Griffith took a step back and raised his arms and said, "Go!" Katherine watched in horror as Thatcher and Livingston started pacing.

"This can't be happening," she said. Everything about it was wrong. She dug her fingernails into her arm to assure herself that she was not still asleep in her blankets, having a terrible nightmare.

She did not wake.

Thatcher had been nothing but kind to her, and she had come to realize that he was not a pirate; he was merely a man of unfortunate circumstance. Whenever she looked on his sad face she hated herself for the moments of pleasure she had taken from this voyage, and lately those had grown far too many.

"We have to stop this," she said to Nathan.

One-Eyed Henry grasped her arm from behind. "Stay your anger!" And then, more quietly, he said, "There's naught to be done. Livingston isn't one to be trifled with. He'll kill you just as swift."

"Do you fear the man, Henry?" she shot back with a glare.

Henry released her arm. "I give advice, that's all," was his humble reply.

Thatcher and Livingston reached ten paces each. Thatcher suddenly spun round with a speed no one would have guessed his cumbersome body was capable of. He took aim.

Livingston turned at leisure.

Thatcher fired.

Livingston jerked. He glanced downward. Thick droplets of blood spotted the sand beside his right foot. His face reddened. "You've shot me bloody shoulder!" he cried.

"I didn't mean to," Thatcher murmured absurdly.

"No, you surely meant for me head." Livingston aimed his pistol at Thatcher's head. "Allow me to show you how it's done, Thatch."

"Please, no!" Thatcher protested, dropping his pistol and shielding his face.

After a pause, Livingston grinned sadistically. "No. It's blades for the two of us." He threw the pistol into the sand and drew his cutlass with the arm that still worked. "Someone give Thatcher a sword!"

No one obliged.

Katherine leaned into Henry. "Give him your sword."

Henry shook his head. "Quiet."

"You bloody coward," she hissed in his ear. He winced, but did not meet her gaze.

Griffith came forward at last and stuck his cutlass in the sand next to Thatcher. He glanced at Katherine. *You could do more than that,* she thought.

Livingston extended his blade. "Wounded or no, I'll still send you to Hell, Thatcher!"

Thatcher grasped the hilt with sweaty hands and pulled it from the sand. He lifted it into the air. The blade shimmered in the sunlight as it trembled in his grasp, scattering silvery shards of light across the beach. "God save me," Thatcher said, briefly closing his eyes.

Livingston charged with his cutlass held high and screamed at the top of his lungs. Thatcher raised his sword and withered behind it. His legs bent and his head sunk into his shoulders and he clenched his jaw and squeezed shut his eyes.

Livingston's blade did not meet Thatcher's. Instead, the quartermaster plunged the blade into the surgeon's stomach. Thatcher's eyes shot open. He gasped hoarsely. Livingston dug the blade deeper into his stomach, forcing him onto his back. Blood spurted in thin streaks across the sand as Livingston ground the cutlass into him. He tilted the blade this way and that, and blood shot up into his eyes. He blinked and persisted in goring Thatcher, who started to wail like a little girl. And then Livingston slid the cutlass out of Thatcher's belly and plunged his fist into the yawning wound that he had carved. Thatcher slapped madly at Livingston's arm and shrieked and wobbled and kicked his feet. The shrieks reached a horrendous pitch as Livingston wrenched a handful of intestine from Thatcher's gut.

Hardened pirates shuddered in petrified silence. Katherine screamed for someone to do something, but no one seemed to hear her. Even Griffith was frozen in place.

Katherine ripped herself free of Nathan's grip and lunged for Livingston's discarded pistol. She dove into the sand and came up with the weapon in her clumsy grasp. As she struggled to aim it, Livingston started to grind Thatcher's entrails into the sand. "Get away from him!" she screamed.

Livingston turned very slowly to reveal a hideous face that was painted in Thatcher's blood. "Put it down, little girl, or I'll gut you next."

Griffith fell out of his stupor. "Katherine!"

She didn't take her eyes off Livingston. "I said get off!"

"I'll have you for this, girl," Livingston said with a ferocious glare, the whites of his eyes made all the worse by the crimson lids that encircled them. "Mark me words, you'll make worse sounds than Thatcher!"

"I'll not say it again," she promised.

"Katherine, please," Griffith urged.

"It's fine," said Livingston. He let Thatcher's intestine fall into the sand as he stood up. He did not remove his gaze from Katherine's.

Thatcher groaned pathetically. "Someone . . . help me."

"Find your stitching kit, fat man," Livingston quipped. "See if you can put your guts back in. You have plenty of time, as that wound won't kill you for hours."

Thatcher screamed something unintelligible and rolled over.

Katherine cocked the pistol. Livingston smiled at her. "Go ahead. Assuming a stroke of luck befalls that shot, I'll die gladly." He extended a hand to the crowd and yelled, "After she's done with me, stick a spit up her cunt. Your next meal is on me!"

The crowd did not cheer. No one dared to utter a word. Livingston gave them a foul look. "What is this?" he cried. "A pack of cowardly whores is what I see! Have you never seen a man's guts?" With that, he leaned over and spit in Thatcher's face.

Katherine stepped closer and aimed the pistol directly at Livingston's head. He moved back. "It's only got one shot," he warned. "You'd best not miss."

"I won't," she promised. She turned, pointed the pistol at Thatcher, and fired. His head snapped back and his brains sprayed across the sand. The echoing report was lost in the crash of a tremendous wave. The water washed up along the beach until it touched the trickling streams of Thatcher's blood.

"YOU BLOODY CUNT!" Livingston bellowed in outrage. He lunged for her, but Griffith was on him before he could get very far. "You cunt! You bloody cunt! I'll kill you! I'll fucking kill you!"

Griffith wrestled Livingston to the ground. He threw a wary glance at Katherine. She lowered the gun and turned away. Pirates in the crowd started to mutter to one another. She heard her name over and over. Whether their comments were good or bad, she could not say, and she did not care.

She met the stern gaze of the tallest of the Seven. He acknowledged her with a slight nod of his bulky chin.

"That fat, foul bastard shot me!" screamed Livingston from behind her. "Someone pry this cursed ball from out me bloody shoulder!"

"Best talk to Henry about that," Griffith replied unsympathetically. "The surgeon is dead."

Before noon, Griffith spirited Katherine back to *Harbinger*, offering no words of dismay or comfort. She suspected that he was angry with her beyond his ability to articulate, but she cared little for his feelings. All that mattered was that Thatcher was out of his misery.

If she'd been gifted with two shots, the second would have found Livingston's forehead. Even so, the quartermaster had done himself in. The stunned silence of the crew was proof enough. Though they were disgusted with Thatcher's stink, no man deserved such an end.

She doubted that Griffith condoned Livingston's actions. Griffith was a killer, but he did not deal out an excess of cruelty unless it furthered his benefit.

When they returned to *Harbinger*, there were only a few pirates aboard who had not been present for the duel. Griffith rushed Katherine into the cabin and slammed the door shut behind him.

And then he unleashed his fury.

He smashed her so powerfully with the back of his hand that she was knocked against the table in the center of the cabin. He moved in for another blow and she momentarily fended him off with a thrust of her legs. He seized one of her ankles and pulled her away from the table. She landed hard on her back. He sat on top of her, straddling her.

"You stupid bitch!" he shouted. For all his anger, there was no hatred in his eyes. He dropped his forehead onto her breast, as though exhausted. When he lifted his head there were tears in his eyes. "He'll kill you."

She ran her fingers through his hair. "You won't let him."

He chuckled mirthlessly. "I can't be everywhere at once, Katherine. Jesus, what have you done?"

"Thatcher was dead already."

"Yes! He was! And you might've let nature take its course rather than wake Edward Livingston's wrath!"

"That man's wrath never sleeps. I could only quicken it. The world is his enemy, and he will kill it one person at a time until someone does the same for him. Are you blind to that?"

"He is my friend."

"The longer you protect me, the closer you are to becoming his enemy. He will murder you if he deems it necessary. He may have tears in his eyes when he does it."

Griffith sighed. "You did right by Thatcher. And I'd wager not a man on that beach, except perhaps Livingston, would disagree."

"Thank you," she said.

He gingerly touched the burning cheek he had slapped. "I'm sorry," he said. "You make me unwise, Lady Katherine."

She nearly gasped, but caught herself.

Lady Katherine.

Clarity struck her like lightning.

Thomas never told you my name; he merely told you the name of his ship. And you guessed my name from that.

When first he uttered the name "Katherine," her surprise had revealed it to be true. The only thing more disconcerting than this revelation was that she had known it all along.

Stupid. So very stupid.

Instead of slipping out from under him and running as fast

as her feet would carry her, she remained under the pirate captain's impenetrable gaze. Instead of spitting hateful curses and clawing his face, as she so intensely desired . . . she smiled.

His fingers found the buttons of her shirt and slowly undid them. He slid off her trousers.

The door was kicked open. Livingston entered. His right side was soaked in the blood that had poured out of the wound in his shoulder. He licked his lips when he saw Katherine, who was naked, save for the unbuttoned shirt. He had a dull look in his eyes, as if drunk, but Katherine guessed that it was due to loss of blood.

Please. Die.

"What's the meaning of this?" Griffith demanded as he stood.

"I fancy a go with your bonny lass," he growled. "She took from me the privilege of Thatcher's screams. For that I'll take me share of her cunny. She's good and ready, from the look of her."

Griffith blocked Livingston's path. "That's not going to happen, friend."

"Friend? Are we still?"

"I would hope."

Livingston sighed. His eyes rolled back in their sockets.

Please. Just die.

Griffith set a hand on Livingston's shoulder. "The shot is still in you?"

"Never you mind!" Livingston snapped, shoving away his hand. He glanced down, staggering drunkenly. The cat was at his feet, rubbing against him and purring. Livingston bent down and snatched the animal by the scruff of her neck. The cat moaned.

"You're hurting her!" Katherine protested.

"Aye," said Livingston. "Maybe I'll take her as me toll for

what you done to Thatcher."

"What I did to Thatcher?" she said, appalled. "I spared his pain."

Livingston's face contorted in disgust. "Spared his pain?"

"Edward," Griffith protested, "it's only a cat."

Livingston smiled darkly. He turned and walked out with the cat in his arms. Katherine brushed past Griffith in pursuit, heading on deck in nothing but an open shirt.

Livingston was waiting for her at the bulwark, gently stroking the cat. "She's a feisty one," he laughed. "Got a bit of her mommy in her, she does."

"Hand her back," Katherine insisted. She was dimly aware of several pirates ogling her, but she paid them no heed.

"She's gotten big," Livingston said. "But still frail, I fear. You give her a name yet?"

"No," she said, praying that the conversation would keep him from doing anything rash.

"Good." He swung the cat by the neck in a great arc and smashed its little body against the bulwark. The animal's screech was cut short as her bones shattered. Livingston tossed the corpse over the edge of the ship and clapped the fur from his hands.

25

CUNNINGHAM

On Jack Cunningham's coattails rode a chaotic torrent of churning grey clouds that had chased him since his parting with Governor Woodes Rogers at Nassau. The storm had been ever-present on the eastern horizon, taunting the little ship with a thunderous fury.

Abettor was a two-masted schooner with a compliment of thirty-two men. Cunningham had disembarked from Nassau's harbor with a crew half as large as when he had entered. All of the crew had been pardoned of their acts of piracy, along with Cunningham. Only half of them agreed to help him seek out pirates that were unaware of the pardon, or arrest those who were strictly defying it, thus acting as officers of Woodes Rogers. The others, while content to accept pardon, openly abhorred Cunningham's willingness to help Rogers, cursing him for a coward as they departed. "Like a dog," one of them called him. "Eager little pup licking his new master's boots for want of affection." Cunningham inwardly acknowledged the truth in their bitter words.

He had watched from the balcony atop Sassy Sally's tavern as Rogers arrived in Nassau on the *Delicia*, flanked by the *HMS Rose*, *HMS Milford*, and a pair of sloops. Only one pirate and his crew had offered defiance. Charles Vane, a brash man who Cunningham thought more despicable than Blackbeard, made an impressive display by setting alight a French ship he had captured. The fires touched the ship's powder magazines, and the blinding blast lit the harbor, as though the sun had risen prematurely. A small cheer went up from several pirates who on the following day would surrender to Rogers alongside Cunningham. A few of the pirates introduced themselves with flippant titles; one man even claimed presidency over a council that Cunningham had never heard of.

Cunningham offered Rogers the firmest of handshakes and his true title: "Captain of the *Abettor*, sir. A fine pirate sloop she was, and now she's whatever you would wish of her." Rogers seemed refreshed by this introduction, for there had been none so honest. As he moved on to the others, many of them adopted Cunningham's honesty, and their plagiarism filled him with resent. *What more should I expect of pirates? They thieve everything, even words.*

Despite a horrifically mangled jaw wrought from a gunshot wound in a past adventure, Rogers was an impressive man to behold. He wore a long jacket, breeches, buckled shoes, a cloak, and a full white wig. But his stout and unchallenged eyes were his most stunning characteristic. Instantly, Cunningham knew that all the fantastic stories heralded of this man were true.

And so he found himself outrunning a storm that snapped at the *Abettor*'s stern with teeth of lightning. Ahead he faced the western horizon, as yet untouched by clouds, and within that opening was a dark green island with a jagged peak at its center, reaching for the heavens.

A familiar brigantine was moored off the eastern beach.

The clouds followed Cunningham in, swathing the island in their impenetrable murkiness. He moored *Abettor* and took a boat to the larger vessel. As he came aboard and shook the hand of his old friend, lightning flashed far above.

"You bring a storm," said Griffith with a welcoming smile.

"Seems it finally caught up with me," Cunningham replied. A crashing report of thunder buckled the knees of everyone on deck, save for the two seasoned captains.

"Best we get inside," Griffith chuckled, "before lightning strikes us dead for our sins."

"It's had many an opportunity," Cunningham laughed. "Thus far we remain un-killed."

On the way to the cabin, Cunningham noted *Harbinger's* broken deck and bulwark. "Your deck looks affright!" he exclaimed. He also noticed far less crew than was customary. "And your crew is scant! Have they all gone ashore?"

"Over a third of them dead and still they're twice as large as yours," Griffith fired back cheerfully.

Cunningham laughed through clenched teeth. There were times when he wanted to strangle Jonathan Griffith for his blithe arrogance, and this was one of those times. Still, his affection for his friend always got the better of him. He let the underhanded remark pass.

"Your crew hasn't been stricken by a plague, I should hope," Cunningham said.

"God no!" Griffith sneered. "I would not have them die so tamely."

The warmly lit cabin was a stark contrast to the dark greys of the outside world, and so was the beautiful woman sprawled across Griffith's bed like a strumpet in a painting. She sat up with a lingering expression of shock. Apparently she was not accustomed to company.

"Katherine," said Griffith, "this is my dear friend, Jack Cunningham."

"Pleasure," she said with a brusque smile. She tossed a glare at Griffith and whipped the sheets up over her impressive mane of curly red hair.

Griffith shrugged. "She won't bother us."

"You've been very busy," Cunningham observed. He tried to ignore the whispers in his head that stressed the significance of the woman's red hair, the British accent that was evident with just one spoken word, and even her name. *What is so familiar about her?*

Griffith's voice cut Cunningham's thoughts in half, like a knife through melted butter. "What brings you to this island, of all places?"

"The wind," he answered with a grin.

Griffith moved to the circular table at the middle of the cabin and slid out a chair for Cunningham. They took seats opposite each other. "I must confess," Griffith said, laying a hand carelessly atop the table, "I thought you might never leave Nassau."

Cunningham ran both hands through his curly blonde hair. He interlocked his fingers at the back of his neck and sunk into a cavalier recline. "And yet here I am."

"Here you are," said Griffith with narrowing eyes. "I'm wondering as to why."

Cunningham suddenly felt unwelcome. "Have I interrupted anything?"

Griffith raised his hand, balled it into a fist, and slammed it down. "Dammit, Jack, I know what's happened in Nassau! Come out with it already."

Cunningham's heart fluttered. *Does he know of my surrender*

217

to Rogers? How could he find out so quickly? Cunningham had set out from Nassau immediately after Rogers made him an officer, and *Abettor* was no slouch in the area of speed. He could not have been outrun.

The beat of his heart slowed as he realized he was jumping to conclusions. The most logical conclusion was that Griffith had heard the news from a passing pirate ship that escaped shortly after the *HMS Rose* was spotted on the horizon. There were more than a few of them.

Griffith studied him intently, making him uneasy. "Jack, you seem to be forgetting that we sailed the seas together and shared many a plunder. I know you well enough. What are you not telling me?"

Cunningham swallowed, his throat suddenly parched. He was acutely aware of the thick humidity of the cabin. He glanced at Griffith's liquor cabinet and glimpsed a long-necked bottle of wine. He wished that Griffith would offer him a drink. He repeatedly directed his eyes at the cabinet as an indication of his thirst, but his old friend was not taking the hint. Perhaps it was too fine a vintage.

"Those days are past," Cunningham said finally.

Griffith regarded him narrowly. Finally he stood and said, "Would you like some wine?"

"I thought you'd never ask."

Cunningham recounted the events at Nassau. With much less enthusiasm he revealed that he had officially abandoned piracy and was presently tasked with seeking out pirates for the new governor. When he was finished, he leaned back and gulped down the rest of the wine while waiting for Griffith's response.

It was a long time before Griffith finally broke the silence. "Why is it you never took on a woman, Jack? I don't believe I so much as saw you in the arms of a whore."

"What has that got to do with anything?"

"Your fondness for this Woodes Rogers fellow makes me suspicious of your inclinations."

Cunningham blinked through a flush of anger. He did his best to preserve a cool tone. "I'm not here to arrest you, Jon."

"Nor could you if you made the attempt," Griffith replied with a dismissive wave of his hand.

"I'm not your enemy."

"That's lucky for you. My enemies are all dead."

"And neither is Rogers."

"That's lucky for him," Griffith retorted snappily, bearing his teeth. "But it seems to me Rogers has made an enemy of all true pirates."

"There are but few 'true pirates' left," said Cunningham. "And do you know why? 'True pirates' sink with their ships and die with their treasures. Have you ever heard tales of a pirate's retirement?"

"Many."

"Truly?" Cunningham laughed. "Lend me their names and residences, so I might congratulate them in person."

"If they advertised their whereabouts, they wouldn't be alive. Just because you don't see them doesn't mean they don't exist."

"I could say the same of mermaids."

Griffith flinched. "One day someone will put a knife in Rogers' spine." And then he smiled, the strain easing from his face as he came to a conclusion. "But it won't be me. I'll take Rogers' pardon, and I'll smile as I do."

The tension fled Cunningham's muscles. He was ashamed for having doubted that his old friend would make the right choice. Through all their years of piracy, Griffith had always been one step ahead of him, and now, for the first time he could recall, Cunningham was setting the path. It was an awkward role that had made him a little nervous.

Griffith slapped his palms on the table and pushed himself to his feet. "Well," he said, "help yourself to spirits aplenty. My cabin is yours. I have duties I must attend to. As you said, my deck is affright and wanting for repairs. I'll return as swiftly as I'm able."

Griffith left Cunningham alone in the cabin. Or so he thought, until the woman stirred in the bed. She had completely slipped his mind. "He leaves me with a man I do not know," she groaned to herself.

"You've nothing to fear from me," he assured her. He poured himself another glass of wine. "Except, perhaps, a bout of drunken philosophizing."

She sat up in the bed, her eyes puffy and her cheeks flushed. "I could not sleep through all your chatter."

"Sleep? It's barely after sunset."

"The clouds make it dark," she snapped.

He could think of nothing to say, so he sipped at his wine. He glanced at her briefly and found that she was fixing him with an ugly glare. He struggled to know why her brilliant mane nagged at his mind. "What was your name?" he asked.

"It 'was' Katherine," she coarsely replied.

"And your last?"

"Lindsay," she sighed.

The name agitated him, for it was so familiar. For the better part of an hour he swallowed entire glasses of wine, hoping to quench this undying need to rediscover some crucial piece of information that had too efficiently been locked away. Whatever it was, it had been inconsequential until now.

And then it came to him at last. The red hair. The accent. The name.

Katherine Lindsay!

She had been here all along in Jonathan Griffith's cabin,

while men in taverns spoke of her as though she were legend, hoping they might stumble across her and seize the staggering reward that her murdered husband's family had promised for her. Most figured she was dead by now, with a lonely grave at the bottom of the sea.

And yet here she was.

"What?" she questioned with a raised eyebrow. A desperate look came into her eyes as she sat taller in the bed. "What is it?"

Steadily he fell back to reality. "Nothing," he said, shaking his head. "It's a pretty name, is all."

The desperation faded from her eyes like a dimming candle. She withered back into the irritable woman that had emerged from the covers. It was unsettling how sourly she twisted so lovely a face. "Yes, it's very pretty," she muttered bitterly. "A pretty name for a pretty girl."

"That you are," he agreed.

She hastily retreated to her hiding place beneath the covers. They spoke not another word to each other. Cunningham returned to his wine and drank until the bottle was dry. So fine was the vintage that he went to the cabinet for more. He poured and drank glass after glass, until dizziness prodded at his brow and threatened to render him cross-eyed.

And still his mind stubbornly fought his arduous attempts to silence it. *Poor girl,* he thought. *Poor girl. Afraid and all alone. Her husband killed. Trapped with pirates. The sort of company I enjoy; not the sort she enjoys. Jonathan Griffith, my dear friend, has made a whore of her. Poor girl.*

When Griffith finally returned, Cunningham sprang from his chair, seized him by the collar, and forced him out of the cabin and onto the deck. It was pitch black, and the air was thick with moisture. A lack of stars told him that the clouds had lingered.

"What madness has taken you?" said Griffith.

"That woman is Katherine Lindsay!"

Griffith balked at the stench of Cunningham's drunken breath, waving a hand between them. "You reek of wine."

"Wine and truth!" he proclaimed.

Griffith stared at him for a moment, and then burst into a painful fit of laughter. With a reddened face and shortened breath he said, "By the powers, Cunningham, I haven't the slightest notion what you're talking about. Let's take you inside where there's far less weather. Rain will fall on our heads any minute. And there's that lightning to consider."

"Are you daft or what are you?" He clutched Griffith's shoulders and shook him. "You've stolen a woman with a high price on her head! Half the sailing world is hoping to stumble across her! She's known from here to Bristol!"

Griffith glanced nervously about. "All right, Jack, I hear you. Just keep your voice down."

Cunningham released his friend's shoulders. "You have to give her up."

"She enjoys her life here," Griffith persisted. "She won't admit as much, but I see it in her eyes. She is not the same woman I removed from the *Lady Katherine*."

"Removed? You *took* her!"

"What's done is done."

"She looks dismal."

"Her pet died."

"You killed her husband!" Cunningham boomed heedlessly. The masts of the ship swayed this way and that. He couldn't be sure if he was staggering or the world was betraying his feet.

"I've killed many husbands," Griffith replied indifferently. "She says nothing of him with my cock inside her."

Cunningham shook his head in disgust and gracelessly tried to turn away. He struggled to keep from faltering, seizing Griffith's arm for balance. "She has a price on her head!"

"Yes, you've mentioned that a few times."

He squeezed Griffith's wrist. "A high price!"

Griffith yanked free of Cunningham's grip and fixed him with an accusatory glare. "*You* want the reward!"

It was rapidly occurring to Cunningham that this was not the same man he had known so many years ago. Bitterness had since tainted Griffith's tongue, and his eyes now burned with avarice.

And then Griffith blinked. He smiled, and Cunningham found the face of his old friend once more. "My apologies," Griffith said. "Our recent plunder was great, but it pales in comparison to her. I'm passionate about her, in a way I've never been about anything. I would guard her with my life, if the need arose."

"Plunder?" said Cunningham. The word was sugar on his tongue.

Griffith tossed a conspiratorial glance about the deck. "Far greater than any mere reward, I'd wager. What if I were to bring you in on a share? Would that stay your tongue, old friend?"

Indeed this was not the man he remembered. Griffith had been altered by his love for a woman, and clearly he would do anything for her. *How lucky for her,* Cunningham thought, *that a man should love her so deeply.* Surely her dead husband had not offered such affection. And why shouldn't he profit from Griffith's love? Cunningham was no longer a pirate, but his lust for treasure remained, no matter how adamantly he had tried to suppress it. What was the harm in taking one final piece of plunder and leaving two lovers to their harmony?

"I see rows moving in those sharp eyes of yours," Griffith noted, teeth showing through his grin. "Have I gotten through?"

It was a fair toll. Cunningham had been forever trapped in

Harbinger's wake. His little ship had merely assisted in several of *Harbinger's* victories. Griffith had once suggested that Cunningham name his ship "*Abettor.*" Cunningham found the name amusing at the time, and used it, but now he was sick of its debasing connotation.

A report of thunder stole away his nostalgic thoughts and rooted him firmly in the present. Griffith was unfazed by the sound; he was keenly awaiting Cunningham's reply with an intense gaze, his convivial grin spread wide. "What say you, old friend?"

"My lips are sealed," Cunningham answered.

"We buried the treasure late last night," Griffith revealed at once, all business. "We must go now, while it's dark."

"The sooner the better."

"Good. Permit me naught but a moment with Livingston. I must contrive a story to account for our absence. My crew cannot know of our dealings."

Cunningham nodded his understanding and said, "I'll wait in your cabin." As he turned, he tripped on a loose plank. Griffith steadied him before he toppled.

They shared a hearty laugh.

By the time the two of them had rowed to the beach, a warm rain was falling in light sheets. They dragged the boat onto the sand and Griffith hefted a shovel and a sack. Cunningham pushed dampened blonde locks out of his face and followed his old friend up the beach.

They plunged into the jungle, which was thicker within than it appeared from without. Deeper and deeper they went, and in Cunningham's intoxicated state it seemed that every twist and turn was the same as the last. Griffith pushed on ahead of him, and massive wet leaves swung back to slap Cunningham in the face. Just as he pushed one leafy branch aside, the next would swing to greet him. The rain fell harder and harder, and the mud they trudged was sloppier with every step.

They came to the end of the jungle, where the ground was rocky and inclined steeply toward the peak. Cunningham leaned back for a look, but the tip was shrouded in dark clouds. Griffith must have spied his grim look, because he said, "Don't worry. We go around it, not up it."

Cunningham sighed. "Thank the powers for that."

And around it they went, on a confusing, labyrinthine path that hugged the mountain. It seemed half an hour before they came to an entrance back into jungle, on what Cunningham presumed to be the western side of the island. They took the downward sloping path into the darkness and walked for a long time. The rain pattered the leaves above, but only a few droplets made it through breaches in the dense canvas.

When Cunningham's legs started aching, he said, "I doubt I would remember this path if I tried."

"That's the idea, my friend," Griffith replied between heavy breaths.

"How much further?"

"We're almost there."

After several more paces they came upon a small muddy clearing where the rain fell openly upon the ground. Griffith handed Cunningham the shovel. "You want *me* to do this?" Cunningham balked.

Griffith shrugged. "I've dug this hole once already, and I will again someday. I don't wish to dig it *three* times."

Cunningham took the shovel and pushed it into the mud. It was another miserable hour, with rain pattering the crown of his head, before the shovel's scoop struck metal. He fell to his knees in the three-foot hole he had dug and cleared mud from the top of the chest. He opened the lid. Even in the gloom the jewels and coins brightly ensnared what little light there was. Never in all his years of piracy had he looked on so abundant and beautiful a treasure.

"And that's only one of thirteen chests," Griffith said from above. He tossed the sack down to Cunningham. "Take as much as will fill."

Cunningham was speechless. Once again, he realized with a knowing smirk, Griffith was a step ahead.

"It's strange," Griffith said, voice suddenly peculiar. "You think naught of treachery."

Cunningham peered up at him. "Why would I expect treachery from an old friend?"

Griffith's face was shadowed, but the curves of his cheeks were expanded in a smile. And then, all around the edges of the hole, six pirates stepped into view. The only one Cunningham recognized was Edward Livingston.

Cunningham realized his folly too late.

He wasn't certain which had been of greater influence, but both alcohol and greed had stolen his wits and successfully conspired against him. The inward admission of defeat did little to quell the rising terror in his gut. "You bring me all this way to kill me?"

Griffith laughed. "You come to me spouting reformed nonsense, with words straight from the mouth of Woodes Rogers, yet here you are digging in the mud like a dog. You should see yourself from up here. The promise of treasure sets a sparkle in your eyes, old friend, and no fool governor can extinguish it. Only pistol or blade may take that honor. You are a true pirate, Jack. Truer than I could ever hope to be. And now you will die like one, with your hands clasped to a treasure you will never spend. When next I come to this island, long after my pardon has been granted, nothing will remain but a wretched skeleton to mark your passing."

Livingston tossed Griffith his pistol. Griffith cocked the weapon and aimed it at Cunningham's head. Cunningham blinked through tears and stinging rain as he strained to see the blackened face of his old friend, Captain Jonathan Griffith, who had forever been one step ahead.

A bolt of lightning struck the island summit and the world burned white. In an instant the light faded and all was pitched in darkness.

26

LIVINGSTON

The shot was muted by a deafening crack of thunder. When lightning flashed again, it cast a ghostly white sheen over Cunningham's tomb, revealing for a split second his dead face, gaping in disbelief. Griffith let the pistol fall into the pit and stepped away. The crewmen that had accompanied Livingston moved in with shovels and began to heap dirt back into the hole.

They had been trailing Griffith all night, per his instruction, after he informed Livingston that Cunningham had bribed him for an unfair portion of the treasure. All through the night Livingston and company maintained a safe distance, so as not to alert Cunningham to their presence. Livingston left the fate of the *Abettor* to the discretion of the crew. He had no doubt that they would take appropriate steps in defending their fortune.

Livingston's foul mood was lessened by the satisfying sight of Cunningham's corpse. He had never cared for this man, and he would have gladly pulled the trigger himself, had Griffith not insisted on having that honor.

Cunningham had been far too feminine in his ways, and there was no place in the world for a man with the fastidious mind of a woman. But far more disturbing was the lingering gaze that Cunningham too often fixed on other men. It had always made Livingston uncomfortable.

After the treasure was reburied, and Cunningham along with it, the pirates started the long trek back through the jungle. Griffith never uttered a word or even tilted his head to look at Livingston. The unspoken soreness between them remained, in spite of Livingston's assistance in the present matter. Their camaraderie had always been one that warranted no apologies, but something had changed. Livingston had little doubt as to who was responsible for Griffith's despondence.

Two headaches removed, he realized. *One left. Harbinger* had been dispelled of Douglas Thatcher's stink, and the sea had been cleansed of Jack Cunningham's unsettling femininity. Only Katherine Lindsay remained. Thus far, Livingston had been deprived of the kills. He would have to make up for that. Ever since the woman had denied him the pleasure of Thatcher's screams on the beach, his mind played out a feast of glorious tortures. The killing of her pet, though gratifying, did little to placate his sweltering wrath. Lindsay had poisoned his blood with rage, and killing her would be the only cure.

A pistol would be too fast for her. A cutlass was a true weapon. It did not murder unless it was instructed to. Perhaps he would plunge it into her nether-region and shuffle it around until it spilled her entrails, without allowing her life to quit.

However, this satisfaction would not be so easily granted while Griffith lived. And though he prayed that he would never lose his friend and captain, with whom he had sailed for count-less years, he feared for Griffith's future. If anything happened to the captain, Katherine Lindsay would weep for death before Livingston was finished with her.

He was thankful for the cover of darkness, as it concealed his growing smile.

Livingston lost track of the time it took them to make their way back to the beach. He began to think that they had lost their way. He was incredibly fatigued, and he wanted nothing more than to fall into a deep sleep and dream of the sweet agonies he could not yet inflict upon Katherine. The rain eventually stopped, but the black cloud cover remained. The air was humid, making him sweat almost as bad as the late Thatcher. His skin started to itch all over.

When at last they emerged onto the eastern beach, *Abettor* was burning.

27

NATHAN

Spars crackled and sails danced as writhing flames raced up *Abettor*'s masts. Heat rose from the decks in shimmering waves that coursed swirling trails of black ash into the starless sky. No rain fell to appease the fires.

The screams of dying men had long since faded, and their searing corpses smelled as sweet as the barbecue of the prior night. It made Nathan's mouth water and his stomach growl, but he was simultaneously sickened by the impulse. From that moment on the luscious scent of sweltering meat would be forever tainted.

He took no part in the scuttling of *Abettor*, or the slaughtering of her crew, thus failing his recently appointed duty as first mate. While the ship smoldered behind them, the crew turned a collective gaze on him and stripped him of his rank with disenchanted eyes rather than harsh words. They blamed him for *Harbinger's* fourteen losses to *Abettor*'s defenses.

He didn't care.

Questions blazed in his mind as furiously as the inferno that steadily ate away at *Abettor*, questions that had not occurred to *Harbinger's* insatiable crew in their homicidal frenzy. And burning brightest, like a blinding spike that divided reason from madness, was the most obvious question of all: how could *Abettor's* crew have possibly known of a treasure that was already buried? Was Jonathan Griffith so foolish that he had revealed the treasure's location to the *Abettor's* captain?

There were no answers to such questions and there never would be. Griffith was a man beyond inquiry. No longer did his crew search for meaning in his schemes. The potency of faith had rendered logic irrelevant.

Slowly the fires chewed through *Abettor* from the inside out, flames bursting from the seams and snaking up the hull on either side. At length she sunk into a shallow grave, and the water sizzled and steamed as it extinguished the fires that touched it. Her keel came to a rest with the water level just shy of her main deck. Blackened masts gave way and came crashing down, smashing through and caving the deck in, and out of that gaping wound exploded a cloud of orange embers that arced outward and cascaded down into the water like the branches of a weeping willow.

The skeletal remains of the ship lurched and settled, and then all was silent and dark, water thinly smoking about the wreckage. Soon the fires would die and the last of the smoke would waft into the clouds above and disperse, and to a stranger it would appear as though the ship had rested there since the beginning of time.

Nathan watched over the bulwark as Griffith and his company boated around the ruin of *Abettor*. Griffith boarded *Harbinger* in silence and vanished into his cabin. A sleepy-eyed Livingston exchanged words with many of the crew.

"Fourteen dead," one of the Jamaicans informed him. The

same man indicated Nathan with an accusing finger and a nasty scowl. Nathan didn't need to hear his words to know what was said.

Livingston approached with an unhappy look. Nathan fully expected to incur the quartermaster's infamous wrath, but he was unable to muster much concern.

However, Livingston walked right past him.

"No lecture?" Nathan asked.

Livingston didn't pause, but under his breath he said, "You're not one of us and you never were." Strangely, there was not a trace of malice in his tone.

Nathan merely nodded.

"I'm going to sleep," the quartermaster said. "Any man who wakes me will get a knife in his belly."

There was a nervous laugh all around that quickly trailed into obscurity. After what had happened to Thatcher on the beach, they were afraid of laughing too loudly at Livingston's jests, but knew better than to remain entirely silent.

Nathan was thankful for Katherine Lindsay. She had done poor Thatcher a favor when others had been too cowardly to step in, but he feared that she had placed herself in mortal danger by doing so. Livingston's bloodlust had been satiated for the moment, but his tenacity would find itself renewed in the coming days, as it always did.

The clouds were dimly illuminated by the dullest of mottled greys. The sun was drawing near on the eastern horizon.

By the same madness that had consumed the pirates on the prior night, a majority vote favored sailing *Harbinger* into the very storm that had tailed the late Jack Cunningham. Perhaps it was the ache of their loins that urged them so recklessly toward Nassau. The promise of a strumpet's bosom was a powerful motivator. Nathan knew this above all others.

Though he missed Annabelle terribly, he did not wish to drown in the attempt to reach her. He had cast his vote in favor of remaining moored outside of the island until the storm concluded, but he was laughed at, spat at, and called a coward.

And so *Harbinger* crested the pinnacle of the tallest wave Nathan had ever looked upon. And as the ship tilted steeply downward, with her bowsprit aimed into thin air and her hull groaning under duress, he closed his eyes and filled his mind with the soothing image of Annabelle's smiling face. He desired more than all the fortunes of the world combined to take refuge in her soft embrace. He prayed to whatever powers were listening to bring him safely to her.

Stinging pellets of rain brought him back to reality. He was blinded by an arcing column of light that struck the deck. He heard the snapping of lines and cracking of wood. Someone screamed, "Get down!" and Nathan turned too late. The splintered end of a shattered spar sailed downward and plunged into the inner bend of his right arm. The force lifted him off his feet and spun him like a ballet dancer being tossed from one to another. There was no pain, just a sweeping nausea as he spiraled through the air. He caught glimpse of the spar stuck in his arm, jutting from his elbow. And then he landed, cheek slapping down hard, and his blood rinsed the deck.

He awoke on the main deck to a blue sky that shone through breaking clouds. He tilted his head and saw that the fore topsail had been ravaged. The hemp was charred and tattered, whipping uselessly in the wind, and the starboard end of the topsail yard had snapped off.

And then, in concurrence with a jolt of pain that peeled his lips from his teeth, he recalled the accident. Livingston was pulling the largest splinter of the yard out of Nathan's arm, with his heel pressed against Nathan's shoulder to secure him. Livingston fell backwards when the splinter finally gave way. Blood spurted all over him.

Nathan shrieked. Two men held him down. The pain was unfathomable. Something shattered inside his mouth as he clenched his jaw, and he felt as though his face had split in two. His head fell back and his skull smacked the deck. His breath caught in his throat as he inhaled, and he coughed up blood and the white chip of a tooth.

"Where the hell is Thatcher?" Livingston bellowed as he tried to force a chunk of wood in Nathan's mouth for him to bite down on.

Griffith stared apprehensively at the quartermaster. He seemed more worried for Livingston than he did for Nathan. "Thatcher's dead, Edward."

The whites of Livingston's eyes surrounded his irises. His pupils were tiny dots. "I know that," he said at once. "You think I don't fucking know that?"

"Of course not," Griffith assured him. He placed a gentle hand on Livingston's shoulder.

"I bloody did him meself," Livingston said, a grin forming. "I remember the stupid look on his face when I took his guts out."

"The arm has to go," came the voice of One-Eyed Henry.

"He's not a yardarm!" Livingston spat. "What would you know of it, carpenter?"

"His arm is useless," Henry replied in the least offensive tone possible. "It will turn black, and the rest of him will go black along with it if we don't take it off."

Nathan glanced at his arm and was horrified by what he saw. He bit down on the chunk of wood and struggled to maintain consciousness. He did not want to wake up minus a limb.

"You know shit," Livingston said, giving Henry a shove.

"Edward," Griffith said. "Calm yourself."

"We have to take it off," Henry insisted.

"Let it be!" Nathan gasped, spitting the chunk of wood out of his mouth. "Let my arm be! It's fine!"

"The boy wants to keep it," argued Livingston.

"I want to keep it," Nathan agreed, nodding frantically.

"He's out of his mind right now," said Henry. "I know what I know. If that arm doesn't come off above the elbow, it'll be the death of him."

"Don't go into the storm," Nathan muttered, in accordance with his thoughts. "Don't go into the storm. Don't go into the storm, I said. I voted. I voted. Remember? Don't go into the storm. I voted. Don't go into the storm."

"Take off the arm," said Griffith. The finality in his order allowed no dissent.

"Didn't vote. Didn't vote." Nathan rolled his head to and fro, and the sky and masts rolled with it.

"Hold him down till I return," Henry said, and he took his leave. Nathan couldn't be sure exactly how long Henry was absent, as he stumbled in and out of consciousness several times. Henry finally returned with a fine-toothed saw and red-hot broadaxe.

Nathan's eyes rolled back in their sockets. Pain washed through him like tides on a beach, and the thought of agony worse than this was incomprehensible.

He fainted.

He awoke to a sherbet sky. Not a single wisp of cloud. The sun had touched the horizon, and was now a giant, misshapen sphere. The storm had passed. *Harbinger* was safe.

Nathan's mouth throbbed and tasted acidic. He swallowed and winced at the sharp pain in his throat. He dug a finger inside his mouth, feeling around until his finger sunk between two teeth into a gelatinous, hollow gum. He withdrew a bloody finger. *I bit my tooth off,* he remembered. *Because of my arm. My arm! They were going to cut off my arm!*

But they hadn't. They couldn't have. The ache of his right arm still plagued him. He sighed in relief and reached to massage it. His fingers grasped air. When he tilted his head for a look, he gazed upon a blackened stump. He screamed and scrambled to his feet, smashing his back against the bulwark. With the only hand he had left he grabbed at the empty space where his arm should have been, unable to clutch it, but still suffering throbs of phantom pain. He screamed and cursed until his voice broke. As twilight fell, he crumpled into a heap and moaned pitifully.

Pirates regarded him with quick, nervous glances as they passed by. As far as Nathan could tell, no one had sustained injuries, aside from minor scrapes.

Just him.

Nathan rolled over on the deck and whimpered, tucking the stump underneath his left arm. He wondered how he could show himself to Annabelle again. He imagined her expression. She would gasp, her lip would curl, and she would turn away and pretend as though she had never known him.

He bent forward and threw up.

28

KATHERINE

Rarely did she realize within a dream that she was dreaming, but as she plunged through the thickening jungle, she knew it could be nothing else. She shuffled through the massive leaves, but they kept coming, tearing at her body one after another and dashing her face like giant paddles on springy green sticks. Passing one leaf meant running into a larger one, and so on. They sliced at her arms, shoulders, and face. She grew furious, slapping at the leaves and screaming, but this only gained her a fresh set of agonizing incisions. She glanced over her shoulder and saw her blood dripping from the tips of the leaves. She shook her head in dismay and pushed onward. *I can't go back, only forward.*

Just when she was beginning to think she would be forever lost in this madness, she pushed through to an empty clearing of white sand bathed in sunlight. The circular opening was no more than twenty paces wide, surrounded on all sides by impenetrably dense jungle. She had no desire to go in there again. *I'll stay here for a while. Rest.*

Streams of blood crisscrossed her arms, legs, and shoulders. She realized that she was naked. Had her clothes been ripped to shreds by the plants? She couldn't remember. She wasn't sure she'd even had clothes on when she entered the jungle.

When did I enter the jungle, anyway?

When you fell asleep.

Ah yes. I am dreaming. But why don't I wake?

Because you don't wish to wake. Not yet.

There was no harm in exploring a dream, despite the pain that her mind made so vivid.

The clearing was totally silent. She couldn't even hear the intake of her own breath, no matter how heavily she drew it. "Hello?" she called, but no sound emerged.

"Hello, darling," came a familiar voice. She turned to see Thomas standing three paces from her, smiling. He looked his finest, dressed for business from head to toe, as though ready to attend a meeting. His hands were in his pockets. His thin hair was pushed back, neatly combed. His skin was a shade paler than she remembered, but his smile had lost none of its charm.

She wrestled with an urge to retreat full speed back into the jungle. *This is a dream,* she reminded herself, and held her ground. Her legs felt like they were about to give out from under her. "What do you want from me?" she managed. Her voice was audible this time.

"You've nothing to fear," Thomas insisted, never losing his smile. "I'm quite dead."

"What do you want me to do about it?" she demanded. She bit her lip, refusing to let herself cry.

This is only a dream. It's not him. It's not your Thomas.

"There's nothing anyone can do about it now," he said with a shrug, smiling away.

Stop smiling.

Her chin quivered. She shook her head, fighting the wave of emotion that threatened to overtake her. She steadied a finger at him. "You stay right there! Don't come any closer."

"I couldn't if I wanted to," he replied, spreading his arms. "I can't leave this place."

But I can. She turned and fled, leaving Thomas and his infernal smiling behind her. She dove into the jungle and crashed through the foliage, ignoring the wounds the plants inflicted. She raced as fast as she could, slamming into the giant leaves, bounding off them, twirling, stumbling, scrambling to her feet and running again. The leaves flayed skin from muscle like a whip, and red shreds of flesh dangled from her arms. She shrieked in pain, but she would not return to Thomas. *I won't have him smile at me again.*

She collapsed into a second clearing. This one was larger than the last, perhaps thirty paces across. Sand spilled into her wounds, grinding into exposed muscle, and she opened her mouth to scream at the sky. As before, no sound left her throat. With pain searing through her body she thrashed in the sand until the grains formed a protective blanket around her. The white grains settled into her wounds and merged together, gleaming like melting glass. The sand forged flesh where it had been stripped bare.

She was healed.

The pain was gone.

She got to her feet, one leg at a time, and found unexpected strength in her muscles. When she breathed, the air easily filled her lungs. She felt renewed, as though a splash of cold water had invigorated her.

"Hello?" she called again, and again there was no sound.

"Hello, Miss Katherine."

She turned slowly, knowing the voice before she saw the

face. "Hello Douglas," she replied cautiously.

Thatcher's lips twitched into an uncertain smile, but it faded quickly. He was as heavy and bald as ever, but he had less cares than she remembered. The skin of his face and arms was smooth and unbroken. He wore a clean white shirt and brown trousers. He looked down and prodded the sand with his big toe, gouging a little hole. "This is my clearing, I suppose."

"What is all this?" she asked. She felt more comfortable in the presence of Thatcher than she had with her own husband, for some reason. *Perhaps it's because he isn't smiling like nothing happened.*

"Is this supposed to be heaven?" she tentatively wondered.

"It's a dream," Thatcher answered flatly.

"I know that," she withered. "I wish to know its purpose."

"It's purpose?" Thatcher considered that for a moment, muttering to himself. "To annoy you with blatant symbolism, I suppose."

"I saw Thomas," she told him, aiming a thumb over her shoulder, "back there, in another clearing."

"Your husband?"

"The very same."

He chuckled softly. "Then I'm not the first dead man you've chanced across."

"Hopefully the last," she sighed. "I'm not sure I can stand anymore appearances from dead friends. No offense."

"None taken."

He avoided her gaze, digging his toe deeper into the sand. She took a step closer, leaning in slightly to see his eyes. "I'm sorry for what I did, Douglas."

"Don't apologize," he said, fixing her with a melancholy gaze. "I'm not Douglas Thatcher. And that man you just left was not your husband. You know this." He pointed to the jungle, opposite the spot she had materialized from. "You must

241

continue on."

"I don't want to," she groaned.

"The jungle won't injure you this time," he said. He looked down at the hole he'd carved in the sand with his foot and studied it intently. "Hmm," he said, stroking his chin. "I wonder how far I can go?"

She moved past him, watching him, but he did not meet her gaze again. She continued into the jungle. The leaves slid about her body, edges coarse and stiff, but they did not break her skin. She grinned and broke into a sprint. *This is much easier.*

It was not long before she came to the third clearing. This one was oval and very far across, maybe the length of a large vessel. In the middle of it stood a man she would not have recognized had she not met him recently. He was tall and sturdily built with a scraggly blonde beard and curly blonde hair. He was dressed all in black. "Katherine Lindsay," he announced with a knowing smirk.

"You know who I am?" she asked, eyeing him suspiciously. *Why am I seeing this man? I met him but once. He means nothing to me.*

"Jack Cunningham knew you," he replied. "But he knows nothing now, as I'm certain you've concluded."

"Griffith killed him?"

"For what he knew," Cunningham said, shaping his right-hand into a pistol and aiming the index finger at his temple. His thumb touched down, and on the opposite side of his skull he flourished the fingers of his left hand, simulating a spray of brain matter.

"You've all died because of me," Katherine blurted. She had finally uncovered the meaning of this infernal dream.

Cunningham grinned, opening his arms wide and bowing. "Very good, my dear. Very good."

"What's the point of this?" she demanded. "I know who has died and why. I need no reminder. Thomas should never have brought me to sea! He would be alive now if he hadn't, and I would be safe in London!"

Cunningham nodded his agreement.

"And *Livingston* killed Thatcher," she continued. "I merely ended his suffering."

Cunningham shook his head firmly. "You ended his life just the same."

"Fine!" she barked. "And you? You died because you were foolish."

"Cunningham was indeed a fool," Cunningham agreed. "But, as I said, I am not Cunningham. This is your dream, Katherine. No one else's."

"Then I'm ready to wake," she proclaimed, pounding a foot in the sand.

"Then wake," he said, as though it was that easy. "Or don't."

"Why wouldn't I?"

"Because there is more to see." He opened a palm to the opposite end of the jungle. "Just a little further, darling."

"Don't call me that." Thomas had called her that. This man had no business doing the same.

He lowered his head in false modesty. "As you wish."

She gave him a wide berth as she made her way around to the opposite side, glancing at him apprehensively along the way. His eyes trailed her the entire time, lips curving in a boorish smirk.

"I'm glad you're dead, Jack Cunningham," she spat back at him. "You didn't even try to save me! All you cared about was treasure!" She ran into the jungle before he could reply.

The trees seemed to open for her when she entered, leaves pulling away from her as she passed by. She stopped to reach out for one and it wrinkled in on itself, shying from her finger.

She frowned and continued on. As she delved further, light spilled in on her from above. The jointed trunks of the trees bent away from her in either direction, opening to reveal thin glimpses of sapphire through the canopy and an occasional flash of sun.

She ran for a very long time, never once grazing a leaf. The muscles in her legs strengthened with every stride, glistening with sweat in the flashes of sunlight. She felt as though she could run forever, and she might have done so if she hadn't come to the fourth clearing.

The jungle vanished on all sides, but no white sand greeted her this time. The ground left her feet and she spiraled through the air into a swirling blue abyss littered with streaks of white. As she spun, she saw the blur of a sheer cliff face. She had run right off it.

She crashed into the water, her back stinging from the impact, and floated on the surface for an instant before sinking. She flailed her arms and legs, suspended underwater with the surface just a few feet above her. She reached for the sun, a glittering orb just beyond the rippled canvas. It dimmed as she sank, and the ripples slowly merged and lost distinction. Just when she thought all hope was lost, her feet touched the ground, sand spreading between her toes. She let her knees bend and then projected herself upward.

She emerged with closed eyes and inhaled deeply. Air filled her lungs. Her eyelids popped open as a sheet of salty water washed down her face. The waves bobbed her body up and down, and beyond each cap she saw a white beach at the foot of the cliff from which she had plummeted. She started to swim.

She swam until her feet grazed sand, and then she stood and waded onto the beach. She collapsed onto her hands and knees, catching her breath as the water washed up around her and retreated back into the sea.

A man's hand fell before her face, palm open. She grasped the hand. *Who is this, now? One last wraith to taunt me?* He helped her up, and when she looked into his face, she recoiled in horror.

"Hello, Miss Lindsay," Nathan said.

29

GRIFFITH

He found Katherine in bed, face veiled by her hair. She had hardly eaten a bite or spoken a word since Livingston killed her cat. Griffith sat beside her and gently massaged her back. He drew her hair away from her face and saw that her eyes were open, staring distantly into space. "You should eat something," he said in an upbeat voice. "There's no reason to sulk about. We have much to celebrate, you and I."

She blinked.

"I'll buy you ten cats and more."

She rolled away from his hand, sat up, and propped herself against the headboard. "A cat?" she said. "That's your solution to everything, is it? Buy me a cat and all my troubles will slip away." Her eyes welled with tears. "Just like Thomas slipped away."

He scoffed. "It's been a year since his passing and still you're on about him?"

"You think me inconsonant all this time because of a cat?"

She shook her head. "I am a foolish woman. There's no doubting it. But at least I am a woman, not a girl. You, Jonathan Griffith, are not a man. You are a boy who mistakes his ship for a toy and the sea for his tub."

He clenched his jaw as he fought through the sting of the insult. This was just a passing phase, he told himself. Women were notorious for this sort of absurdity, at least once a month.

"You're a child," she went on, "and that's well and good, because I shall never give you one. You need only look in a mirror."

He lashed out, seizing her hand and twisting her wrist sharply. She whimpered pitifully, her face flushing with color. "Watch your words, woman! It's a small miracle if a child does not already grow in your belly."

Her lips curled into a wicked smile, distorted by the flicker of candlelight. For a bracing instant he was reminded of the fiery demon of his nightmares. "There are no miracles," she said. "I cannot produce children."

He released her hand and stood. He turned his back on her, hiding the grief that contorted his face. He heard the rustling of sheets and the creak of the mattress, and then he felt her hot breath on the back of his neck. Her tone was overly cheerful, trickling like water over a brook. "Why is it you never asked if I had a child?"

"I did not care," he replied. In truth, he had not wanted to know. He had felt vindicated in parting a wife from so foolish a husband, but he had no desire to part a mother from her child. He had banished the possibility from his thoughts.

"I have no children," she said. "And I will never give you any."

"You lie," he sneered.

She snatched his hand and pressed it to her belly. "Nothing! How is that possible after all this time? I've had you inside me more times than I care to count. It is no lie. And I don't need to look into your eyes to see that it devastates you."

Heat coursed in his veins. He spun on her, grasped her by the arms and shoved her onto the bed. Instantly her bravado withered, and she let her head fall to one side. A tear spilled from one eye and dotted the quilt.

"I hate seeing you like this," Griffith said. He meant it. Since her capture she had blossomed into a formidable woman. Looking on her now, he recalled the skinny ruin he had dragged from *Lady Katherine*.

"Your desires are at odds with one another," she murmured, her voice as distant as her gaze.

"What has put such a fire in you?"

She glared fiercely. "'She says nothing of him with my cock inside her.'"

Griffith frowned, not following. It was jarring to hear that word come out of her pretty mouth.

"That's what you told your friend, Jack Cunningham."

And then it came to him. Outside the cabin door, he had been trying to keep Cunningham quiet while the fool drunkenly revealed his discovery. *She heard us.*

"Yes," Katherine said, nodding with a scathing smile. "I heard you."

Griffith's mouth was suddenly very dry. "They were little more than boorish words spoken in jest to an old friend. Men speak coarsely when absent women."

"You murdered your 'old friend' to keep me a secret."

Griffith swallowed, and the sound was embarrassingly loud in his throat. He found it difficult to look her in the eye, but he managed, even as he said, "I would murder half of the Caribbean to keep you secret."

She nodded. "For once, I believe you."

He expected her to turn away, but she remained right where

she was, studying him apathetically, as though he were an oversized weed that needed plucking. When he could stand her gaze no longer, he hastily took his leave.

The humidity of night air tasted faintly of the recent storm. The glow of the waxing moon cast a shimmering stripe across the calm waters, illuminating the decay of *Harbinger*. Her decks were ravaged, her sails tattered, and her lower decks diluted. The battle with the galleon and the assault on *Abettor* had reduced her crew by half. The surgeon was dead, the first mate was maimed, and the quartermaster was quickly losing himself to madness.

However, those were distant cares. Nassau was drawing near on the horizon, and Griffith would sail *Harbinger's* rotting bulk into the harbor under British colors. He would greet Governor Woodes Rogers with a smile and a handshake, and he would claim his pardon. In the jungle paradise of New Providence he might loiter for a month or two, keeping Katherine close by his side at all times, until *Harbinger* was fully repaired. And then he and the surviving members of his company would set sail for the unnamed island where their treasure was buried. He would retrieve his share and part ways with *Harbinger* and her crew, leaving the madness of Livingston and the imprudence of pirates behind him. He would settle on a plantation with Katherine, living out the rest of his days in serenity. The future was near enough to taste, a fine vintage that teased the tip of his tongue.

However, his vision had been irrevocably altered. He no longer saw children laughing and running about the green hills of his plantation. He wanted to believe that it was a lie, but he had seen the truth in Katherine's eyes. She would never bear him children. As terrible as that was, he felt worse for his mistreatment of her. It was not her fault, merely an unfortunate stroke of fate. How dreadful of him to blame her for something she had no control of.

I must tell her I'm sorry. Beg her forgiveness. She is everything.

And with a surge of confidence, he affirmed that he would march back into the cabin and offer his sincerest apology. If necessary, he would prostrate himself before her.

He straightened his shirt and combed his fingers through his raven hair. As he started off, a chill born of enlightenment shuddered through him. Captain Jonathan Griffith, bane of the North Atlantic and Caribbean combined, had fallen madly in love.

Livingston intersected his path, face darkened by twilight. "It's the woman, isn't it?" he said, voice flat and lacking the usual respect afforded a captain. "Who else could paint such a foolish grin on your face?"

"Watch your tone, Edward."

"We're pirates," Livingston replied with a shrug, "and our captain makes an ass of hisself, prancing about the deck with a queer grin."

Griffith felt his teeth grinding.

"Am I wrong?" Livingston persisted, glancing around. He snatched a passing deckhand by his arm and drew him near and asked, "Am I wrong?"

"No, sir," the pirate replied instantly, without the slightest clue what the quartermaster was going on about. Livingston released the man and watched him scurry off.

"You see?" Livingston said. "They all know. Women belong on land, not on a bloody ship, and certainly not in a captain's bed."

"You want one of your own?" Griffith said, hoping to calm Livingston's nerves with humor.

"No! I was always smarter in that regard. Never let a whore cloud my judgment."

"Is my judgment truly clouded?" Griffith demanded. "Have I led us astray? Have we not plucked our fortune from the sea, as I always said we would?"

"A boy lost his arm."

"And you murdered a doctor."

"Thatcher!" Livingston spat, tossing a dismissive hand at the sky. "He weren't no proper doctor!"

"And Henry is?"

"Thatcher would've taken the lad's arm just as quick. Would've smiled as he did it, that fat bastard."

"Perhaps. We'll never know."

"Thatcher would be alive if he hadn't murdered one of our crew in the first place!"

"True," Griffith conceded with a heavy sigh. "Everything we do comes at a price. Was that never clear to you? Did you think there would be no casualties? At least the boy is alive and will see his arm compensated for. Thatcher, he's just dead."

"Excuse me while I weep," Livingston snickered. He turned away, setting his palms on the bulwark and chewing his lip.

Griffith moved beside him. "What do you care about some boy, anyway? Compassion does not suit you, Edward."

"No more than marriage suits you," Livingston shot back. He paused to discern Griffith with his eyes. He leaned forward suddenly, feeling about the captain's waist. "Where is it??"

"What in the world are you doing?" Griffith said, slapping Livingston's hands away.

"Where's your bloody pistol?"

"Dunno. Suppose it's in my cabin."

"With *her*?! You bloody fool!"

Griffith's hand balled into a fist involuntarily. He smashed Livingston in the nose, feeling a satisfying crack of cartilage behind the blow. Blood spurted from both nostrils, dribbling down Livingston's mouth and chin. He clasped a hand over his face, eyes wide in disbelief. Griffith looked down at his fist, which had seemed to move of its own accord. His blood-soaked knuckles started to throb.

"You broke my nose," Livingston declared stupidly, black droplets of blood collecting on the deck.

Griffith resisted a second blow while the man was stunned. "Consider yourself fortunate I'm absent my pistol."

30

KATHERINE

Her hands trembled as she pressed the cold ring of the barrel to the underside of her chin. *It would be so easy.*

Griffith had forgotten the pistol on his desk, and it was loaded. It was the first time he had been so careless since he first left her alone in his cabin, with the swords. She had waited for this moment for so long, and had nearly given up hope that it would ever come. He had been so careful.

Her finger hugged the trigger, but she did not squeeze it just yet. It seemed the easy and sensible choice. She would never be free of Griffith. There was no love in her heart for him. The physical attraction had dissolved, and now she saw a wraith of a man, desperately clinging to a future that had long since eluded him.

She was bound to a man she abhorred, and only death would release her. Tiny beads of sweat collected at the edge of her jaw and dripped onto the barrel of the pistol. Her chin quivered and her teeth clacked. She licked her lips. Her finger was moist on the trigger.

She caught a glimpse of her reflection in an aft window. She looked positively idiotic aiming a gun at herself. Morbidly, she wondered what her head would look like after the deed was done. Would the gawking gentlemen in London find her so attractive then? She pictured Griffith stumbling in on her corpse, with her skull yawning and her brains splattered across the bed.

She saw a smile spread across the pretty face of the woman reflected in the window; the first genuine smile in what seemed an age. She was pretty, she realized. She was beautiful, in fact.

She tapped the trigger repeatedly, her finger refusing further commitment. *This is stupid,* she realized. *Only a man could concoct so silly a notion as suicide. Better I should use the gun on Griffith.* The image was so vivid in her mind that she could see the blood running down his nose from a neat, smoking hole between his eyes.

Of course, killing Griffith would only be another form of suicide, and she would endure prolonged torture before being allowed to meet her maker.

Before she could govern these clashing thoughts, the door opened and Griffith stepped in. His eyes went wide in horror at the sight of the gun in her hands. "Katherine? What are you doing?"

She looked down and realized she was still pointing the gun at herself. She resisted chuckling. "What does it look like?" she replied as casually as possible. Pulling the trigger had proved more difficult than she ever imagined, but she wasn't about to let Griffith know that.

"It looks like you're about to do something stupid."

"If only an intelligent option would present itself," she sighed, "I would seize it as eagerly as I seized this gun, which you so graciously left behind."

Griffith paused for a moment, his eyes darting back and forth, searching frantically for the correct approach. He raised his hands slightly, letting her know he intended no sudden intervention. "Let's talk about this," he said calmly.

"We *are* talking," she said.

"Why don't you point the gun at the deck?"

"So you can leap at me and wrestle it from my grasp? I think not, captain."

He winced at the formality.

"I either point this at myself," she continued, "or I point it at you. Which would you prefer?"

He was clearly at a loss for words. She liked him this way. Unfortunately, he always found something to say eventually. "I prefer neither."

"You must prefer one or the other."

"Is your life so terrible here?"

"Not always," she admitted. "But I hate myself for thinking it anything but."

"You think too much," he said, rubbing his temples and closing his eyes in exasperation.

She kept the gun level, for she knew he might spring to life at any moment. His lazy gestures could easily be part of a ruse. "If only I could turn off my brain as easily as you and your crew." She was enjoying this banter, despite knowing it was the last they would ever have. That notion did not sadden her; it empowered her.

Griffith droned on. "You think you don't deserve to be happy, but you do!"

"I deserve every happiness except this one," she said, jerking the gun accusingly.

He raised his hands defensively, and she wondered briefly if the shot would pass right through his palm. "Be careful with that," he begged. "You would kill us both with a single shot."

She snickered bitterly. The implication was clear: shoot me and you'll seal your own fate. "What does it matter? If I can't live with myself, why shouldn't I take you with me?"

"Because the men outside will kill you very slowly."

"Point taken," she said, shoving the nozzle deeper into the underside of her chin.

"I mustn't lose you now," Griffith pleaded desperately. "You've given my life purpose. I'm so close now, Katherine. *We're* so close."

"So predictable," she said with an extravagant roll of her eyes. "You've taken everything I have. You care nothing for me. You care only for the way I make you feel. You expect me to continue living like this? This isn't living. It's a long and slow death."

"Life is never what we expect it to be," he said, spreading his arms wide in an encompassing gesture. She thought he looked rather silly. "It is never the perfect future we pictured as foolish children."

Her arm was quivering from the weight of the weapon. She allowed it to fall slightly. Griffith misinterpreted this as an opening and took a step forward. She tensed her arm and pressed the nozzle harder into her chin. He halted, but stayed exactly where he had advanced. He was making progress.

"If you truly care for me," she said, choosing her words carefully, "you will release me at Nassau. Tell Governor Rogers that you rescued me from the last pirate ship you plundered. I will corroborate your story. No one need know otherwise. Take the reward for yourself."

A way out for both of us, she realized. *Please, Jonathan. Please take it.*

"I will do no such thing," he said. "I do care for you, but that very concern prevents me from releasing you. I'm sorry. I know you don't understand right now. I hope that one day you will."

That made her laugh. "You speak boldly to a woman with a loaded weapon."

"A woman who possesses no intention of using it."

"What makes you so certain?"

"You would have pulled the trigger by now."

She blinked, and her vision was instantly blurred by tears. The gun was shaking in her grasp, its weight tugging at her arms. She wanted nothing more than to let it fall to the deck.

Griffith took another cautious step forward. He smiled softly and outstretched a hand, fingers slowly uncurling. His hand resembled an overturned spider, slowly waking from a feigned death. "Let me have that," he said.

"No," she replied. "There's no other way."

"There's always a way," he hissed, abandoning tact. "You just have to look a little further. This ship will not be our lives forever, don't you see that? We're so close now. So very close. If you end it now, you'll rob yourself of what might have been."

She pictured Nassau port, with its lush trees, and its pirate-hating governor. *So close.*

"Yes," he said, eyes gleaming hungrily, hand outstretched and beckoning her. "There is always another way."

"You're right," she nodded. She aimed the gun squarely at his head.

The gleam left his eyes and his cheeks went a shade paler than his heavily sunned skin normally permitted. "What are you doing?"

"You've convinced me."

"Convinced you?"

"Only one of us will leave this cabin, captain. Sweet of you to bargain so diligently for my life over your own. You see, I don't really want to die. I never wanted to die. But I cannot

257

suffer another minute of this world with you in it. In order for me to live, I must kill you."

"My crew will slaughter you."

"Maybe," she shrugged. "Whatever happens to me, that silly expression on your face is more than worth the trouble. When I am reunited with my husband in the next life, I'll relate to him just how pathetic you looked when I killed you."

All kindness vacated his face. His features contorted, clenched teeth showing behind snarling lips, cheeks blooming a homicidal shade of red, a single vein bulging from his forehead. "You ungrateful little whore!"

She squeezed the trigger, but it required more pressure than she was prepared for. It didn't budge, and Griffith saw his opening and lunged at her. The next few seconds seemed to stretch into long, sluggish minutes in which she viewed the events distinctly and without distortion. Griffith was no longer pathetically comical; he had twisted into some kind of merciless animal. She finally glimpsed what his enemies must have seen before he killed them. Muscles rippled beneath his clothes as he thrust himself at her. His face was bright red now, his bulging eyes threatening to explode from his skull, saliva frothing from his mouth. His hands stretched before him, fingers splayed and gnarled like claws.

He had advanced within two feet when she heard a metallic snap, followed at once by a deafening blast. Something stung her eyes, forcing them closed. She blinked rapidly, cleansing her eyes with tears. An impenetrable cloud of white smoke was suspended before her, obscuring Griffith.

And then, over the ringing in her ears, she heard his blood-curdling shriek. A pair of clammy hands grasped her arms. His face passed through the smoke. She gasped and dropped the gun. It landed with a distant clunk.

The shot had ruptured his left cheek and exited behind the

ear she had bitten on their first meeting. Blood spewed from each end. The gaping, smoldering hole revealed shattered molars. He tried to say something, but only blood spilled out of his mouth, like water from a faucet.

Katherine tore herself away from him. He staggered after her with frenzied desperation in his eyes, wailing and clasping at his cheek. She moved around the table as he followed. His arm swept over his liquor cabinet, toppling bottles of rum and wine. In her hectic retreat, Katherine's legs hit the foot of the bed and she nearly collapsed. She rolled out of the way as Griffith advanced, his blood-soaked hands pleading to her. He loosed a final, mournful wail, and then he collapsed face-first onto the bed and lay still. Smoke wafted from the hole in his ear and blood soaked into the sheets.

Katherine moved without thinking. She snatched the smoking pistol from the deck and threw it onto the bed beside Griffith. Not a split second later, Livingston, One-Eyed Henry, and five other crewmen piled into the cabin. They gawked in silence, slowly approaching the bed. Thick smoke collected above them, trailing steadily from Griffith's head.

Katherine sat on the desk, staring at the corpse, hoping that the joy welling inside her was not written plainly across her face. Fortunately, she still had a few tears in her eyes, facilitated by the stinging smoke.

Livingston loomed over the bed for a long time. When he finally turned, she was surprised to see him smiling. "Tell me he shot hisself," he said calmly.

"He shot himself," she replied in a shaky voice. When she looked at Griffith again, the little plume of smoke seemed to be thickening. The hole in his cheek was illuminated orange from within and dimly flickering.

Livingston's teeth showed as he grinned. "I'm glad you said that, Katherine."

"What's to be glad about?!" cried One-Eyed Henry. "He's bloody dead, he is! Don't make no difference how it happened! He's dead, and dead is dead! That's the end of it! Oh, bloody hell!"

"He shot hisself," Livingston said sarcastically as he moved slowly toward Katherine. "Our dear captain, who just made his life's fortune, shot hisself. I suppose he weren't known for his smarts in latter months. Truth be told, there be more brains spread about those sheets than I wagered he had in his thick skull."

As she gazed into Livingston's abhorred face, a strange calm swept over her. "He shot himself," she repeated.

"And that might very well be the truth of it, strange though it be!" Henry wailed. He was crouched over Griffith, closely examining the hole.

Livingston guffawed, slapping his thigh. "Henry fancies hisself a doctor now! Probably thinks he can patch up that hole and send Griff on his way."

Henry's cheeks bulged and he covered his mouth, convulsing over the smoking corpse. "Oh Christ, someone get a bucket of water. His tongue is on fire."

In spite of herself, Katherine started to chuckle. The utter absurdity of the situation, of these pirates, of life in general, had overtaken her. The tremors in her belly gave to laughter, and soon she was cackling hysterically. Livingston scowled, and that made her laugh all the harder. She pointed at him and laughed, and then she pointed at the corpse of Griffith and howled.

Livingston seized her by the hair and shook her violently to make her stop, but she couldn't have stopped even if she'd wanted to. Laughter flowed out of her until she was at a loss for breath. And even then she didn't stop. She laughed until her face was bright red and her voice was broken.

One of the crewman said, "Somebody plug that bitch's hole!"

Out of sheer exhaustion her laughter finally died, but still she chuckled like a little girl who has stayed up far past her bedtime.

"Feel better?" Livingston asked with an arched brow.

"I really do," Katherine admitted with a luxurious sigh.

Livingston shook his head in bewilderment and said, "We'll do this on the main deck, where everyone can see."

31

LIVINGSTON

Livingston straddled her waist and, with his cutlass drawn, spread his arms to the gathering crowd. "No guns for this bitch!" he bellowed. "Not till the very end! She's taken from us our dear Captain Griffith!"

There was a collective gasp from the many that did not yet know.

"Very convincing," Katherine said. "Even I almost believe you care."

Livingston had to admit, this woman's nerve impressed him. There was not a hint of fear in those pretty eyes. But he knew better. "I know what you want, Lady Katherine. You won't have it. In the end you'll beg me to do it. And even then, I'll keep you alive a little longer."

If this terrified her, she did an admirable job of not showing it. "I know what *you* want, Edward Livingston," she taunted back with an infuriating smirk. "You won't have it."

"Kill her!" came a shout from someone in the crowd.

"No!" Livingston said, wagging a finger. "Slowly she did him! And slowly we'll do her! She took one piece at a time from our dear captain! We owe her the same!"

Some random cheers rose from the crowd, but there was also a low, underlying hum of dissonance. Livingston ignored the timid naysayers. His chest heaved, and with each breath he felt larger, like a god perched atop a mortal. "What piece did she take first? Is there any man here who remembers?"

"His ear!" someone cried. "She bit off Griff's ear!"

Livingston lowered his gaze to Lindsay and parted his lips in a macabre grin. He set down his cutlass and stripped off his shirt, revealing a hairy, muscular chest glazed in sweat. Still she offered no hint of distress.

"Leave her be!" came a feeble cry from the crowd. The voice was familiar.

Livingston frowned and glanced about. His eyes narrowed when he found the culprit. He smirked. "Best stay out of it, Nathan! You won't be saving her with one arm! You had enough trouble with two!" The majority of the crowd roared laughter, but Livingston silenced them with a fierce glare. "And any other man tries to stop me will get a shot betwixt his eyes!"

"Do it already!" someone shouted.

"Get on with it, Livingston!" exclaimed another.

"For pity's sake," came a much weaker voice, "she's only a woman!"

"Do what you done to Thatcher!"

Livingston took a deep breath, reared his great chest, and then fell on Lindsay. He jerked her head sharply to one side, pressing her left cheek against the cold deck, and enclosed his mouth over her right ear. He licked the inside of the lobe, letting her squirm beneath him. He then retracted his tongue, took a breath, and bit down. He gnawed through her flesh, twisting his head this way and that, until his teeth clamped together. He came up with blood bubbling out of his mouth and streaming down the sides. He spat the ear at the crowd. A pirate snatched it out of the air and held it aloft for all to see. Most of them cheered. Some fell silent, as they had done when Livingston tortured Thatcher.

Lindsay's shrill screams carried into the night, long after the cheers had faded and only wayward moans of disapproval remained. The crowd stared in collective shock, startled by the grisly sounds that came out of her. Livingston felt vindicated. "You lied, Katherine. You've given me exactly what I wanted. Thank you."

She freed a hand and slapped it to her head, her fingertips scraping the gooey, curdled surface where her right ear had once been. A steady gush of blood splattered her palm and poured down her head, mixing nicely with her red hair.

Her screams gradually dissolved into pathetic whimpers. Livingston glanced about the crowd and glimpsed an uneasy anticipation on their faces. "Is this not what you wanted?" he demanded. "You feel sorry for her, is that it?"

There was a minor delay before someone half-heartedly yelled, "Never!"

"Good!" Livingston replied, scanning for the man who had shouted. He couldn't find him. "This is what they do! They wake sympathies we didn't know we had! Sympathies are best left on land, where they belong! They rob us of our ambitions! They make us forget that the sea is our only true mistress . . . and she does not suffer women! Neither must we!" He pointed toward Nassau. "Women belong there! On land! Our dear captain forgot that, he did. And he paid for his infidelity with his life."

Several of them started to cheer, but the riposte felt forced and unsatisfying. They were frightened of him, Livingston realized with a smile. *Good,* he thought. *Let them be frightened.*

He would soon be their new captain, after all. Who better to run this ship? And what better way to newly christen it than with the blood of the bitch that had murdered the previous captain?

Livingston looked down on her and snarled. "You're not done, missy. You're not done yet." He took up his cutlass. "There be Griffith's sliced up arm to consider. I think it was the left one, yes?" He pressed the blade to her left arm and gave it a brusque tug. She merely flinched, and Livingston inwardly cursed himself for starting so ambitiously with her ear. A sword slice was probably just a sting compared to the ache pulsating through her head right now.

There was a distant look in her eyes, which were directed past him, to the stars. He shifted, obstructing her gaze. She turned her head to look away, but he squeezed her cheeks between thumb and forefinger, angling her head toward his. He would not allow her to see anything but him. Her eyelids fluttered as she shifted her gaze sharply to the left.

The fire in this bitch!

She had been nothing more than a bony, whimpering waif when Griffith first dragged her aboard. Livingston allowed himself a moment of respect, taking in the fiery red halo splayed about her head. Her bosom, now full with the added weight she had acquired over the past year, heaved between his legs, cleavage mashing together. He felt his manhood struggling against the inseam of his breeches. He reached down and took hold of her shirt, tearing it open and freeing her breasts. He bent over to suck at a nipple. She moaned, probably from the pain of her absent ear, but he pretended she enjoyed his mouth. And maybe she did, in spite of herself. "Little whore," he muttered as his tongue circled the areola.

"Jesus Christ!" he heard Nathan exclaim.

"Leave him to it, boy," came One-Eyed Henry's voice.

"He'll kill you. He'll kill us all."

No one was cheering now, and that annoyed him. He sat up long enough to scowl. "I don't hear any bloody—"

A shot rang out. The crowd split at the center to reveal the tallest of the Seven. He held his pistol high, barrel smoking. He fixed Livingston with a deadly glare that would have chilled lesser men into humble grovelers. In harsh, tentative English, he managed to utter, "End. This. Now."

Livingston was in awe. He hadn't expected any opposition, and certainly not from one of the blacks. "What is your name?" he asked, condescendingly sounding out each word.

"My name," the huge black man said, "is Minkah."

Livingston scoffed. "Someone fucking shoot this overgrown monkey."

There was a long, awkward silence. Just when Livingston was about to take matters into his own hands, a shot rang out and struck Minkah in the forehead. He stiffened, was frozen in place for a moment, and then collapsed to the deck with the weight of a boulder.

In an instant, *Harbinger* was hurled irrevocably into chaos. Another of the Seven, who were now four, loosed a deep cry of protest. Pistols fired, cutlasses clanged, and feet hammered the deck. Pirates fell dead and wounded, howling in pain.

Livingston shrugged and returned his attention to Lindsay, "Where were we?"

Something exploded behind him, and a wave of heat seared his back. He fell over Lindsay, who remained limp and lifeless. The sounds of battle had ceased, for the moment anyway. Livingston looked up and saw the crowd's slack-jawed faces lit in amber hues. He peered over his shoulder, shifting his weight atop Lindsay but not allowing her to weasel out from under him. A fiery blaze had ripped through the door of the captain's cabin, clinging to the overhead and rolling under the top of the doorway. Embers ascended into the night sky to join the stars. There was nothing beyond the door but blinding yellow light, as though the sun had materialized within.

Livingston remembered Griffith's smoking corpse. No one had put him out. "Get in there and douse that blaze!" he ordered. Only five of them obliged, while the majority resumed their fighting. The water merely fueled the fire, which was growing steadily, burning through to the deck above.

Livingston returned his attention to Lindsay, who was gazing curiously at the blaze, as though she welcomed it. She looked at Livingston and grinned, her teeth glinting from the fire, her red, blood-streaked hair shimmering vibrantly. He could have sworn he was staring down at Satan himself.

Or herself.

His cock felt like it was going to burst in his trousers. He fumbled at the laces, tugging them away. "I'll have you right here," he said, nodding self-assuredly. He shoved a hand down her pants, fingers squirming. "Is your cunny hair red too?"

"Ask Griffith," she sneered.

"Would that I could," he replied. "I'll just have to find out for meself. Maybe I'll flip you on your belly and go in the back way, how does that sound?"

She was still smiling, which both excited and frustrated him. But she wasn't looking at him; she was looking slightly past him again. He saw the reflection of a man in her eyes, standing over him. He turned too late. A plank cracked the side of his head, splintering. The impact sent him tumbling off Lindsay, and the world tilted dizzyingly until his back crashed against the deck.

Nathan stood over him, brandishing in his remaining hand a smoldering plank of wood that had probably been part of the captain's cabin door. "I said that's enough!" he exclaimed through heavy gasps.

Before Livingston's mind could register what had happened, Lindsay crawled on top of him and straddled his waist with surprisingly strong thighs. She brought the blade of his cutlass to his throat and grinned triumphantly. A thin line of cold steel pressed against his Adam's apple.

"Nathan," Livingston growled. His head felt as though it had been filled with tar. The stars twirled in the night sky, leaving white, arcing trails. "Nathan, get this bitch off me, lad."

Nathan didn't move. He dropped the plank.

"Nathan," Livingston pleaded. "I forgive you. You're a good lad, I know that. I'll give you first go."

Nathan said nothing. His face was an indistinguishable blur.

The captain's cabin ruptured violently, a massive ball of fire rolling out of it and taking several dueling pirates with it. The blaze engulfed them, and only their shrieks were heard from within. They emerged burning and flailing madly, until one by one they collapsed to the deck. The fire spread swiftly from their bodies.

Katherine Lindsay was silhouetted in flame, the edges of her face highlighted orange as she looked down at Livingston. "You've gone and pissed yourself," she said. He glanced down to see a yellow pool spreading about his waist.

"Please," was all he could think to say.

Lindsay took a deep breath, her exposed breasts rising. She lifted the cutlass into the air, aiming its tip downward, and brought it down slowly. The tip touched his belly, and he drew in his breath to prolong the inevitable. The tip punctured the skin and sank into him. His belly expanded as he convulsed and gasped for air. Lindsay leaned on the pommel. The blade sheared through him like a bolt of lightning, exiting his back and sticking him to the deck like a pig on a spit. He grasped at the sharp steel, struggling to wrench it from his body, but only succeeded in slicing his fingers. He sucked for air, but something caught in his throat. He tried to scream, and a bubble of blood erupted from his mouth, bursting in his face.

Lindsay stood, leaving the cutlass in its place. "The fire comes for you," she said, aiming a finger at the blaze. He looked to the left and saw the flames lapping along the deck, sliding toward him. The pirates were in a frenzy, screaming and running about. Some of them were scrambling over the bulwark and leaping off. Distantly, between tremors of pain that surged unremittingly from his belly, Livingston wondered how things had gone so wrong so quickly.

This bitch killed us all.

He attempted another scream and failed, sucking blood into his lungs. His arms flailed, fists banging the deck at his sides. His abdomen slid up and down along the blade, fluids seeping out of him.

"It comes for you," Lindsay repeated, her voice hideously broken. "You will pass into the sea nothing more than a blackened scaffold, and your dark mistress will not recall your name, for she has swallowed a million of your lecherous kind before you, and she will swallow a million more before she's done."

Her hair was a translucent meridian, wreathing her head in fire. Her shadowed expression was impossible to see, but he knew she was smiling.

The slithering fire touched his legs, and Edward Livingston found his scream at last.

32

KATHERINE

Livingston was stubborn even in dying. His violent throes lasted far longer than she could have hoped, even after the flames encased his body and licked at his face. His twisted lips shriveled and peeled away from his teeth, blackening his gums. One of his eyes burst in the socket and liquid flowed out, sizzling as it ran down a smoldering cheek. His skin sank into the hollows of his skull until nothing was left but a charred, grimacing death's-head.

"We have to go," Nathan insisted, pawing at her shoulder. "There's an HMS on the starboard beam, no doubt spied the fire from Nassau. If we swim ashore, they might not see us."

Katherine, satisfied that Livingston was thoroughly dead, faced Nathan. She set a hand on his shoulder and said, "Thank you," as genuinely as she could manage, despite her ravaged voice and throbbing skull.

Nathan nodded humbly. "What was I to do?"

Katherine clutched her shirt over her breasts and took in

her surroundings. She looked aft and saw the cabin bursting with flames. Several men who had been dueling on the quarterdeck were suddenly consumed as the beams gave way beneath them. Whites and blacks alike sunk to their deaths, claimed by billowing flames that fed off fresh oxygen.

"It's Hell," Nathan said.

"It's beautiful," Katherine heard herself say, in a voice barely recognizable to her.

The fore-and-aft sail caught fire. The blaze leapt to the mainmast and quickly took the main topsail.

"We have to go," Nathan said again, tugging at her. He pointed starboard. There she saw the massive sails of a steadily approaching HMS ship. It was a man-of-war.

"Can you swim?" she asked, staring at the space where his arm had been.

"Maybe in circles," he admitted.

She allowed herself a small chuckle.

"I don't care much for fire," he said, glancing nervously about. "Given a choice of deaths, I'd just as soon try my hand at drowning, if it's all the same to you."

"Water is the easier death," she said, watching a man slap at the flames ascending his shirt.

"Aye."

It was just then that two pirates, one white and one black, both engaged in a duel, collided with Katherine and Nathan. Katherine was hurtled a good distance away, where she was overtaken by a rolling cloud of smoke. She covered her mouth to keep from coughing. Bits of ash singed the fresh hole in her head. Her agonized cry was drowned out by the roar of fire and the wails of dying men.

Swords clanged and feet thumped the deck. She could see nothing through the smoke. She moved carefully, pirouetting and sweeping her perimeter, trying to take in all directions at once. Her fingers brushed the cold steel of a cannon barrel. She followed the barrel to the bulwark, where the smoke was pouring over the side like mist over a waterfall.

"Nathan!" she called, making her way around the cannon.

She crashed into someone. Hands seized her arms and steadied her. The man smiled broadly. "So happy you're quit of Livingston!" One-Eyed Henry exclaimed. He was drenched in sweat from head to toe, clothes matted to his skin.

Katherine slipped from his grasp and regarded him incredulously. "Thanks to Nathan," she said coldly.

"Yes, well, I was just as imprudent as he in my youth. Age makes cowards of us all."

She glanced down, eyeing the pistol fastened in Henry's belt. "What was it you said, Henry?"

"Beg pardon?"

She moved closer, fully aware that her shirt had come open and her left breast was exposed. The pain surging through her skull invigorated her. "'Leave him to it, boy.' That's what you said."

Henry gave a timid chuckle that sounded like the squeak of a dying mouse. "It all happened so fast," he said. "Who knows what came out of my mouth?"

"I know," she replied. "Lately, I just can't forget little things like that."

"What was I to do? Livingston would have murdered every last one of us, given the chance."

"And yet he's dead by a woman's hand."

"Eternally grateful for that, I am," Henry laughed. "I ought build you a house, when we get to Nassau."

She continued her advance until her breast grazed Henry's chest. He tittered nervously, his lone eye wandering downward. She slipped the gun from his belt and backed away, aiming it at him. "Nice of you to reload it for me."

"Don't shoot!" He thrust his hands skyward. "Please! I done nothing!"

"That's no lie, Henry. You've done nothing. You and nearly every other pirate on this damned ship, with the exception of Minkah."

"Who?"

"A black man. The one you shot, in point of fact."

"What?! I shot no one!" A bead of sweat trailed the middle of his nose and hung at the tip, expanding in size.

"Livingston didn't see who did it, even though you were trying so hard to impress him, but I saw you. You smiled when you did it."

The bead of sweat fell. "Fine," Henry sighed, dropping the innocent act. "You saw me shoot a nigger."

She lowered the gun a few notches, and Henry breathed a sigh of relief, mistaking her intent. She squeezed the trigger. Henry's right kneecap was blasted into a fine crimson mist. He crumpled to the deck and shrieked like a little girl.

She tossed the gun at his side and left him there. "If the fire doesn't take you," she called back, "the gallows will."

She finally found Nathan crouched and coughing at the starboard bulwark near the forecastle. "Thought I'd lost you," she said as she helped him up.

So thick were the flames and smoke that she couldn't see to the stern. Only a few dueling pirates remained, scattered here and there. Why they continued to fight when clearly they should have been swimming for their lives was beyond her. Men had their priorities, and she supposed pride stood taller than all the rest.

She shook her head and purged her thoughts of them. "It's time to go," she said.

"Aye," Nathan agreed.

She helped him onto the rail. He struggled out of his shirt, which would only hinder him in the water. It proved difficult to remove with a single arm, and she helped get it over his head. He nodded his thanks and she pushed him off. She watched him touch down with a quiet splash. He immediately started swimming.

Katherine followed, not sparing another glance at *Harbinger* or the folly of its crew.

33

NATHAN

The shouts of pirates and the cracks of gunshots and the clashing of swords grew fainter and more intermittent as Nathan paddled toward the beach. The ache in his remaining arm had given to a pleasant numbness. He developed an effective method for paddling, swishing his arm beneath his body rather than to the side, and relying heavily on his legs. Adrenaline carried him further than he would have thought possible.

He inhaled deeply as often as he could, his head bobbing above and beneath the water. The waves surged him forward as he neared land. He swept his arm below for another stroke, and his fingers raked sand. His legs lifted suddenly into the air and he was thrust forward with startling velocity. The massive wave deposited him carelessly onto the beach like an oversized fish, bits of gritty sand filling his mouth. He rolled onto his back, panting heavily. Water swept onto the beach around him. Silhouetted palm leaves fluttered gently in the breeze, partially obscuring the starry sky.

When Nathan caught his breath, he perched himself on his elbow. *Harbinger* was completely engulfed in flames. Its form was warped and indistinct, like a log in a fireplace that had burned too long. The sails were gone and only the mainmast remained. Nathan no longer heard the cries of men or the sounds of battle.

The HMS was circling closely, dwarfing the fiery brigantine. Tiny officers stood at the bulwark, probably staring in disbelief. Nathan allowed himself a smile. The king's fleet never got the chance to take down *Harbinger*; they could only watch as it destroyed itself from within.

Something stirred in the water. Nathan shuddered as a shadow rose before him, eclipsing *Harbinger*. Her hair was matted to her head, glistening dark red, like wine through a murky bottle. Her torn shirt hung loose, a breast carelessly exposed, and her breeches were taut against the lean muscles of her legs. She treaded through the waves, never swaying in the current, until she stood before him, face concealed in shadow. "You swim faster with one arm than I with two," she said.

Nathan laughed. "You frightened me."

She offered a slender hand. He took it and she lifted him up easily. They came face to face, and Nathan was surprised to see a smile. After an awkward pause, he said, "You're finally quit of pirates."

"Suppose so," she replied casually. "What now?"

"There's someone I must see. And I'd wager there's a certain Governor Rogers who wants to meet you. Your family will be relieved to know you're alive."

Her smile faded. She took a step back and turned to look at *Harbinger*, which was already starting to sink, with the water bubbling around it. Her eyes glinted with the reflection of the burning ship. "Yes, I suppose they will."

Nathan placed his hand on her shoulder. "You've nothing to fear from them now," he said.

"I know," she replied, not taking her gaze from the dying ship. "They were only men."

"Griff figured he'd live forever, I think."

"It was him or me." There was no detectable emotion in her voice.

"Then you made the right choice," he said, squeezing her shoulder. The muscles slowly eased of tension under his grasp. "We should go, before any men of authority show up."

"I need to watch this," she said, shrugging his hand away.

Nathan avoided looking directly into the blaze. "Seen one fire you've seen them all."

"It's beautiful," she mused. It was the second time he'd heard her say that, and it made even less sense to him now. "It purifies whatever it touches. It's funny."

"I don't think it's beautiful or funny."

"Not the *laughing* kind of funny."

"Didn't know there was any other kind," he said with an exasperated sigh. This wasn't the ideal moment for prolonged cogitation. "We really should—"

"I'm not stopping you," she snapped. She looked at him, instantly repentant, and smiled again. "Go, Nathan. Go find your woman." Nathan was shocked she knew his intention. "I'm sure she's wonderful."

He lowered his head. A tiny white crab was scuttling along the edge of one of his footprints. It rapidly burrowed a little hole in the sand and disappeared. *Smart creatures.*

"Nathan," Katherine said, her voice lifting his gaze. "Don't let them find you. They'll hang you."

"Thank you, Miss Katherine. But I'm more concerned about how you're going to convince Governor Rogers you are who you are. Begging pardon, but you look different from when I first saw you tied to our mast."

"That's my problem, Nathan."

"Well, I was formulating a plan on the swim over."

She laughed. "I would have thought you'd be more focused on sculling with one arm."

"That wasn't so difficult as you might think," he replied with a chuckle. "I was thinking you and me see Governor Rogers together. I can vouch for your identity." He studied her face, waiting for a reaction.

"Nathan, Rogers will string you up faster than—"

"Not if you vouch for me as well."

She bit her lip, eyes darting back and forth. "How would I do that?"

"You tell Rogers I was a deckhand on your ship. I'd wager there's no record of someone as unimportant as me turning pirate."

She hesitated. "What if Rogers has the *Lady Katherine's* log at his disposal?"

"I doubt that!"

"It's a possibility. They've been searching for me, after all. There's a reward out."

"Logs are tricky things," Nathan shrugged. "They're always missing someone. Point is, if you vouch for me, there's no way they can hang me."

"Rogers can hang whomever he likes," Katherine said. "I've been gone a long time. For all we know, some wench may have tried to claim my identity already. They may be expecting a scheme, especially from a pirate. And no offense, but you look like a pirate." She tapped the stump where his right arm had been.

His cheeks filled with heat. "Any sailor can lose his arm! And you look half a pirate yourself, Miss Katherine!" He waved a hand over her missing ear, careful not to brush the wound.

She merely smiled. "Your plan is well intended, Nathan. It's also foolhardy. I have no intention of meeting with Rogers. I have no way to prove who I am, and even with your word, he will suspect us both of subterfuge."

Nathan couldn't believe what he was hearing. "It's the only way! He won't hang you if there's even a chance you are you. Women don't hang so easily as men."

"There's an irony," she chuckled.

He wasn't sure what she meant by that. He couldn't believe she wasn't taking this more seriously. Her life was at stake. Why couldn't she see that?

"Go to your woman, Nathan. Do not linger in port for more than a day. Spirit her and yourself somewhere safe. And don't worry about me. If it's not obvious by now, I can take care of myself."

She leaned forward and kissed him lightly on the cheek. Wet strands of hair touched his face. "Goodbye, Nathan."

Only three emaciated whores loitered within the Strapped Bodice. Two brunettes and one blonde. They all raced hungrily to Nathan's side as he entered, like starved dogs soliciting their next meal. Having recently emerged from the sea half dead and minus an arm, Nathan must have looked affright, but none of them seemed concerned. He shied away from them and said, "Is Annabelle here?"

The three of them exchanged uncertain glances and then simultaneously said, "That's *my* name!"

Nathan shoved past them. He walked up the stairs to the private rooms. After checking in each room, he discovered only another skinny, ugly whore engaged in sweaty relations with a bearded fat man. "Don't go nowhere, love," she called over her shoulder. "I'll get you next!"

Time seemed to slow to a halt. As he walked down the stairs with his head cast downward, insignificant details in the wood stood out. The swirls in the crooked planks of each step took on intricate shapes. He saw a ship with three masts in one step, cresting a wave. He saw a cutlass and a pistol in another, crossed at their midsections. He saw a massive, swelling wave that descended into a field of fire. Finally he saw a woman standing over the corpse of her dead husband. Her eyes glared accusingly at him. The swirls seemed to bend as her gnarled fingers came forward, reaching out to him.

"Are you okay, dearie?" said the blonde whore when he reached the bottom floor. She touched his shoulder. Perhaps this was only a strategy to lure him into her bed, but a quick glance at her big doe-eyes revealed genuine concern.

The two brunettes studied him from a dark corner.

"Where's Charles Martel?" Nathan asked.

"That rat hasn't been round for months," the blonde said. "Heard he left for Tortuga."

"I heard Teach got him on the crossing," the taller of the brunettes said. She had an obnoxiously loud voice.

"That's nonsense, that is," replied the blonde. "Charles had nothing that would concern Teach. Lost all his coin, he did. No more pirates round these parts."

"I see one here," said the loud one, aiming a long finger at Nathan.

"I'm no pirate," Nathan said.

"Begging pardon, sir," she said, glancing at his stump.

"What happened to Annabelle?"

"I don't know no Annabelle," said the blonde.

The loudmouthed brunette stepped forward. "No point looking for that one, dearie. She went with Charles to Tortuga, she did."

"Tortuga?" Nathan repeated despondently. There had to

be some mistake.

"She's got nothing to offer a strapping lad like you, anyway. Not no more."

"What?" Nathan couldn't make sense of anything this bitch was saying. He suppressed a sudden urge to smack her.

"Someone worked her over good, they did."

His mouth felt numb, and he wasn't sure if he was talking or thinking the words as he repeated, "Worked her over?"

"A bald man with a terrible temper. What was his name?"

"Edward Livingston," answered the blonde. "Benjamin told me it was his ship what burned up just off shore."

"Right, that's him!" the brunette said. "Sliced up her face and other parts best left not mentioned. She weren't so pretty after that." She shrugged. "No matter. The clients still fancied her curves better than the rest of us, and Charles saw fit to take her and leave us behind. Suppose it was for the best. Either she's been pillaged by Blackbeard or she's right this very second perched atop whoever Governor Rogers hasn't strung up by their balls, and no woman wants those cocks inside 'em. I'm happy right where I am, thank you very much."

The blonde scoffed. "You stayed here because Charles took only his finest girls."

"There's plenty of men happy with my cunt."

"They don't have a choice, do they?" said the blonde. "Men will stick it in a goat when they run out of women."

"Oh, is Benjamin telling stories again?"

"He's a fine man, he is. He's gone respectable."

"No respectable man would stick it in you!"

The two whores were at each other's throats as Nathan walked out of the Strapped Bodice and into the night air. He moved slowly down the steps, staring at them as he had done before, but unable to find any images within the wood for all the darkness. He stopped on the last step and craned his neck, taking in the stars.

There was a hollow feeling in the pit of his stomach, but he knew no amount of food would appease it. He absently rubbed the stump where his arm had been.

Annabelle was gone. Why hadn't she waited for him? Had she been afraid to show him her face, after what that monster Livingston had done to her? Did she not realize that she would always be beautiful to him, no matter what? She couldn't have given up on him so easily. Perhaps Martel had given her no choice.

Or mayhap she's dead, killed by Edward Teach. But why would Teach bother with a ship full of strumpets? Teach loved strumpets as much as the next pirate, but he wasn't fool enough to take them aboard his ship.

No, she is alive. I can feel it.

His only hope of finding her would be to charter a ship to Tortuga, but how would he do that without coin? Could he steal a ship? He looked out across the bay and saw the HMS in the distance, silhouetted black against the dim cobalt horizon. There were several other ships in the bay.

His shoulders sagged. How would he steal a ship without help? A one-armed man couldn't hope to row a boat, let alone captain a crewless ship. He was as penniless as the day he had joined Griffith's crew, with absolutely nothing to show for his time as a pirate, aside from a missing arm. And now he was stuck in the last place a pirate wanted to be, with a governor that would gladly string him up with anyone else who had been unlucky enough to survive *Harbinger's* demise.

34

HORNIGOLD

"Where is she?" Benjamin Hornigold asked the black-skinned man who was vehemently sweeping the floor of Sassy Sally's tavern. Hornigold wasn't sure why the man was so intent upon his task when the place was completely empty. The near-to-spotless floor appeared as though it hadn't seen many visitors of late. The sweeper shook his head, pointed to his mouth, and muttered something in gibberish. Hornigold seized the man's broom to halt his incessant sweeping and said, "No English?"

"No," the black man replied.

"A girl," Hornigold said, and he emphasized the point by cupping his hands before his pecs and moving them up and down. The black man grinned and nodded knowingly. He pointed upward.

Hornigold released the broom and said, "Have your cook bring a bowl of turtle soup upstairs, and tell him if he spits in it again, I'll split him from cock to apple." The black man frowned. Hornigold formed the shape of a bowl with one hand

and dipped a phantom spoon into it with the other. The man nodded his understanding and retreated to the back.

Hornigold climbed the dark stairway to the second floor, which beheld a lovely open view of the colony and harbor. Apart from a few children, merchants, and sailors, the streets were mostly empty. A lone dog roamed the beach.

Hornigold spotted his beloved sloop. Her clean white sails shone brilliantly in the unobstructed sun, nearly blinding him. A hulking HMS was moored in the distance beyond, unable to proceed further into the shallow bay for fear of running aground. He wondered if the combined might of the two ships would be enough to scuttle Edward Teach's flagship, *Queen Anne's Revenge*. He cursed his naiveté in handing Teach the *Concord*, which Teach subsequently bestowed with that ghastly name, setting her upon the British vessels that Hornigold had been wise enough to avoid.

He turned from the view and focused his attention on the task at hand. He was, after all, Woodes Rogers' man now. Blackbeard would soon be dead, one way or another. The age of piracy was nearing its end; Teach simply hadn't caught on to that fact. *History may recall your name,* Hornigold thought, *but I will see you dead, Teach.*

He rapped on the door of the first room. When no answer came, he moved to the second. After a moment, a female voice said, "Who's there?"

"I'm Captain Benjamin Hornigold," he answered.

"I don't know you," came her muffled reply.

"I know *you*," he called. "Can we talk for a moment?"

"I don't think so."

"I imagine you're hungry," Hornigold said.

He waited. The door opened. The light spilled in on the wildest mane of red hair he'd ever seen. The face within was beautiful, but clearly exhausted and pained. Her lips were cracked, her left cheek was bruised, and blood stained her torn shirt, which she was holding shut with a clenched fist. She squinted in the sun, squeezing one eye closed.

Hornigold offered his hand. She regarded it suspiciously for a moment, chewing on her lower lip, and finally took it. He guided her to a little round table and offered her a chair. She pulled away and sat down. She tossed her hair out of her face, and for a moment he glimpsed her right ear, or rather the hole where he ear *should* have been, before her hair fell back into place. He held back a gasp of revulsion.

"What do you want?" she asked as she looked out across the harbor. Her hoarse voice broke on the last word.

Hornigold took off his long maroon coat and hung it over his chair before sitting opposite the woman. He brushed annoying specks of dust from his white shirt and adjusted the white handkerchief that hung loose around his neck. Finally, he revealed his intent. "I'm looking for Katherine Lindsay."

If that name meant anything to her, she managed not to show it. "I don't know who that is."

"She went missing a year ago." Hornigold crossed one leg over the other and rubbed annoying smudges of sand from a polished leather boot. "Her husband was killed by pirates. The family is looking for her."

"That's sad," the redhead said, her incredulous expression betraying no hint of emotion.

"She was kidnapped by an elusive pirate named Jonathan Griffith. I knew him briefly. A generally decent man."

Her right eye twitched, but Hornigold couldn't be sure if that was a reaction to the sunlight or the sting of his baiting. "Griffith perished last night, just out there," he pointed to the bay. "Perhaps you saw the fire?"

"I did," she said. She looked at him. "You take the time to personally inform every resident of this?"

Hornigold smiled politely. "Most of the pirates on that ship are dead. Those few that were caught will hang very shortly. However, a one-armed young man named Nathan Adams presented himself to Woodes Rogers yesterday."

She blinked.

"Seems this Adams fellow is eager to claim the reward for Lindsay's safe return. He claims that he served as a deckhand on Lindsay's ship and was taken hostage along with her. He claims that Lindsay and he escaped from Griffith's ship last night and swam to shore."

"That's a wild story," the redhead said with a smirk. "Does Rogers believe everything he hears?"

"Certainly not," Hornigold said. He realized that he had been idly stroking his moustache, and promptly jerked his hand away from his face. It was an annoying habit he had never been successful in smothering. "However, it's a claim worth investigating while young Adams sits in a cell awaiting execution." He studied her for a reaction.

"He's going to hang?" she said, her chin quivering very slightly. She looked into the wind, hair sweeping past her face.

Hornigold resisted a smile. He had found his woman, for a certainty. "Only if he's lying," he said.

Sassy Sally's portly cook ascended the stairs and lumbered up to them. He set a bowl of turtle soup before Hornigold and glared at him. Hornigold seized the man by his collar. "Bring me a second bowl, minus your saliva."

The cook shrugged innocently. "I dunno what you mean."

"Listen to me, you shit, the soup isn't for me, it's for the lady." The cook's eyes darted from Hornigold to the woman. "Now bring her another bowl or I will split you from cock to—"

"Yes," the cook nodded frantically, "'Cock to apple.' I heard you say this inside! My mistake! I thought the soup was for you." He pulled away, retrieved the soup and shuffled off.

Hornigold sat back down. The redhead merely raised an eyebrow. "Chivalry is alive and well in the Caribbean, I see."

"They don't like me here," Hornigold explained. "It seems I've stifled much of their business."

The cook returned rather swiftly, depositing another bowl on the table, this time in front of the woman. He bowed slightly and smiled nervously. "Apologies," he said, and threw Hornigold another nasty look before scurrying away.

The woman stared uncertainly at the murky contents of the bowl. "Eat," Hornigold insisted. "You appear famished." She greedily seized the spoon and slurped up the soup. Her shirt fell open and Hornigold shifted to one side, hoping to catch sight of a nipple. Unfortunately her damnable hair deprived him from this angle. When she emptied the bowl, she tossed the spoon in, slid it back to him, and returned her sight to the bay.

"You are Katherine Lindsay, are you not?"

"I am not," she replied easily.

"That's unfortunate," Hornigold said. His hand inevitably drifted toward his moustache as he wondered if he should return with guards to seize this woman. "Might I ask what your name is, then?"

"Kate," she replied, and for the first time, she actually smiled.

"Kate?" he said, astonished at the nerve of this woman.

She tossed a cavalier hand in the air. "It's a common name."

Hornigold winced as his fingers absently gave his moustache a fierce tug. He dropped his hand to his lap and held his wrist firmly in place. "What's to keep me from dragging you before Governor Rogers?"

Her lips parted, revealing clenched teeth. "It would be very foolish to present a false woman to Lindsay's family."

"Oh, you are most certainly false." Hornigold proclaimed, standing and slipping his coat back on. It had grown a tad chilly for his liking, and this conversation was nearing its end. "But you are also Katherine Lindsay."

"How much are you willing to wager on that, captain?" She stood and circled the table. Her blood-soaked shirt hung loose, hair covering her breasts. Her trousers were tight against slender, muscular thighs. She was smiling confidently.

"How much is at stake?" he asked nervously.

"More than Katherine Lindsay is worth," she replied. "More than your little ship is worth."

Anger swelled in his chest. *The nerve of this bitch!* He started at her, hand poised for a crushing blow, but he managed to stop himself.

She didn't flinch. "I may not be Katherine Lindsay, but I did swim here from Griffith's ship, before it sank."

He pulled away from her. "Then you're a pirate."

"As were you, I imagine," she retorted.

"I am no longer!" he protested bitterly. "I am a privateer! I have always been so! Sometimes a man must resort to extreme measures in extreme circumstances, but I have never attacked my own people. The dog they call Blackbeard twisted my crew against me and took it upon himself to attack good British sailors."

"Then you're a smart pirate, but a pirate nonetheless. There are far worse than *you* roaming these waters."

"One less, it would seem." With finicky fingers he adjusted the black collar of his red coat.

"You mean Griffith?" she sneered. "It's my understanding he was not the worst of the Caribbean's troubles. The man burned down his own ship, for heaven's sake!"

"Did he?" Hornigold said. "I would've guessed he'd had help. Perhaps from a vengeful woman whose husband he'd murdered. Terrible luck, bringing a woman aboard. Or so I've heard. Most pirates know better."

"Very terrible for Griffith," she said. She was closing on him again. Whatever exhaustion had plagued her earlier completely faded. "Not so terrible for you."

Some silly part of him felt like leaping over the balcony to get away from her. "You're insane, do you realize that?"

"I'm alive," she said. "Griffith is dead." She sat on the edge of the table, folded her arms, and crossed a leg over the other. "And I can make you a very rich pirate hunter." She raised a finger to correct herself. "Privateer."

Hornigold wrenched his eyes from her and set his fists on the balcony railing. He swept his gaze over the bay, trying to avoid the white sails of his ship, but they were far too bright to be ignored, pervading his peripheral vision. "Those be virgin sails," Blackbeard had once said, mocking Hornigold's tidy ship. "Afraid to get dirty."

He turned to find her smirking at him, her tresses moving softly in the wind. He caught another glimpse of her mangled ear. "What was he like?" he asked.

"Who?"

"Griffith."

"I don't remember," she answered without haste.

He chuckled. "Was yesterday so long ago?"

Again she unveiled that pleasing smile that softened her face. She was very beautiful, but her sun-touched skin, lean muscles, the bloodstains on her shirt, and fleeting glimpses of that recently lost ear reminded Hornigold that this woman was not to be trifled with. He had never met a woman like this, and he suspected that if he left now, he never would again.

Her reply was methodical. "Not so long that I cannot recall the location of Griffith's greatest secret."

"Let me hazard a guess. Is it buried treasure?" Hornigold

loosed a boisterous laugh.

She spread her arms. "Is it so farfetched out here?"

"Yes," he replied. "A pirate rarely parts with booty until he reaches port, where it is exchanged for coin and swiftly fumbled into the willing arms of strumpets. Buried treasure is almost always a myth, conjured over a bonfire under influence of spirits."

"Almost always," she agreed. "Griffith did not part with his booty. He merely secured it in order to accept a pardon from Rogers, claim the title of pirate hunter, and retrieve it at a later date."

Hornigold frowned. The scheme was sensible enough. He would have done the same, had Blackbeard not stolen his crew and the majority of his bountiful plunder right out from under him. "And you know the location? Can you produce a map?"

"I can draw you a map," she said, tapping the side of her head. "It's all here."

"I find that difficult to believe."

"As a woman who resided in Captain Griffith's cabin for a year burdened with nothing but an abundance of time and unrestricted access to his charts, I can assure you, I know many things I should not."

Hornigold pushed himself off the railing and approached her. She gazed up at him but did not rise. He pinched her chin and studied her eyes intently. Having served with pirates since 1713, he knew a liar when he saw one. There was no lie in this woman's intelligent eyes.

He released her chin and turned away. If the treasure was as real and lucrative as she claimed, Hornigold might ease in his obligation to hunt pirates. More specifically, he might abandon his search for Edward Teach, who had earned nothing less than a bloody demise at Hornigold's vengeful hands. Yet, he had always known that hunting Blackbeard was at best a fool's errand. Teach had warned him not to follow, and in issuing that warning he had deliberately galvanized Hornigold into doing just that. The monstrous bastard ached for a final battle at sea between the two of them. And surely, if Teach won, he would allow no one else the honor of killing Hornigold. The last thing Hornigold would see would be Blackbeard's grinning face swathed in the smoke of that terrible burning beard.

Hornigold felt the woman's eyes on his back. He turned to find her regarding him with a shrewd smile. "Your thoughts are at war," she said. "Who's winning?"

"Money always wins," he replied.

"Not always," she said, setting a hand on her leg. "Just ask Griffith."

"I can't," Hornigold chuckled. The wood groaned as a heavy gust of wind tugged at the balcony. The trees swayed all around, and for a moment the entire island seemed to be moving. "What's it like to take revenge?"

The wind tossed strands of the woman's hair in front of her face, but her eyes did not flutter as they held his. "I wouldn't know."

Hornigold deeply inhaled the salty air. "Intensely gratifying, I should think."

She shrugged pensively. "I would think it too swift and final to be satisfying. A man can only die once, when a thousand deaths would serve him."

Only one thing remained now. Hornigold had no wish for an innocent boy to die, but who was to say Nathan Adams was truly innocent? *Lady Katherine*'s crew had not reported a deckhand missing. By their account, only Katherine Lindsay had been kidnapped. "Shame about the boy," he said. "He was so very convincing."

She opened her mouth as if she wanted to say something, but closed her lips.

"To your knowledge," Hornigold pressed on, "did the boy willingly commit acts of piracy?"

"What?"

"Is Nathan Adams a pirate?"

Her eyes flickered away. "What does it matter if he is? Have your governor hand him a pardon and make him one of your crew. You can do that, yes?"

Hornigold proceeded cautiously. "If the boy is a pirate, he has attempted a perverse deception against 'my' governor, and any pardon he may have otherwise received is null."

Her lip curled in disgust, but still she avoided eye contact. "Nathan would *never* have received a pardon, even if he had surrendered himself without subterfuge."

"Then you admit that he is false."

"Rogers will kill him no matter what I admit."

"That's not true," Hornigold insisted. "You will be safely returned to your family, and Adams' life will be spared." He smiled. "That is, if you are, in fact, Katherine Lindsay."

Her brow creased. Her head sank and she let out a slow sigh that was barely audible over the wind.

"Your thoughts are at war," Hornigold echoed.

She set one hand in the other and rubbed her palm with her thumb. She didn't seem to recognize the lines she saw there. She lifted her head and held Hornigold's gaze. "I won't pretend I'm someone I'm not."

"Then the boy will hang," said Hornigold.

She looked to the bay. Her gaze was impossibly distant, as though her vision stretched beyond the horizon and sailed the curve all the way to the end of the world. A single strand of hair trailed in front of her face, swaying gently, and she made no attempt to remove it. Hornigold followed her gaze to the horizon and saw a grey patch of clouds he hadn't noticed only moments ago. The clouds appeared small from this great distance, but they were ominously dark. He couldn't be sure if the clouds were approaching or diminishing.

The red-haired woman's raspy voice cut into his thoughts. "I'm ready to leave when you are."

COMPLETE THE TRILOGY!

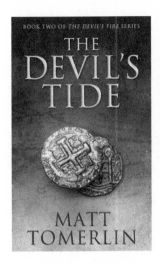

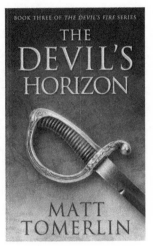

Available at Amazon.com
and other stores

facebook.com/thedevilsfire

TheDevilsFire.com

CPSIA information can be obtained
at www.ICGtesting.com
Printed in the USA
BVHW01s2322191217
503277BV00001B/20/P